DEVIL'S INTERN

JAYME PHELPS

Editors: Allie Doherty and Borbala Branch

Proofreading: Rachel Talavera of Yours Truly Book Services

Cover: Emily's World of Design

Formatting: Dawn Luocus of Yours Truly Book Services

Lake Country Press & Reviews

"I believe I am in Hell, therefore I am."
— Arthur Rimbaud

For my husband Brett, who supports every dream I want to chase, thank you for being my biggest fan. For Kristopher, Justin, and Tyler, who are my Sun, Moon and Stars, I love you all. Thank you for your love and support.

CHAPTER 1

The warlock stood across the bar from me, narrowing his dark, beady eyes as he worked himself up enough to confront me. His inky black hair fell in a limp sheet around his scrunched face as he stared with distaste, and I knew he was going to be trouble.

My jaw clenched as anger bubbled inside of me. *This is the last thing I need.* Ever since vampires started killing supernaturals in the city, the witches and warlocks were even more hostile than usual, coming into the bar and ordering drinks only to complain I had under-poured or overcharged. *What's it gonna be this time?* Because the Goddess only knew what kind of bullshit this one was going to sling. *Where are those old Gods when you need them?* After all, I could sure use one now and again to smite someone, like the asshole standing in front of me.

"Give me what I paid for, you incompetent *void*," the warlock spat, his foul-smelling breath packed an even bigger punch than the weak slur he used. Though, if he meant to piss me off, he was on the right track.

His claw-like fist slammed the glass he was holding down onto the counter with a thud, and the fact that it was empty told me he had liked it enough to drink the damn thing before complaining.

My shoulders tensed. "Want another one?" I asked through gritted teeth.

"I want you to give me the Hennessy I paid for, not the house crap you poured last time," he complained, causing the patrons around us to look our way.

He pushed the glass toward me using more force than necessary, and it slid easily across the smooth surface I had just wiped down. Then I watched as it went crashing to the floor, where it shattered at my feet.

Irrational fear gripped me. My heart skipped a beat, and my throat constricted at the sound of the shattering glass that, to me, was ten times louder than it was in the noisy room. My mind raced, and I was hurtled back to the moment that brought me to Idir in the first place, the image suddenly crystal clear as it flashed before my eyes...

Searing panic coursed through me as I pressed my palm against the hole in my chest. The tall, thin, blonde man kneeling in front of me was waiting for me to respond to him, but I couldn't remember what he'd said. *Don't scream, don't panic, you're gonna be okay,* I thought as another shot rang out, turning the window above our sanctuary into nothing more than a glittering blanket around us. The gunmen robbing the bank had given up on escaping without incident and were shooting with abandon at the police surrounding the building on the street outside.

My vision blurred, going black around the edges as blood oozed from the wound—I was losing too much blood.

"I can save you right now," he soothed, unfazed by what was happening. "But... you'll owe me a debt." His face was a mask of calm seriousness, and I tried to focus the last of my energy on him as I clung to my remaining threads of consciousness.

I'll give you anything you want as long as I live through this. I have to survive for Alex and Isabella's sake. I won't leave them. I thought of my twin brother and sister as I gave a weak nod. My heartbeat ratcheted even higher as he reached his hand inside his jacket and pulled out a neatly folded sheet of heavy cream-colored paper.

"You'll have to promise me your soul."

My soul? Is that a contract? Who is this guy, the Devil? I must be delirious. Either way, I was dying, and I needed to believe I would somehow make it out of there, so I gave another nod.

Taking my hand gently in his, he slid the paper underneath. "You have to do this on your own; I can't do it for you. Just press your thumb down if you agree," he explained calmly. So, without another thought, I pressed my sticky thumb against the heavy paper.

The electric shock of it in my memory was punctuated by a thud that brought me crashing back to reality. The warlock with his stupid thin-lipped scowl had slammed his fist down again and was leaning even closer over the counter, his face less than a foot from mine.

"I didn't realize you were also mute. Can you talk, you stupid *void*?"

Now he had done it. I might be what the magical community liked to refer to as a "void," because I lacked a soul, but that didn't give warlocks like him the right to destroy property and insult my intelligence.

I reared back, the muscles in my shoulder flexing as I wound up to punch the asshole square in the jaw. His expression morphed from smugness to outright shock, and it was in that split second he realized I meant business. But before I could strike, Matt stepped up behind me, grasping my elbow firmly between his strong fingers.

"What's going on, Anna?" he asked, and if he hadn't been the boss, I would have shaken him off.

"I'll tell you what's wrong. Your bartender served me house liquor instead of what I asked for. She's probably keeping the difference, too," the warlock sneered.

Arrogance rolled off him in waves as he stood there, arms crossed, staring down the bent bridge of his nose at me while he awaited a response.

"Anna's a good bartender—one of the best I've had in years. If she poured you the wrong drink, I'm sure it was an accident," Matt replied as he let go of my arm and shot me a knowing look.

I knew he understood, but I wished that just this once, he would've stepped in a second too late, allowing me the satisfaction of breaking that stupid beak of a nose on that smug face.

"Stop harassing my bartender, Derek, or you'll have to find another place to drink," Matt said, interrupting my daydream.

Matt was a lot of things, but a pushover was not one of them. The slightly pointed ears and lyrical voice might fool some at first, but fairies were known to have a wicked mean streak, and Matt was no exception.

He turned to me, placing his hand lightly on my shoulder. "Pour the man another drink, then close his tab for the night." Glancing over his shoulder, he gave Derek a pointed look, waiting until he received a frustrated nod of agreement before returning to the other end of the bar.

I took my time pulling the bottle down from the shelf behind me, whistling a tune as I poured another shot of Hennessy. Then I stared directly into his eyes as I plastered a smile on my face, making sure to slide the glass back to him just hard enough that some of the dark amber liquid sloshed over the side, leaving behind a wet trail. His face contorted into a mask of pure hatred, but he knew better than to complain again lest he wanted to be banned. Shooting back the drink, he slammed the glass down and stomped away, muttering insults under his breath.

Once he was gone, I wiped away the sticky trail of alcohol and glanced at the clock on the wall, groaning inwardly. *Only eleven-thirty. Crap*, I thought. And the bar was getting even more crowded by the minute.

Normally, that wasn't a bad thing. It meant tips would be pouring in, despite all the hostility I had received recently. Tonight, however, I just wanted my shift to be over. I wanted to curl up in bed in my crappy little room, pretending it wasn't Halloween. But since Nate, the only other bartender in the place, had taken the night off, Matt needed me more than ever. That meant at least two and a half more hours of watching actual pixies swarming the room sporting gaudy fake fairy wings. The irony of it all almost made me laugh.

The appeal was lost on me, but according to our head wait-ress, Nina, it was still the only time of the year the magical community could be who they were without fear of persecution from humans. After all, the Salem witch trials might have seemed like a long time ago, but to anyone in the magical world, it was like it had happened yesterday.

I turned to the woman sliding onto the stool in front of me, glad to see a smiling face for a change as she ordered her drink. But the sound of the door crashing open against the wall had every eye in the place turning, curious to see who was about to enter.

Are you freaking kidding me? He took the night off only to end up back here with his latest fling. I rolled my eyes at the thought as Nate came through the door. He was half carrying, half drag-ging a drunken witch I had never seen before.

"What's up, my Supes!" She squealed from the still open doorway as she sauntered in, an arm swung casually around his neck.

She was done up in all black, sporting fishnet stockings, a skin-tight short black halter dress that flared at the hips, and knee-high boots with a wicked stiletto heel. She finished off the look with a comical little witch's hat balanced precariously on top of her mess of short dark curls framing her heart-shaped face. I gave a wave of my hand toward Nate, returning my attention to the woman in front of me who had been waiting patiently for her whiskey sour. Then I watched from my peripheral as he steered the woman into the last empty booth.

He deposited her gently onto the cracked, black vinyl seat before weaving his way toward me through the tangle of bodies. "Hey, Anna, please tell me you've got some coffee brewed." He sagged against the bar, and I shook my head at him, laughing internally at his plight. *Serves him right for making me endure this mess alone.* I scowled at him, my brow cocked, lips pursed as I leaned forward on the counter. Then I took a moment to really look at him. Unfortunately, the bags under his dark brown eyes and the way his sandy brown hair stood on end had me feeling sorry for him, and I found myself hurrying through the swinging door into the modest kitchen.

This was the third random girl he'd brought into the bar this week. He was definitely a player, but I had known that from the moment I met him. And in those few years, he had slept with every waitress that had the bad luck of ending up in his sights.

Which wouldn't bother me, except for the fact that they would come back to work the next day, nursing a broken heart after their one-night stand. He was the sole reason for Idir's high turnover rate, which is why I no longer bothered to learn the new girls' names.

Nina, however, was the exception. She'd been around longer than Nate and me both; and for whatever reason, he didn't even bother with her. She joked it was thanks to the locket she wore around her neck, saying it held a rune of protection against anyone like him. But I was pretty sure it was because she was a succubus. No matter how insatiable Nate might be, he couldn't handle her, and he knew it.

The door to the kitchen swung closed behind me, bringing with it a slight breeze that did nothing to fan away the nearly rancid smell of stale oil hanging heavy in the air. I could swear I felt it coat my skin as it flooded my nostrils, and I had to squash my gag reflex before I had another mess to clean up. *Would anyone even consider eating those onion rings if they could smell this place?* My face scrunched as I stared at the basket of overcooked rings next to the fryer, and my stomach grumbled loudly.

"Hey, Bruce," I greeted the cook with the friendliest smile I could muster as I reached for the pot of coffee.

I had to use the bottom of my apron to wipe off the greasy handle so I wouldn't drop it before emptying the last of the dark liquid into one of our few stained ceramic cups. He gave me a grunt of acknowledgment, then frowned before turning his back on me once again.

"I suppose you want me to make another pot of that, too," he grumbled.

"You're the best, Bruce." I couldn't help it when the corner of my mouth lifted, and I smiled to myself as I placed the pot back because I knew deep down, he was a total softie. Bruce only looked grumpy on the outside. It's the way trolls were, after all. Backing through the door, I dodged Matt, making sure not to trip over the giant rubber floor runner that flanked the bar, while holding the mug in one hand and a bowl of creamer in the other.

"You're a lifesaver," Nate sighed.

"Tell me something I don't know," I replied with a sarcastic grin, but his silence told me he wasn't in the mood for banter. "That bad, huh?"

"This one is awful when she's drunk," he confided. "Until her probation is over, and she gets her magic back to full strength, she's as bad as a human. All it took was one margarita and..." he trailed off as he motioned with his arm toward the booth where she sat sobbing with our most recent hire.

His response surprised me, making me furrow my brows at him. He made it sound like he knew her on a personal level, which was all kinds of weird for him. Especially because I had learned during the past few years that he was more likely to remember the color of a woman's panties than her life story.

"Is she your *girlfriend*?" I wiggled my brow at him as I leaned in, resting on my forearms so our heads were closer together.

He shot me a withering look as he reached forward, his strong, thick fingers pushing my shoulder back hard enough that I almost face-planted into the solid slab between us.

"What did I say?" I joked.

"You're ridiculous." He held out his hands, and I shook my head, handing off the heavy white mug and creamer to him. I was curious, but not that curious.

"Well, good luck with that," I called as he walked away.

Unfortunately, most of the other people in the place weren't as friendly as my coworker. But thanks to Matt's supportive touch on the small of my back as he passed by every so often, I was able to hold it together. Plus, the never-ending line of people coming in and out kept me busy enough to stop me from acting on any impulses I might have had.

CHAPTER 2

The minute the lock on the door clicked, I let out a breath of relief. All the tables had been wiped down, and the only thing left to do was drag the mop across the sticky floor. Thankfully, that wasn't my job.

Every part of my body hurt from the tension I was holding all night, and I could feel the ache in my muscles as I plopped down into the creaky wooden chair at the nearest table. A shiver raced down my spine as the air hit my sweat-slicked skin, and I pulled my thick red hair into a ponytail, securing the long waves with the thin black hair tie I always kept around my right wrist. I hated wearing it down, but the patrons seemed to like it, and I always made better tips when I did. I just wished I had taken the time to straighten it. Maybe then it wouldn't have been so tangled.

"You okay?" Matt took a seat across from me, a stifled yawn escaping his lips as he settled in, and I knew when he asked, he wasn't asking as my boss—he was asking as the guy I sometimes shared a bed with.

I sat back in my chair, reaching for his hand across the table. My shoulders relaxed as he laced his strong fingers through mine, and settled my feet across his knees, effectively bridging the gap between us as I thought about the day. He knew this was the anniversary of the day I had made the deal that would give my soul to the Devil, landing me here in my own personal Hell on Earth, and that's why I normally stayed holed up by myself on Halloween. But I had already hashed that out with him a long time ago, so I didn't want to talk about it again. Two years had passed, and nothing I said was going to change where I was, so there was no use in talking about it.

"I would've felt a lot better if you let me punch him." My mouth quirked to the side as I half joked with him.

He shook his head, a smile forming on his full lips as he patted my calve with his free hand. "Believe me, I considered it. But it would have been more trouble than it was worth, for both of us. Why don't you stay here tonight? I have a bottle of Morgan upstairs calling your name," he said with a chuckle. It amused him to no end that I wasn't a top-shelf kind of girl. I preferred my alcohol like my lodgings: affordable.

If you only knew, I thought. The only reason I drank cheap liquor when I was mortal was because it did the trick to get me drunk. But after I "died", I could no longer enjoy the feeling of drowning in oblivion because then it wouldn't be Hell, right? Even if I did get to serve my sentence on Earth.

Shaking my head at him, I got up and rounded the bar, pulling down a bottle of Fireball. After pouring us each a double, I raised my glass in a toast to the ending of another year of confinement. He tilted his glass toward me in response before we both tipped them back, draining the contents in one gulp. The burn of the alcohol was almost soothing as it blazed a trail of fire down my throat, where it pooled in a warm puddle in the pit of my stomach.

"I know Halloween is tough for you, but this year seems worse. You wanna talk about it?" He picked up the bottle and poured us each another one as he looked up at me through his long lashes. His thick, wavy hair brushed his shoulders, and I reached out, tucking a strand behind his ear as I fought the urge to cry.

"I hate this town, Matt. I want to leave." I rubbed the back of my neck, blinking away the tears that were stinging the corners of my eyes.

What I didn't tell him was how much I was missing Alex and Isabella — the twin siblings I was forced to leave behind. My heart ached every day for my brother and sister, who had to fend for themselves once I was gone. It was bad enough losing both of our parents at the same time. But then they lost me, too, the only family they had left... and I had no idea if they were even okay or how they got by these past few years without me.

Three states, three measly states were all that separated us. Yet, thanks to the ridiculous boundaries of my sentence, it might as well have been another planet.

"So, take a break. Go somewhere, anywhere, ... get out of here and see something you've never seen before."

"Don't you think I've tried?" I sighed, throwing my hands up in frustration before tipping back the shot to try to calm my nerves. "There's no way out for me. It's like the town is some kind of supernatural dead end that leads right back here the minute I try to cross through the city limits, thanks to my contract."

"Well, Silas does know his way around a magical contract," he said with a sympathetic shrug. "But is it such a bad thing? I mean, he basically chose you to be immortal. You get to live for eternity with no consequences, no fear of death. From where I'm sitting, you're lucky." He looked far away for a moment, then shook his head at the thought before pouring us yet another.

"No, Declan *chose* me... for whatever reason, and now I'm stuck in this place where people hate me, and I can't even get drunk, for fuck's sake." I couldn't help but laugh at how stupid it all was. *I wish someone had told me that Heaven and Hell aren't what humans think.*

I reached out, picking up the glass up in an automatic

response, and I held it to my lips, inhaling the spicy scent of the cinnamon before setting it back down with a thud. *What's the point?*

"You don't get it. I'm stuck. For eternity, in this place where people loathe me. And regardless of what you see, for me, this is literally nothing more than a fancy prison."

"I know that warlock got under your skin," he said, bringing the flashback that altercation had caused to the forefront of my mind. Shaking my head, I closed my eyes and let out a shaky breath. Matt thought it was about the warlock, and I would let him believe it. Because I didn't want to admit, even to myself, that the trauma from making my deal cut me deeper than I realized.

"It's fine. I just need to shake it off."

"Well, for whatever reason, today was an especially bad day, I know that. But you'll feel better tomorrow—you'll see. And as for the witches and warlocks, they're just lashing out because they're worried about everything that's been happening recently." A shock of disbelief went through me. I knew he was only trying to be helpful, but I was too emotionally raw. *So, this is out of character for them, and I'll be fine tomorrow, huh?* I thought as I gave an incredulous snort and walked away, leaving him standing there alone to gape after me. I couldn't believe that he was dismissing my feelings and their behavior like they were both something recent.

From the moment I walked into this place when I started my sentence, I was shunned. I hated this city because no matter how much freedom I appeared to have; I knew that it was nothing more than a cell without bars. I was thrust into a world I knew nothing about and had to come to terms with the fact that I was surrounded by things I thought were a fairy tale.

Up until the day I *died*, I'd had no clue that there were supernatural beings walking the streets of every city in the world. Now, I was one of them. Well... sort of.

Sitting down at the desk in Matt's tiny office, I dropped my head into my hands, pushing my palms hard against my eyes to stop not only the tears welling in my eyes but those images of the moments that had landed me here. The ones that still haunted me almost daily.

"Anna," Matt said, interrupting my downward spiral as he gently laid his hand on my shoulder. He had learned the hard way not to spook me, as I had developed the habit of lashing out anytime I felt cornered. "Tell me what I can do."

"I'm just tired," I lied. I was ready to go home and be done with it all, but my brain lingered just a moment longer on the image of the man's face. His blonde hair, blue eyes, and Adonis-like features may have made him look innocent, but I knew better now. That day in the bank was the first time I met Declan. I was grateful that I had only seen him one other time since then because I might have killed him, or at the very least, given it my best shot.

Slipping my bag over my shoulder, I let go of the image of Declan, then winced at the brief phantom pain in my chest that only ever appeared when I thought about that day. Regardless of the fact that the whole thing had happened years ago, I was still more than angry. So instead of taking it out on Matt, I decided to kiss him lightly on the cheek and walk away.

I breathed a sigh of relief when he didn't push the issue and ask me again to stay. I knew I would regret hurting his feelings tomorrow, no matter how good it felt to lash out at him tonight.

CHAPTER 3

T he cool air smelled damp when I stepped out into the empty street. Goosebumps lined my arms, causing the short hairs to stand uncomfortably on end, reminding me that fall was in full swing. Even though it wasn't nearly as cold in the desert as it was in my coastal hometown, it was still chilly enough that I would soon need another layer.

I found myself jogging down the familiar side streets leading home, my sneakers treading lightly over the crumbling pavement while I thought grudgingly again about the man that would forever haunt me. Declan may have saved my life that day, but I had hated him every day of my afterlife. He had preyed on me in my moment of weakness, knowing that, like just about anyone, I would give anything to live.

But that was in the past, and I needed to try and leave it there, especially because there was nothing I could do to change it. As I rounded the next corner, I could see the cluster of buildings surrounding the old town plaza in the distance. At this time of night, the park would be illuminated by the soft light of the street lamps, bathing it in a warm, welcoming glow. Though experience told me that there were always bad things lurking, even beneath the street lights.

"Stop it, Derek. I told you I didn't want to do this here. This place is gross."

The feminine voice cut through the night air, bringing me back into the moment at hand, and my heart skipped a beat at the realization I wasn't the only one on the street. Her voice was low and pleading as I approached the next alley, and I lowered my head, determined to just keep walking. The last thing I needed was to get involved in whatever was going on, only to find out they were role-playing or something weird like that. But when I reached the next building over, the sharp crack of flesh on flesh stopped me in my tracks as the woman yelped in pain. The awful sound was followed closely by a series of whimpering sobs I couldn't ignore.

Just leave it alone. This isn't your problem, I reasoned, releasing a breath through my pursed lips. *Walk away.* But I knew I couldn't do that, so I snuck back to the edge of the building, peering through the dark for a moment before working up the courage to move closer. I skirted around empty coffee cups and pieces of trash to keep as quiet as I could before peeking my head around the edge of the giant green dumpster in my path. I figured it was probably best to survey the situation before just rushing in blindly.

A few feet away, I saw a man pressing up against the woman I was sure I had seen at Idir with Nate just a few hours before. Her curls were a mess, and the tiny witch's hat that had been artfully balancing there when she had waltzed into the bar earlier now hung on by only a few strands of hair.

I breathed deeply, steeling myself for a moment before making my way a little closer to be sure. It was definitely the girl from the bar, but it wasn't Nate she was with. I watched only a second longer as she pushed against him, clawing at his hands and arms while he pulled at her dress, trying to find the easiest access to what he wanted. *I don't think so.* My blood boiled watching her struggle, and neither one of them noticed me as I stood from my hiding place and strode toward them.

Reacting on instinct, I grabbed his shoulders, feeling the

warmth of his magic flooding through my palms as his power began transferring to me in a matter of seconds. *Oh shit! What in the hell did you just do?* I cursed myself, realizing too late that I had let my guard down in my panicked state, and without meaning to, I sent some of the magic back toward him. He was a low-level warlock at best, but there was enough power coursing through me that I was able to give him a jolt of his own magic before he realized what was happening.

An audible groan escaped my lips as he turned on me, and I recognized him as the very same warlock I'd been itching to hit at the bar. As if that weren't bad enough, the faint light from the distant streetlamp reflected off the shiny metal pin on his breast pocket. I wasn't sure how I had missed it earlier, but now there was no mistaking the silver emblem of the Guard—nine small stars, one representing each of the coven groups, surrounding the Celtic symbol of protection.

My eyes closed momentarily, and I gave a shake of my head as I took a short step back. "I don't want any trouble," I said, raising my hands in front of me, palms out in surrender.

I shouldn't have been surprised, yet I couldn't help but feel blindsided when he took advantage of my momentary shock and reared back his fist the way I had earlier. Only there was no one there to stop him before he punched me right in the jaw — sending me staggering a few steps back.

"That's for getting me kicked out of my favorite bar," he snarled as he continued his assault, his other fist pounding into the soft flesh of my abdomen. My knees hit the ground from the force, and I was suddenly grateful I had decided on jeans instead of the shorts I'd been wearing earlier in the day. "And this is for interfering in Guard business." He wrapped his hand around the fabric of my thin black cotton t-shirt, giving me a split second to close my own hand around his wrist before he reared back once again.

This time, I dropped my guard completely, allowing enough

energy to flow into me to purposefully channel it back into him, knocking him out cold before he could take another swing. Once he hit the ground, I gulped in a deep breath of cold air, feeling the sting in my lungs as I waited for him to move again. When he didn't, I crawled my way toward him, trying to ignore the pain as tiny chunks of gravel bit into the soft flesh of my palms.

My jaw tensed, sending throbbing pain shooting through my teeth, but that was the last thing on my mind. *Don't let him be dead, don't let him be dead,* my brain screamed as my eyes scanned their way over his body. There was no movement, no blood I could see, and he didn't seem to be injured at all, but I hit him with enough of his magic that I was worried I might have actually stopped his heart. So, I reached forward slowly, pressing my fingertips to the pulse point on the side of his throat. My hands shook as I was overcome with the reality of what I had done, and I almost cried out in relief when I felt his pulse beating strong beneath my fingertips.

A sob escaped my throat as I sat back on my heels. "Thank the Goddess," I cried out to the darkness before falling back onto my butt unceremoniously. It was then that I realized the woman was still there, watching silently, her mouth hanging open in shock.

"Are you okay?" I asked, using the wall to help me stand. *Shit, that's gonna leave a mark,* I thought as searing pain shot across the length of my jaw. She nodded at me, her dark curls falling in a pile across her forehead. She pushed them back quickly with a sweep of her hand before scooting back away from me, almost as if she were more scared of me than the Guard officer who had just attacked her. She had seen what I could do, and thinking back, I couldn't remember anyone ever seeing that happen before, not even Matt. I didn't often take others' magic, and when I did, even accidentally, I always let it dissipate. I had never used it against its owner, though possibly because I didn't realize that it was something I could do. Plus, when it had happened in the past, it was in such minuscule amounts, no one ever realized.

As a *soulless*, I was like a sponge. I could absorb other supernatural powers, but they were finite, and I couldn't manifest them without taking them first. At least as far as I knew.

"Don't worry, I'm not going to hurt you," I reassured her as I reached out my hand to help her up.

"I thought you were a *void*," she remarked, ignoring my hand until I awkwardly let it fall back to my side.

Adrenaline still coursed through me, but I forced my shoulders to relax, my eyes rolling as I shook my head. "Soulless," I sighed, aware of the annoyance that colored my tone. I wasn't sure what irked me more—her use of that slur after I took a beating for her, or her wariness toward me as if I'd been the one to attack her in the first place. *My jaw is probably fractured, but no problem. Glad to have stepped in,* I thought, irritated as I watched her use the wall to haul herself to her feet. Her stockings were torn, boots scuffed, and somewhere during her struggle, she lost the headband completely. The officer near her feet gave a slight moan, and the two of us glanced at each other before high tailing it out of the alley.

A few blocks later, I slowed down to a walk. I figured he wasn't coming after us, and I needed to allow the pinch in my side some time to subside before it got any worse. The adrenaline was fading, and fatigue was setting in, reminding me of the late hour. I was shocked when she slowed down with me, giving me no indication that she wanted to part ways anytime soon.

"What happened to Nate?" I asked curiously as I massaged my jaw lightly with the tips of my fingers. I knew he wasn't really a second date kind of guy, but it didn't seem like him to abandon a drunk woman, either.

"Derek... the Guard officer, we used to date. He offered to

take me home, and I told Nate it was okay, or he wouldn't have let me go."

"I thought you were on a date with Nate tonight." I looked down at the sidewalk, surprised by the slight judgmental tone I heard in my own words.

"No, we're just old friends," she laughed. "We know a lot of the same people, and sometimes we hang out."

I had to admit, I was a little blown away to find that Nate was capable of being friends with a woman, but I kept my mouth shut. I would be in enough trouble if she told him I beat up a Guard officer. I definitely didn't want him pissed at me for making fun of him, too.

"Where are we going?" Her brow furrowed as we crossed through the park in the center of old town.

"I'm going home. I need to put something cold on this jaw. I might pour drinks for a living, but I still need to be able to talk tomorrow," I shrugged, then gave her a wave before opening the gate beside me.

"You live in a church?"

"I live in the rectory," I corrected. Luckily, Father Miguel took pity on me when I got myself kicked out of the sleazy halfway house I was forced to live in at the start of this ridiculous sentence.

I was sleeping on a bench in the park across the street from the church when Father Miguel found me. I tried explaining to him I was not exactly human anymore, but he brushed it off. He said *God loves us all—even the lost and the broken—*and he would help me as long as I followed the rules. I agreed, and for the past year or so, I occupied a tiny bedroom on the second floor of the rectory, with the understanding that I could stay as long as I helped clean the church once a week and didn't bring male company. Which was only one of the reasons Matt and I stayed at his place above the bar.

"Weird," she said, her face scrunching up as she continued

to judge me. "And I thought you were strange before, so that's saying something." She stood there for a second, hand on hip, shifting from one foot to the other while she turned something over in her mind before giving a shrug. "I'm Rachel, by the way." She offered me her hand, and I shook it quickly, letting it fall before absorbing more than a tiny amount of her warm, earthy magic.

"Anna."

"Well, Anna, if you want to, you can come with me to my place, and I can fix up that bruise for you." She gestured awkwardly toward my swollen face.

Okay, so apparently, I look like crap, I thought grumpily.

"It's fine; I'm already here. I'll just put some peas or something on it." I shrugged, though, in all honesty, I had no idea if there was anything even remotely icy on the premises.

"I'm a witch. I just need a few things, and you'll be good as new."

I had to admit I would rather not see what my jaw looked like after a few hours, even after icing it, especially if she could really fix me up the way she claimed. With a shrug, I closed the gate behind me and followed her. We walked in comfortable silence for another few blocks —well, if a throbbing jaw could be counted as comfortable. Shortly after, Rachel rounded a corner, leading us to a modest apartment complex.

Her place was a cozy two-bedroom with exposed wood beams in the ceiling and natural wood floors. Plants lined the front window in handcrafted dark wooden boxes, slim enough not to hang over the edge of the shallow sill. I settled into the armchair in the living room, feeling more comfortable than I should have in the presence of a witch. But I pushed the thought away as I waited.

I watched as she carefully cut pieces from the leafy green plants in the boxes before dropping them into the bottom of a dark stone mortar. She settled herself on a stool behind the kitchen counter, where she drizzled oil over them before taking the pestle to the whole concoction and grinding away. The rhythmic sound of stone scraping against stone was soothing. I was surprised by how comfortable I was in her presence, so I settled further back into the chair, content with the smell of fresh herbs and relative silence.

I couldn't say I was pleased with the pungent green paste she smeared along my jaw. However, the numbing feeling that came along with it was a welcome one. *Well, this is handy. I wonder if she would teach me how to make this?* The thought floated through my sleepy mind, and I didn't complain too much as I lay my head back, allowing my eyes to drift shut while I waited until it was time to wash it off.

CHAPTER 4

The crick in my neck was the first clue that I wasn't asleep in my bed; the other was the residual smell of the ground herbs still plastered to my face. I rolled my head from side to side, stretching my arms out above me while I took in my surroundings in the fading daylight. The half sheet of notebook paper on the coffee table in front of me caught my eye, alerting me to the fact that I was alone.

Had to run some errands and didn't want to wake you. Thanks for saving my butt. Don't worry about the mess. I'll swing by Idir to check on you later.

Glancing at my watch, I realized I would barely have enough time to take a quick shower before work if I sprinted the few blocks to my own place. I felt bad for leaving the green stuff smeared across the cushion of the chair, but she did say not to worry about the mess. So, without stopping to wipe the gunk off my face, I twisted the lock on the doorknob and took off at a full sprint.

I reveled in the blissful emptiness of the rectory, taking the stairs two at a time in my rush to the shower. *Damn it, those were my favorite jeans,* I thought as I examined the holes in the knees after peeling them off. But there was no time to cry about it, so I kicked them to the corner and stepped into the steamy shower. Thankfully, the scalding hot water made quick work of the green goop along my jawline, and I breathed a sigh of relief when I looked in the mirror to see there was no sign of bruising.

I guess there's a silver lining after all. Though I was still running late, so I pulled on a pair of jean shorts and a black polo before racing out again. I was pulling my thick red waves into a ponytail when I strolled into Idir only five minutes late to clock in, happy Halloween was over, and work would be back to normal again.

"Hey," Nate said when I approached the bar. His expression, uncharacteristically sour, stopped me in my tracks. My gaze followed his involuntarily as his eyes moved from me to the other side of the bar top, where two burly-looking men sat unmoving across from him. *Weird.* I opened my mouth to ask, but the almost imperceptible shake of Nate's head told me not to say a word. When his eyes met mine, it was clear this was going to be a bad situation, and I had to tamp down on my urge to turn tail and run.

The two men got to their feet in tandem, both reaching for their front left shirt pocket to bring attention to the Emblem pinned there. They were Guard officers, and there was only one reason they would be there flashing their badges at me. *Shit, shit, shit, what do I do?* The instinct to run washed over me again, but instead, I planted my feet on the floor, knees shaking while I waited to hear whatever it was they had to say to me.

"Anna Westfall, were you the female bartender on duty last night?" The first officer asked. He was tall but round —a huge contrast to his short, thin partner, and his mustache reminded me of a fuzzy brown caterpillar sitting on his top lip.

Are you the only two idiots around who don't know that I'm the only woman who tends bar here? I gritted my teeth, biting back the snarky remark before it could pass my lips.

"Yep, that would be me," I replied, placing my hands on my hips and pulling back my shoulders to stand taller.

He grimaced, taking a step toward me as he looked me up and down, assessing how much of a threat he considered me to be. I stepped back, placing myself just out of arms reach, and he cocked his eyebrow. "We need you to come to the station with us for some questions."

His hand shot forward, his fingers constricting around my wrist, but I shook him off, pulling back, out of reach. Blood rushed up his neck to his cheeks, coloring him beet red, and my heart hammered in my chest.

I bit my lip, tasting the metallic tang of blood. *Stupid, Anna, you shouldn't have done that.* What if they mistook my movements as an attempt to escape like the robbers from my past? I couldn't go through that again. Phantom pain shot through my chest with the memory of the bullet, and I could almost feel the blood filling my lungs again, the coppery taste choking me. Swallowing it down, I cleared my throat and feigned ignorance.

"What's this about?" I knew good and well that it could only be related to what happened the night before, but I wasn't about to implicate myself.

"One of our officers was ambushed near here, and he's filed a complaint against you. The High Priestess wants your official statement."

"Are you kidding me?" Nate scoffed. "Does she look like she could beat up a full-grown warlock? And an Officer of the Guard, none the less." He slapped his hand down on the bar, punctuating his point while the men continued drilling holes in me with their eyes, neither joining in on his laughter.

"It's fine. I'll come with you." I lifted my hands in a show of surrender, knowing I would end up going one way or another. At least this way, it would be on my own terms. As much as it could be, anyway.

"Don't worry, Anna, you didn't do anything wrong," Nate said, leveling the two men with a glare but knowing better than to interfere in official Guard business.

Turning on my heel, I headed back out the door just in time to see the last rays of sunlight slip below the horizon. My stomach sank right along with it because, deep down, I knew there was no way they were going to go easy on me.

Beads of sweat broke out across my hairline as I slid into the back seat of the waiting sedan, jumping in the seat when the door slammed, locking me inside. *Breathe, just breathe, you're okay, it's okay. It's only questioning,* I reminded myself as I continued to dig my nails into my palms. Thankfully, we didn't have to go far, and I couldn't help but breathe a sigh of relief when the thin guy opened the door, releasing me from the car. After all, I didn't think I was claustrophobic, but the idea of being trapped in that back seat had me second guessing that.

The Guard station was an unremarkable red brick building downtown. It was nestled a few doors down from the human police station where the Guard kept up on what was happening in the non-magical world without raising suspicion. To a human, a Guard officer looked like any other security officer around town, and no one thought twice about seeing them around.

No bars covered the windows of the building, inside or out, telling me they weren't worried about prisoners escaping. Whatever means they used to keep prisoners in line were sure to be used on me since I had injured one of their own. My entire body shook as I walked behind them, keeping some distance between us but making sure not to fall too far behind. My throat ached from the sob that pushed its way insistently up my windpipe; my eyes stung from the unshed tears threatening to fall. As we continued down the sidewalk, I scanned my surroundings, trying to take stock of the situation.

They didn't carry any weapons other than the tiny capsules in the satchel at their hip holding stunning or containment spells. It was a dead giveaway; they were still new to the Guard because the capsules were only carried by warlocks in training who had a hard time casting without the focus of the container.

That made me feel a little better. It told me the Guard didn't see me as enough of a threat to send anyone more skilled. After all, the higher-level warlocks could cast with just a few muttered words that were rarely spoken loud enough to understand.

As we entered through the double doors, I was surprised by how reminiscent it was of a human precinct. There were several officers milling about while others sat behind desks, but very few of them even looked up at us. They were all immersed in their own work, some gathered together in groups laughing and talking, while others sorted through stacks of paperwork.

Look at them, talking and laughing while I march to my demise. Maybe I should make a run for it before I'm trapped in a room. But it was too late for that.

The two officers led me down a bright, sterile corridor to a meeting room at the end. Inside sat the High Chair of the Southwest coven, Melinda Farrington, the Local Head Officer of the Guard, Henry Matheson, Derek, the officer from the bar and alley the night before, and Rachel. My heart skipped a beat at the sight of her there, and my palms began to sweat when she didn't look up at me as I entered the room.

Taking a seat in the chair opposite Melinda, I noted the room smelled of sage, licorice, and sandalwood. The magic of the herbs permeated the air to encourage everyone present to tell the truth. My nerves calmed a bit, knowing that if they intended to *force* me to tell the truth, they would have required me to ingest a mixture of the herbs instead.

"Ms. Westfall, do you know why you're here?" Melinda asked. Her thin lips pursed as she looked me over with distaste, and I briefly considered how to respond. *Options, options, options... I could lie, tell the truth, or feign ignorance. Hmmm...* Unfortunately, none of those seemed like a good idea, but I didn't have much of a choice. Finally, I decided ignorance was the safest path.

"I'm not sure, High Priestess," I answered, using her local title over her regional title in hopes of conveying enough respect. My response flowed easily past my lips, and she seemed pleased enough with my answer and use of her title that she decided to continue.

"Officer Martin has filed a complaint against you," she stated, pausing only a moment for me to interject. *Of course, he did. That little weasel.* My lips pressed together tightly; I knew better than to say that out loud.

When I showed no signs of objecting to what she had to say, she continued on. "He has accused you of assaulting him within the walls of the fairy owned establishment Idir, and again in a nearby alley later the same evening. He claims that you stalked him and without provocation, assaulted him, interrupting a private moment of discussion between himself and Ms. Rachel Gomez, a member of my coven. What do you say to these charges?"

"Do you really think I could have beaten up a trained Officer of the Guard and escaped without a scratch?" My words came out slightly strained, each one being weighed by the magic before fighting their way out. *Damn it, just calm down and breathe.* The magic sensed my evasiveness as I failed to answer.

"You didn't answer my question, Ms. Westfall. Besides, Ms. Gomez has already admitted to healing your jaw. I suggest you amend your statement."

Hmmm, let me think about that...no, I would not like to amend my fucking statement; I just want to leave. But I guess I don't have a choice, do I? I sighed and shot an annoyed glance at Rachel, who still refused to even look at me, hoping beyond hope that she had told the truth with the exception of how I had knocked Derek out. I took a deep breath, allowing the mingling herbs to permeate my lungs before speaking again.

Fuck, Anna, what did you do that for? Are you trying to get your-self tortured? I closed my eyes and shook my head at myself.

"Okay, yes. The officer and I exchanged words at Idir, where he used some pointed slurs and accused me of pouring him the wrong drink. The issue was resolved, and the owner of the bar asked him to leave. After closing, I was walking home when I heard what sounded like a slap, followed by a woman's voice begging someone named Derek to stop. I went into the alley to make sure she was okay and found Officer Martin trying to tear off Ms. Gomez's clothes. I intervened. He punched me in the jaw, pinned me down on the ground, and I pushed him off long enough to get a hold of a nearby board I used to knock him out. I made sure he was still breathing and then escorted Ms. Gomez to her apartment where she healed my injury."

The words rolled off my tongue, almost eager to get out, and though it was not the complete truth, it was close enough that no one noticed the pause when I forced out the lie about using a board to knock him out. Melinda placed her hands on the table, lacing her fingers together as she nodded, accepting my story as truth before looking to the Head of the Guard. His face was red with fury, his dark brown eyes mere slits as he stared at me from across the wood table, and I could swear they had a red tinge to them, too.

"That's ridiculous. There's no way a respected member of the Guard would stoop so low as to fling casual slurs at an insignificant bartender or assault a known member of the Farrington Coven. This woman obviously has a vendetta against my Officer, and I want to see her placed under arrest," he demanded vehemently.

After listening to his spiel, the High Priestess looked to Rachel, who might as well have been invisible up to that point.

"You already heard my side of the story, High Priestess. You know what she's saying is true."

My breath came out in a quiet whoosh. She still wasn't

looking at me, but it didn't matter anymore because she had vindicated me to the only person in the room who had any real power. Now I just had to cross my fingers that Melinda was fair, regardless of how much she looked down on anyone who wasn't a part of her coven.

"Are you kidding me?" Derek spat. "You're going to listen to the word of a criminal and a... *Soulless*... over me? Rachel is on probation—her powers have been all but stripped for crimes against the Coven, and she's not even a living being," he said, pointing his finger to me.

"Are you finished, Officer Martin?" Melinda asked, cutting him off before he could go any further. "I'm well aware of Ms. Gomez's past transgressions, but her actions are not in question here today. And while I agree that there must be some form of punishment for assaulting an Officer of the Guard, I believe the Prism may be too harsh considering the testimony today." The authority emanating from her voice was unquestionable.

The two Officers were nothing less than furious, but neither uttered a word. Instead, they sat silently, looking as if they'd sucked on a lemon.

It's about damn time someone put you in your place. I crossed my arms over my chest and shot a smug look across the table.

"Ms. Westfall, while your actions were admirable, I do not condone vigilantism. Therefore, I am confining you to the local prison where you will be held for three months, as punishment for your attack on Officer Martin,"

Wait, what? Oh, Goddess, no. I doubled over, my chest constricting as I attempted to force air into my lungs. Everything around me started going fuzzy, blurring around the edges. I forgot how to breathe. *I'm going to be sick.* The acrid taste of bile rose in my throat, and my knees turned to jelly. *I'm in hell, and now I'm going to jail. All for helping someone in need. How is that fair?*

"High Priestess, if I might make a suggestion," Rachel interjected, using Melinda's more casual title and breaking through my thoughts as I started to spiral into a full-on panic attack. The High Priestess nodded to encourage Rachel to continue.

"I can't help but feel responsible for the predicament Ms. Westfall finds herself in, and I would like to propose six months house arrest with work release instead. I will take personal responsibility for her and her actions during that time."

I waited, not daring to take more than a few shallow breaths before the High Priestess gave a terse nod of her head in agreement. "I hope you know what you're doing, Rachel," she warned, and just like that, I was evicted from my life at the rectory and forced into confinement with a woman I barely knew. My eyes met Rachel's, and I swallowed the hard lump in my throat. *It beats jail time, right...* Suddenly, I wasn't so sure. Behind the pity in her eyes shone the glower I was used to seeing from the supernatural's. *Maybe a jail cell was the better option.*

"You've got to be kidding me!" Derek slammed his fist down in a fit of rage. A sheen of sweat beaded at his hairline as heat crept up his neck to his face.

"Mr. Martin, in the future, it would serve you well to remember to reign in your temper. I have no qualms with removing you from your post." Melinda addressed Derek before turning to the Head of the Guard. "And as for you, I expect better behavior from the Officers under your command."

Mr. Matheson gave a terse nod but didn't speak up. Instead, he shot a glare at Derek and avoided looking at Rachel and I altogether.

Melinda left the room first, patting Rachel lightly on the shoulder before sweeping past me without another glance. The two Officers followed on her heels, both fuming mad, but they knew better than to question the sentence again. As far as Melinda was concerned, justice had been served.

Rachel and I sat in stunned silence, neither of us daring to speak for a few more minutes, letting it all sink in. *What in the hell just happened here?* I asked myself, my head spinning. I was sure she was questioning her decision as much as I was at that moment.

"Well, I guess we should go get you moved in." She got to her feet, looking somewhat dazed. "Unless you have to work tonight, and then we can get you moved in tomorrow morning." She lifted her wrist, checking at the time on her watch, and I mimicked the gesture, shocked to see the whole proceeding took less than an hour. Nate was sure to have filled Matt in by now. Not that either of them could do a thing to rescue me from my newest hell.

"I have to get to Idir, but I'll be at your place after my shift... I guess," I said, hurrying out the door. The whole thing was awkward enough without me prolonging it, and I didn't want to drag it out any longer, especially if we were going to have to talk about it later.

"Our place," she hollered after me, and I could have sworn I heard her mumble much quieter, "at least for the next six months."

CHAPTER 5

"Are you planning on leaving the couch today, or are you going to continue to punish me for saving your ass from a prison cell?" Rachel grumbled as she picked up the half-eaten bowl of Ramen from the coffee table.

I shrugged before stuffing a handful of potato chips into my mouth and chewing as loudly as I could manage in an effort to drown her out and soften my own guilty feelings. *What's the point?*

"It's been a week. Have you even checked in at Idir?" She dropped the bowl into the sink with a loud thunk.

My stomach knotted with remorse as I recalled the last conversation I'd had with Matt before I stormed out of work a week ago. He'd been sympathetic about my punishment but chastised me for knocking out the stupid Guard Officer.

I knew he was right—I was ready to punch Derek in the face that night, but I only did it later in an attempt to help Rachel. Him giving me the third degree about it only pissed me off even more. In response, I spent the last five days in the same pair of pajamas on the couch in front of the TV as punishment. Now I had no idea who I was punishing anymore: Rachel and Matt, or myself.

I know, I know. I'm dead weight. Literally and figuratively. My eyes closed, blinking back tears that were stinging my eyes.

Five, four, three, two, one... I let out a long sigh, heaved myself from the sofa, and left the bag of chips behind before stomping down the hall to the bathroom that, of course, had a tub with no shower.

"Why couldn't I be stuck in a place with a shower?" I grumbled too quietly for her to hear me. I filled the tub with hot water, dropping in one of Rachel's homemade peppermint bath bombs. The large, round ball fizzed in the water, and I watched mesmerized as the tiny bubbles spread across the surface. At first, I used them to tick her off because misery likes company and all that. But it seemed like she had a never-ending supply, and they helped me calm down, so I would continue to use them until she asked me not to.

Climbing into the tub, I allowed my muscles to relax as I breathed in the soothing minty vapors. I was so relaxed as I sank into warm water, I had to convince myself to scrub clean before changing my mind about going in to work after all. Matt wasn't expecting me, but I was sure he would be happy to have me there, nonetheless. I finished up quickly, drying myself off with one of the fluffy gray towels from the shelf before pulling on a pair of skinny jeans and a faded black tee. I could hear Rachel shuffling around in her room, so I took the opportunity to sneak to the front door while she was distracted. I couldn't handle her pitying glances. And part of me wanted her approval, so I grabbed my hoodie from the coat rack and headed out the door.

Once I crossed the threshold, the inside of my wrist warmed up, reminding me I wasn't free to just come and go as I pleased. But the sensation wasn't uncomfortable, and it faded after a few moments. My sneakers crunched over the loose pavement as I hurried down the street and examined the little black X inked on the soft flesh of my wrist.

"It's the rune Gebo," Rachel had explained when she placed the mark. "It represents balance and harmony through self-sacrifice. Specifically, it balances the terms of your sentence with the sacrifice of my energy so that we remain connected," she explained. "Please don't test it because it'll be uncomfortable for both of us, to say the least."

I wasn't sure how it worked, but I knew I didn't want to chance it because it would send pain shooting through my body if I strayed from my path for more than a few minutes. It would also alert the matching rune on Rachel's arm. "Why didn't you just stay out of it?" I chastised myself as I pulled my sleeve back down to cover it. *Now I really am a prisoner in every way.*

I pushed through the heavy wooden door of Idir a few minutes later, winded from the exertion after spending so much time on the couch. "Anna!" Nate hollered from behind the bar. His enthusiasm brought Matt dashing in from the office, and he wrapped me in a bear hug, not letting go until I returned the gesture.

The warmth of his body enveloped me, and I couldn't help but melt into his embrace. "I'm glad you're back," Matt said, pulling back too soon. His eyes roamed over me before he leaned down, his lips pressing lightly against my forehead.

"Me, too." I sighed, pulling him close again and burying my face in the crook of his neck where I breathed in the piney scent of his body wash. I was only gone a week, but I already missed him and the comfortable routine of being behind the bar pouring drinks.

"So, how are things with your new living situation?" he asked. I didn't get the chance to answer before a hearty laugh rang out behind him. We turned, our eyes locking on Nate, who was attempting to stifle another bellow only to let out a snort instead. I raised an eyebrow at him, and he put both hands up in mock surrender as he shook his head.

"What? It's not my fault you're an awful roommate. Don't blame me."

"Seriously?" I asked, placing a hand on my hip. "You're the reason she was in the bar to begin with."

"Hey, she called me." He laughed, but it was short-lived as I leaned across the bar top and whipped the nearest towel forward, catching his thigh with the end of it.

"Ouch!" he growled, his eyes flashing yellow for a split second before he turned away. It was easy to forget he was more than human because he rarely let it slip, but he had grown comfortable enough with me over the past year to be off his guard.

Nate, being an unaligned Wolf, kept a very low profile when it came to revealing his true nature. He was only one of three in the whole city, thanks to prejudice from the witches and warlocks. Before me, Matt was the only one who knew what Nate was. He had told me in confidence one night when the three of us were drinking after hours. Probably because there really was no one for me to tell, seeing I had no friends or ties other than the two of them.

"That's for being nosy," I said through gritted teeth before striking at him once again. He danced away from me, barely dodging the end of the towel before Matt snatched it from my hand.

"Tell me you're not being difficult." Matt sighed. "She stuck her neck out for you. You could be in a cell right now." His words were like a punch to the gut, but I knew deep down he was right. *I know that, and I feel like shit for it without you reminding me.*

"What did you want me to do?" I threw my hands up, feeling the sting through my jeans when they came back down, slapping me in the thighs. The groan that escaped my lips turned into a choked sob, and the bar grew unusually quiet around me — the only sound coming from the dull drone of the television in the corner as all eyes landed on me and Matt. Seeing we had an audience, Matt grabbed me by the elbow,

35

steering me toward the stairs in the back, and tossed Nate an apologetic look over his shoulder. But I was the one who deserved an apology if you asked me.

I climbed up toward the second floor to his apartment, crossing the room in only a few strides to stand against the island in the kitchen that doubled as a dining table.

"I'm sorry," he apologized, closing the door before leaning against it as he looked at me, his mouth turned down at the corners with regret.

"For what?" If he was going to apologize, I wanted a detailed list of offenses.

He moved over to where I stood and placed his hands on my hips, his warm brown eyes meeting mine as he held me at arm's length.

"For being angry with you. I know you were only helping Rachel when you intervened, but..."

Anger bubbled through me once again. "You're right; I was only trying to help, and look at what that got me." I let out a huff and closed the space between us, allowing my forehead to fall against his solid chest.

"I'm happy you're not in prison. Though I have to admit that I'm a little jealous I wasn't there to offer you house arrest with me," he smiled slyly. I laughed as I pulled away from him, punching him lightly on the shoulder. He grinned a big toothy grin at me as he pulled me back against his chest, where he buried his nose in my hair, inhaling the scent of my lavender shampoo. As I relaxed into his warm embrace, he released a long sigh pulling me even closer still.

I wanted to hold onto my anger, but he was silent, like he was working up the courage to actually say what he was thinking. "There's something I've been meaning to tell you." I knew from his tone he didn't want to look at me. I stood there, wrapped in his arms, my forehead pressed against his collarbone, afraid that if I moved, he would completely lose his nerve.

"There's a way to get out of your contract with Silas." The words spilled out in a rush, and it took a second for me to register what he said.

Pushing away from him, I moved around the island until I was standing opposite him. "What do you mean there's a way out of my contract?" I asked, turning to face him again. I leaned forward, resting my forearms on the counter, looking him straight in the eyes, and waited.

His fingers raked through his long, dark waves before he placed his palms flat on the counter, leaning forward until his hips settled against the edge.

"There was someone like you before, a Soulless. They were able to get out of their contract with Silas. I don't know any more than that, just that if anyone will be able to help you, it will probably be someone from the Coven."

"And you're barely telling me this now?" My reaction was immediate and harsh, and I regretted it the moment the words left my mouth because it wasn't his fault. He gave a frustrated shake of his head, then turned and strode across the room where he dropped onto the small love seat.

My brain was reeling as I tried to grapple with the knot of guilt forming in the pit of my stomach, while at the same time trying not to let this revelation overwhelm me. *Could it be possible that there's a way out of this? Do I dare to even hope?* My heart beat frantically in my chest as my emotions warred inside of me —excitement battling fear and hope as I paced across the kitchen.

Maybe the answer isn't the witches, maybe it's something to do with the contract itself. I chewed my bottom lip as I considered this because even though Declan had been the one to make my deal, the true owner of my contract was Silas, the Devil himself.

So maybe that was the loophole. But then why wouldn't I need to go directly to Silas himself? Or even to Declan?

"Why someone from the Coven?" It was bad enough that I had just landed myself in trouble with the witches. Now I needed their help with something else. How convenient.

"They know more about supernatural contracts than anyone. When this happened, they were the only ones uninterested in how or why Silas would release a soul, which makes me think they might have had something to do with it," he trailed off.

"Why not Silas? Or even Declan?" I asked.

"Do you really think either of them would willingly tell you how to get out of your contract?" He cocked his eyebrow skeptically at me. *Dammit. He's right; neither of them would do that.*

I just hated that the witches were my only option.

"How long have you known this?"

"Since before you came to work here, but I hadn't thought about it until the night you told me how much you hate it here," he admitted. My heart constricted in my chest, knowing that my honesty had hurt him. "You can ask your new roommate, but I think you're going to need someone much higher up to find the answers you're looking for."

I crossed the room and sat down in his lap, draping my legs over the arm of the couch. His body heat invited me to bury my face into his broad chest while he wrapped me in his strong embrace. My head spun with all the new information. I was confused...and dumbfounded—unable to process it all. Matt, however, was a comfort, and I needed all the comfort I could get in the moment.

"Thank you," was all I could say.

As I snuggled in deeper, the erratic beat of his heart hammered against his ribcage, echoing in my ear. The blood pumped, almost in morse code, spelling out his worry of what I might do with this newfound information. But I wasn't sure if it was because he thought it might get me into more trouble than I was already in, or if he was scared, I might break my contract and never come back.

"Hey, Matt." A sharp rap on the door had us both jumping as Nate called out, interrupting the moment. "Have a minute?"

"Duty calls," I sighed, planting a soft kiss on his lips before getting up and heading toward the bathroom. "I'll be down to help in a minute." He nodded and closed the door behind him, giving me some privacy.

Ugh, how is it that after all of that, I have more questions than answers? Why does everything in this place have to be so damn complicated? I swear it would have been easier if things were as black and white as I thought they were when I was human. I stood in front of the white porcelain sink in the bathroom, letting the water run cold before splashing some over my face. After giving myself a once over in the mirror, I decided to pull my hair up, then took a deep breath, centering myself before I made my way back to the bar, hoping my outburst from earlier was long forgotten.

"Good to have you back," Nate remarked. He nudged me with his shoulder, and I gave him a lopsided grin as we fell into a comfortable rhythm. Nate and I were so used to sharing the cramped space, the two of us danced around one another in perfect harmony, twisting and side-stepping in sync, until the final call rang out for the night.

I wasted no time wiping down the bar and tidying things up before high-tailing it out of the bar, barely stopping long enough for a goodnight kiss. I had no time to waste in this pseudo-life anymore. The sooner I got to Rachel, the sooner I would be on track to breaking my contract and tasting real freedom for the first time since I died.

"Good luck," Matt yelled after me. Of course, he wasn't surprised by my disappearing act after sparking my intrigue.

I ran down the dark street toward my new home, slowing as

I approached the apartment complex. Suddenly, I was less than sure how I was even going to broach the topic with Rachel. I hadn't exactly been the model roommate, so I could only cross my fingers that she would be willing to help me out.

If there really are any Gods out there, I could use an assist right about now. I sent out a silent prayer into the ether, then strengthened my resolve.

CHAPTER 6

You've got this, Anna. No matter what happens, just don't get weird and defensive. A thick layer of sweat clung to the back of my neck, and my thighs tingled with fatigue as I slowed to a stop at the front door. I couldn't remember the last time I'd ran anywhere, and now I knew why.

I turned the doorknob, still wary of the fact that it never seemed to be locked. When I passed over the threshold, the vibrations of Rachel's protective wards offered little comfort, brushing my skin with a surge of soft magic prickles she swore would be fatal to an intruder. If they could get past them, anyway. But despite her promises, I wasn't confident her magic couldn't be overridden.

After all, it had taken some time for me to wrap my brain around the fact that there was a whole supernatural world I knew nothing about, living right under my nose my whole life. And all it took to discover it was dying, so the learning curve was steep, to say the least.

The lamp in the living room glowed softly as I entered the cozy space, and I noticed Rachel had cleaned up after I left. She was sitting at the kitchen table working on something when I closed the door behind me. *She's probably pissed at you for being such a jerk earlier. You need to stop doing that,* I chastised myself as

I stood silently near the door, watching her focus on whatever she was doing.

It took everything I had not to just spill my guts and tell her everything Matt told me. But I knew I needed to try to clear the air between us because as much as I hated to admit it, I wanted her to like me more than anything. I wanted a friend.

"Hey." My stomach knotted, and my foot began tapping out a nervous beat as I waited for her to say something, anything.

She didn't look up at me, but the pen in her hand stilled for a moment. "Hey."

I let out the breath I was holding, feeling the air rush past my lips. "Sorry about earlier. I have this way of being kind of an asshole when I'm feeling sorry for myself. Kind of a hold-over from my human days." I bit my bottom lip and stuffed my hands into the back pockets of my jeans, relaxing a little when her shoulders shook with a quiet laugh.

"I get that. How was work?" she asked. It wasn't the response I wanted, but at least she was talking to me.

"Good. It was nice to do something normal." I slid into the other chair at the table, my heart beating fast in my chest as I watched her scribble notes into the pocket-sized leather-bound notebook in front of her. I took a few calming breaths while I worked up the courage to ask her about my contract with Silas. She was so engrossed in what she was doing, I didn't think she even heard me respond to her question, so I decided to try a different tactic before giving up.

"What are you working on?" My voice was much louder than I had intended, causing me to blush as my knee began to bounce up and down. It was a dead giveaway that my nerves were starting to get the better of me.

"Do you need something?" She looked up, cocking her perfectly shaped eyebrow at me. She slowly closed the book around the slender fountain pen she was using, holding the flap closed so she could focus her full attention on me.

"Why did you bail me out?" I blurted out, surprised by my own question, but it had been on my mind since that night. I just hadn't gotten around to asking.

"You helped me out of a bad situation. It was the least I could do." She shrugged at me, her eyes meeting mine, and for a moment, I could have sworn they flashed red. *Damn, all this stress has me seeing things.* I shook my head, blinking my eyes a few times for good measure.

"But I'm a 'void.'" I rolled my eyes at my own use of the slur.

"Yeah, well, I'm a witch on probation. I guess we make a good pair."

I laughed, nodding in begrudging agreement. I wasn't positive I could trust her yet, but she did go to bat for me with Melinda, so that counted for something. It also didn't hurt that I needed to ask a witch about my contract, and as luck would have it, I happened to be living with one.

"What do you know about contracts?"

"Not a lot. It's not my area of expertise. Why?"

"There are areas of expertise?" I asked, taken aback by this new knowledge.

The slow nod of her head coupled with the quizzical look on her face said, 'Duh, what rock have you been hiding under?'

"What's yours?" I countered, realizing I didn't know that much about witches, or her in general, for that matter.

"Hexes," she shrugged.

"Are all witches like that? Only focused on one thing?"

"Most, but there are some of us who dabble in a little bit of everything. Why the twenty questions?" she asked.

"Curiosity."

She opened her book again to pick up where she'd left off. She obviously didn't want to discuss witch background with me. "The High Priestess."

"Huh?"

"She knows everything there is to know about magical

contracts, but I'll tell you right now, she's not going to be of any help to you." Her pen hovered above the page for a second before she continued on, her tone very matter of fact. "You're not a witch."

Ouch. I was taken aback as her words hit me like a slap to the face, but instead of lashing out, I took a deep breath, releasing it in a long stream as I tried to keep myself composed. *Let it go, just let it go...You need to talk to Melinda, and you can't go without her.*

"What if you went with me?"

She snorted, shaking her head. "Why? She's not going to lift your sentence. She was already more than lenient with you. In fact, I'm surprised she went along with this whole house arrest thing in the first place. I'm sure it was only because she doesn't like Henry Matheson."

My leg bounced triple time, and I bit down hard on my tongue, the sharp sting bringing me back to my senses. I refused to lose my temper. I had a feeling she was being short with me because of the way I'd acted over the past week.

"I can't go without you. You know that as well as I do."

"Yep, and I have better things to do than annoy Melinda with your inane questions. So, thanks, but no thanks." Her lips pursed as she released a loud annoyed breath through her nose. *Fuck it.* I laid my palms flat on the smooth wood grain surface between us and leaned as far into her space as the table would allow.

"I don't care about any of that. I just need to know if there's a way out of my contract with Silas," I admitted. Her sharp intake of breath told me she hadn't been expecting that, but she composed herself quickly, smoothing her face into a mask of indifference. She closed the book once again, placing her chin in her hand, and stared off into space as she contemplated.

Yes! Now I've got her attention. I sat back in the hard wooden chair, allowing my shoulders to release some of the tension.

Her mouth twisted as she thought about it, her pen tapping against her chin. "I don't think it's possible," she replied with a shrug after a few minutes.

"It is. I have it on good authority. But I need to talk to her about it."

"Fine, I'll take you in the morning," her curiosity had been piqued, and it gave me hope that maybe Melinda Farrington would feel the same. "Get some sleep. We need to be there just after dawn—it's when she's most receptive to requests." She picked her things up from the table and headed to her room without another word, leaving me alone with my anxiety.

I dragged myself to my room, feeling the emptiness of it and wishing Matt was there to keep me company. A glance at the clock on the bedside table flashed big red numbers at me, and I flopped down on the bed face first.

Two-thirty. Go to sleep. I rolled over and stared at the wooden beams running across the ceiling as I kicked off my shoes and socks. *If I go to sleep now, I can get a solid three hours.*

I wasn't sure when I dozed off, but about two minutes after I woke up, my alarm went off. I slid my finger across the screen, silencing it just as I rolled out of bed. The wood flooring was cold on my bare feet thanks to the cooler nights, so I hurried to get changed and made sure to grab my hoodie on my way to the bathroom. Unfortunately, a bath would take too long, so I swiped on some deodorant, brushed my fingers through my long waves, and swished some mouthwash before making my way to the living room.

Rachel was already waiting for me, and she handed me a tumbler on our way out the door.

"You are my hero right now." I practically moaned as I accepted the proffered cup, ready to drink it black if need be. It wasn't like me to wake at the crack of dawn, I was more of a night owl, so the steaming cup of liquid smelled delicious.

We stepped out into the crisp morning air, and I looked

toward the mountain, my jaw dropping at the sight in front of us. *Wow! Note to self... get out of bed early more often.* More than a dozen colorful hot air balloons floated lazily across the clear blue sky, and I couldn't help but stop and stare at the sight. I had heard about them but had never seized the opportunity to see them before now.

"Are you seeing this?" I pointed at the closest one, a bright green and blue striped balloon floating close enough to hear the flame as the pilot lifted it even higher above us.

"Only every day." Rachel was unimpressed by the sight as we climbed into her little blue Hyundai. I took a tentative sip as she navigated her car toward our destination, and I was thankful she had added cream and sugar.

"Thanks," I took another drink from the cup, allowing the coffee to warm me from the inside. "How did you know I take cream and sugar?"

"I had no idea. But I take cream and sugar, so I figured if you didn't want it, I would still be able to drink it." She laughed, and I couldn't help but join in. It was pretty genius, after all.

"So, what made you decide to take me to see Melinda?"

"Are you kidding? There might be a way to get out of a deal with the Devil. Obviously, I want to know if it's true." She was clearly excited, but I just shook my head at her. Of course, it was nothing to do with me and everything to do with her own curiosity.

We pulled up outside a charming, stuccoed house settled in near the mountain, but instead of going to the front door, she led me around back to a large wooden barn. The doors were wide open, revealing an expansive space void of the stables I had expected. Instead, the interior had been converted, so it no longer looked like a place that once housed animals.

To one side was a spacious workout area complete with hanging bags, sparring mats, and every kind of fitness machine you could imagine. In the opposite corner at the back of the room were several rows of shelves stacked with bottles and jars, each with a neat handwritten label across the front. Above the shelves were lines of hanging herbs, all in various stages of the drying process. Near the entrance, long, wooden tables with benches were laid out, and I looked toward the sound of stone grinding against stone, to find Melinda mashing something in a large black mortar. It was the ultimate functional space for coven needs.

As we approached, I decided to wait for Rachel to do the talking since I was unfamiliar with coven protocols. My knowledge of Melinda began and ended with her title, and the last thing I wanted to do was piss of the person with the key to my magical cuffs.

"Good morning, High Priestess," Rachel greeted her brightly, flashing a dazzling smile as she bent her head respectfully.

Melinda took a breath, her chest heaving as she closed her eyes momentarily, clearly centering herself before looking up at us. She looked different in her own space than she had in the conference room at the Guard station. More vulnerable maybe, or a little less threatening. Her light brown hair, pulled back into a braid, fell over one shoulder, and I noted the fine lines between her eyes and across her forehead deepened when she scowled at the sight of me.

"Rachel, what brings you here?" Moving the pestle to the side, she wiped her hands on the pristine white apron she wore, leaving light green and brown streaks from the fresh herbs.

"Anna has something she'd like to ask, and you're the only one in the Coven who might be able to answer her." Rachel smiled, dipping her head slightly in a show of respect. *Hmmm, I guess I'm not the only one who doesn't want to piss her off.*

Melinda's mouth formed a tight line, but she didn't say a word as she turned expectantly toward me, a look of disdain coloring her features before she smoothed her expression into a mask of indifference. Blood rushed to my face, the sound of it beating loudly in my ears now that I had her full attention. The last thing I wanted was to be rude, but I didn't think she would appreciate me wasting time by beating around the bush, so I decided to get right to the point.

"I want to get out of my contract with Silas."

"Not possible," she replied without skipping a beat, her expression void of any clues as to what she might be thinking before giving a decisive shake of her head. Just like that, she dismissed us, picking up the pestle once again, resuming her work.

Are you fucking kidding me right now? That's it? Not even an explanation or anything? I was dumbfounded. Her response was so absolute, so final, it left no room for discussion or argument, and I almost turned tail and ran. I allowed myself to hope, and Melinda had crushed my dreams like a bug beneath her shoe without a second thought. My eyes burned with the unshed tears that were threatening to fall, but I refused to give them release. The idea that my afterlife belonged to Silas with no way out had me ready to scream — and I would have if not for Rachel. Her soft touch on my elbow grounded me, giving me the strength to hold it together for a little while longer.

"Thank you, High Priestess. I know how busy you are. I just thought, since you're the most knowledgeable person I know, you might be able to help. But if it's above your expertise..." Her voice trailed off like bait on a hook. The grinding of stone on stone stopped, and I knew Rachel had struck a nerve. "Then, of course, we understand. Thank you for your time." She bowed her head again, then shot me a look that said, 'wait for it...'

"Breaking a magical contract of any kind comes with consequences. But breaking a contract with Silas is nearly impossible and far too costly. You should know that better than anyone, seeing you've already given him your soul." Her eyes were judgmental as she looked me over, but the sadness lacing her voice told me she knew exactly what that cost was. "The only advice I can offer is to let it go." She bent her head over her work, turning her back to us, and before I could insist that she help me, Rachel tugged insistently on my arm.

The angry crunching of the gravel underneath my sneakers matched the annoyance that had built up inside my chest from our brief conversation, and the only person within close proximity for me to take it out on was Rachel.

"What the hell?" I demanded once we were back in the car. "She knows it can be done, and how to do it, too."

"I know that," she seethed, turning the car around to head back down the dirt drive.

"Then why did we leave? She might have told us if we had persisted."

"You don't know her like I do." She sighed. "Once she's given her answer, she's done talking."

I crossed my arms and settled back in the seat, trying to keep my features as neutral as possible. I couldn't do anything about it now. I needed to come up with a plan of my own to convince her later.

"Why are you in trouble, anyway?" I was curious, and it seemed like as good a time as any to ask her about it. She told me before that she was on probation, and Nate had said the same thing the night he brought her into the bar, but neither one of them said why.

"Selling hexes to humans." She shrugged like it was no big deal, but the way she turned away from me to look out the side widow had me wondering.

"You mean like cursing people?"

Please tell me you're not some psycho witch that goes around hurting people. She mentioned the night before that her specialty was hexes, but I had no idea what that meant.

"No, like spells, but not black magic," she snorted.

"But isn't a hex a curse?"

"No, it's just a spell. But most people tend to associate that word with something nefarious. It's a common misconception outside the magical world."

"Well, that doesn't seem so bad," I said, feeling a little sorry for her. "And you got your powers taken for that?" It seemed the witches were even stricter than I first thought.

"No, I got probation for that. My powers were stripped down to their very basic form because the human I sold it to used it on a man who became so obsessed with her that he almost killed her," she admitted. Her face was etched with regret, and I wasn't sure if it was for the woman or for getting caught.

"How is that possible? I thought magical potions and spells were a fairytale."

"Of course you did. Humans aren't supposed to know about magic. That's the point."

I nodded as I thought about it for a minute, then decided I didn't need to know more. I was in enough trouble and needed to focus on figuring out how to get more information from Melinda, not get involved in Rachel's stuff. Besides, there was nothing I could do for her, and I felt like I owed her enough as it was.

The rest of the drive was silent but quick thanks to the fact that we were headed in the opposite direction of the rush hour traffic.

"If you don't mind, I'm just gonna drop you at home, okay? I have some stuff I need to get done." She pulled to a stop at the curb outside the apartment, though she didn't put the car in park as she waited, basically letting me know she was in a hurry. I got out without another word, but before she pulled away, she rolled down the passenger side window, causing me to pause. "Sorry that didn't go the way you wanted it to." She frowned, and I could tell she meant it.

I shrugged, not knowing what so say to her, then watched as she pulled away, leaving me alone in the apartment that still felt foreign to me.

Well, I guess I'm stuck here. At least for the time being, so I might as well make myself more comfortable. I pulled the boxes I'd brought with me out from the bottom of the closet, shaking my head at the crazy mix of things stuffed into each one. *This is what happens when you're forced to move unexpectedly.* I threw my head back and groaned, then started to neatly fold my clothes before arranging them in the drawers of the dresser. I didn't have much, but it was enough to make the space feel lived in.

The last thing I did was set the framed picture of Matt and me on my nightstand, smiling to myself as I thought about the day I took it. Matt wasn't big on pictures, so I'd had to sneak in a selfie of us while he was still sleeping one morning. He still didn't know I had it. In fact, I couldn't remember seeing a picture of him anywhere, which made mine even more special.

I wiped my dusty hands on my jeans, pulled my phone out of my pocket and headed for a quick soak in the tub, glad I had wasted enough time to justify going into Idir. My shoulders ached as I settled into the steamy water, a reminder of all the tension I held during our chat with Melinda, and I soaked myself until the water was nearly cold, then needed to rush to finish up. As I dried off, I rolled my shoulders, then stretched my neck from side to side, annoyed by the fact that even a bath wasn't enough to relieve my tension. After striking out with Melinda, my patience was worn thin, and frustration built in my core even thinking about it.

The urge to let off some steam beckoned to me like a seducing whisper, and I bit my lip as the image of Matt and me wrapped in his sheets sent a shiver of desire through me, urging me to get a move on. I didn't think the house arrest spell would stop me from being at the bar any time, but I hadn't tested it out yet. *Hmmm, maybe it's time to see how flexible this magic leash of mine is.*

I dressed quickly and added a little bit of mousse to my hair, hoping it would help the curls dry neatly and not end up frizzy after seven or more hours of sweating behind the bar. Finally, I swiped a thin layer of lip gloss across my lips before I headed out the door.

The new waitress, Jessica, waved when I walked in, but she didn't stop to chat. Instead, she headed to a table in the corner near the TV, where she switched out an empty glass for a full one.

I rounded the bar as Nate came through the door to the kitchen, leaving it swinging behind him, and I had to jump back to avoid him as he hefted three crates of glassware onto the counter. Grabbing my apron, I picked up a clean towel from the shelf next to him and started to help him dry all the rocks glasses.

"You *know* Rachel, right?" I asked Nate as I slid the glasses carefully onto the shelf.

"Yup."

Really? Yup? Please tell me that getting information from you isn't going to be like pulling teeth. I closed my eyes, then summoned as much patience as I could muster.

"How well?" I set down the glass I was drying and gave him a pointed look.

"I haven't slept with her if that's what you're asking," he said with a chuckle.

I rolled my eyes at him, shaking my head at his nonchalant attitude. His brown eyes sparkled with amusement, but he just shrugged as if to say, *what did you expect?*

"Tell me about her."

"What do you want to know?" He turned toward me, giving me his full attention.

"Anything. Everything."

He laughed. "That's vague."

"Well, she's my new roommate, and I know nothing about her," I shrugged and picked up another glass.

He turned back to his work, and I assumed he was shutting me out like Melinda did, but instead, he began talking while he dried the glasses in front of him.

"Rachel is...well, let's just say she can be naïve. She trusts everyone, even when they prove they can't be trusted."

"What are you getting at?" I stopped polishing the glass I was holding to shoot him a glare.

"Leave it to you to take that personally."

Leave it to you to be an asshole, I thought but decided to let it go. I knew I was overreacting, and it had nothing to do with him.

"Anyway, she's also really loyal. Once you're her friend, you're her friend for life, and for a witch, that's a long time."

He picked up his empty crate and headed back to the kitchen, leaving me with no more than I already knew about her. I narrowed my eyes in his direction. I had a sneaking suspicion he wasn't telling me everything. Maybe I was paranoid, but hell, I could be after all of this supernatural shit had snuck up on me and bit me in the ass. Or maybe he knew as much about Rachel and the witches as I did.

"Can I get some service here?" A mellifluous voice called from behind me. I turned to find a tall, slender woman sitting a few stools down, and wondered how I had missed her as I made my way toward her.

"Sorry about that; I didn't see you come in," I apologized. Her chestnut hair was pulled up into a smart bun reminding me a little of an elementary school principal. Her features were sharp but not unattractive, and I would have guessed she was in her late forties or early fifties based solely on the fine lines at the corners of her eyes.

"It's fine." She waved off my apology with a casual flick of her wrist. "I actually wanted to chat with you."

Wariness settled like a rock in the pit of my stomach, but I laid my towel on the bar and waited patiently for her to continue.

Leaning forward, she beckoned me to do the same with a crook of her long, slender finger. "I overheard you talking with the High Priestess today," she whispered.

"Okay..." The wheels in my head turned, flipping through images of the barn, but I failed to place her anywhere. I couldn't remember seeing anyone else there with us. But no one had ever accused me of paying too much attention to my surroundings. I'd miss my own damn reflection if I walked too fast past a mirror.

"I know how you can get out of your contract."

Holy shit! This is a dream, right? I must be sleeping. The skin on my arm stung when I pinched myself, and I sucked in a breath. *Okay, I'm not dreaming.* My heart skipped a beat before it resumed thudding quickly in my chest, but instead of throwing a dozen questions at her, I bit my tongue and waited. *Stay cool, just keep it together. Don't let her know how bad you want this.* There was only one reason someone would come to me with this. She wanted something.

"What's the catch?" I asked warily when it was apparent she wasn't just going to divulge all the details there and then.

"You have to use the information I give you in a very specific way." She shrugged, lifting her hand to examine her nails under the dim lights, and I knew she was trying as hard as I was to come across casual.

"Like how? Will I have to kill someone?" I leaned forward to whisper as my eyes darted around the room, making sure that no one was paying any attention to us.

"No, nothing like that."

"Fine. What do you want me to do?" I figured I could

handle whatever it was she wanted, as long as it got me back to my old life and I didn't have to get my hands dirty.

"You need to make a deal like the one Silas made with you," she started. "But with that witch over there." She motioned with her eyes toward a nearby booth so as not to draw attention to herself.

You're joking, right? I wanted to laugh, but the look on her face said she was dead serious. *Oh my Goddess, she's fucking serious. What in the hell am I supposed to say to that?*

"You want *me* to make *her* a deal?" I scoffed, the words sticking in my throat. I forced them out in a low, stuttered whisper, feeling the bile rise, burning the back of my throat. "And how exactly am I supposed to do that?" I stood up tall, crossing my arms over my chest as my foot tapped out a panicked rhythm on the thick rubber mat beneath me.

"Figure out what it is she wants, and then..."

Anxiety built in my chest as I watched her sit there unconcerned while I had a mental breakdown. *Who do you think I am, lady, a fairy Godmother? Do you see a magic wand?* I was skeptical, to say the least, especially since it was Declan who had made my deal, not Silas. Then there was the fact that I had no magic of my own and no idea how all of it had even happened in the first place.

"I was dying," I scoffed. "I doubt she's going to make a deal like that."

"You might be surprised." She cocked her eyebrow at me as she shooed me away with her hand, gesturing with her head toward the young woman who looked to be around my age. Now I would be twenty-three forever.

With a sigh, I made a whiskey sour and carried it over to the booth where the woman sat. She was slumped over her phone, her long, blonde hair framing her face like a curtain. She looked tired and worried as she read through the text on her screen, and my heart sped up as I approached her. I wasn't sure if my palms were sweating from my nervousness or slick from the condensation on the glass, but either way, I would lose my nerve if I didn't make my move immediately.

"Looks like you could use another one," I smiled as I set the glass down on the table.

"Thanks." She slid her empty glass toward me, pulling the new drink closer without looking up. "Just add it to my tab."

I stood next to the table, feeling awkward before deciding to dig my heels in and try another tactic. "Are you okay?" I needed to at least get her to talk to me.

"No, but unless you have a genie in a lamp, there's nothing you can do." She sighed.

Without prompting, I slid into the booth across from her and wiped my damp palms on my thighs.

"Are those actually real?" I asked curiously.

"Genies?" She gave me a puzzled look, to which I gave an enthusiastic nod.

"Well, the stories have to come from somewhere, right? I mean, witches and fairies are real. So, who knows."

"Well, I don't have a genie in a lamp, but I may be able to help," I said, my voice wavering. She looked at me, her green eyes curious as she tried to decide whether or not to take me seriously.

"And how are you going to do that?"

Good question. I sat up taller, sucking my bottom lip between my teeth, where I gnawed on it for a moment.

"Well, why don't you tell me what's wrong, and then I'll tell you how I can help. Be as specific as possible."

What if this doesn't work? Or worse, what if it does? Will she be soulless like me? The beating of my heart felt like a humming-bird trying to escape its cage. But rather than dwelling on it, I brushed the feeling aside and leaned forward, resting my folded arms on the table, giving her my full attention.

"Can you stop vampires from hunting one of my siblings?"

she asked, her perfectly arched eyebrow cocked as she sat back against the bench.

"Sure." I gulped, trying to swallow past the lump in my throat as I searched my memory for how this should go down. I had no idea if I could make good on anything I promised. But I needed to try, especially if this might be my only shot. "You'll just owe me."

She scoffed, but as I sat, unflinching, I could tell she was starting to wonder. *I'm going to burn for this, aren't I?* My brain conjured an image of me tied to a pyre, and I could swear I felt the heat across my skin as flames licked me. I shuddered at the thought, knowing I would feel every excruciating minute of that without the sweet release of death.

She shifted in her seat, the vinyl creaking beneath her as she sat up and stared me straight in the eyes. "Okay," she drawled. Her stiff posture told me she was unsure, but all of a sudden, I felt a sort of magical pressure building around us, urging me to keep going, so I did.

"I'm dead serious right now. I can guarantee that your siblings will be safe from vampires, but you have to give me your word that you will owe me."

Reaching my hand across the table, I waited patiently for her to agree, hoping with everything I had that this would get me what I wanted. "What do you have to lose?" I asked, knowing she was right on the verge of saying yes.

"Okay, deal." She reached out, clasping my hand in hers, and we both gave a slight gasp when we felt the snap of magic sealing our deal.

Remorse dropped like a stone into the pit of my stomach, and I wanted to hurl, but I could tell by the jelly-like feeling in my legs I wasn't going anywhere soon. *I hope it was worth it.*

"What happens now?" Her voice cut through my thoughts, and she pulled her hand back to cradle it against her chest. Her eyes were wide with fear as she realized I wasn't kidding, and I wondered if my expression mirrored hers.

"Nothing. Go home and stop worrying." I tried to portray a look of calm confidence despite the anxiety clawing at my insides.

I took a breath, filling my lungs until they burned, then willed my legs to hold me as I stood up from the booth. I grabbed the glasses from the table, pausing for a split second before deciding to head back to the bar without looking back. My hands shook as I set them in the rack to wash, thinking belatedly about the woman who had started the whole ordeal. But when I turned around to find her, she was nowhere to be seen.

"Damn it!" I cursed under my breath. *What did I do?* I lifted my hand, examining the pale flesh under the dim fluorescent lights. We had both felt the sting from the electric snap of the magic as it sealed our deal, but there were no marks of any kind. I had no idea what it meant and no one to ask. I had jumped blindly into something I had no idea about with the misguided notion that this would somehow fix all of my problems. Now, the only thing I had accomplished was adding one more thing to my ever-growing pile of crap, and no way to know what the consequences were for what I had just done.

"What did Selene want?" Nate asked, reaching around me for a Collins glass as I stared at the door, dumbfounded.

"Who?"

"The witch." He gestured toward the now empty stool where the woman had been.

"She wanted to send a drink to someone," I said, letting the lie slip through my teeth.

"Hmm." He shrugged, letting it go as he turned away to deliver the drink he was holding.

What am I supposed to do now? I grabbed a towel from the bucket of sanitizer beneath the counter, ringing it out before running it across the smooth surface of the bar. My mind wandered back to my earlier vision of Matt and me tangled up in bed. But as much as I wanted that release, I was too worked up to even imagine it, and I didn't want to ruin his night because I was too distracted for anything else. I needed to talk to Rachel. See if she had any ideas about what transpired. Unfortunately, that meant I wouldn't be testing out my magical leash tonight.

Thankfully, the bar was dead, and Nate could handle it himself. So I pulled my phone out of my back pocket and sent a quick text to Matt, letting him know I needed to leave early. The second I got a reply, I headed out the door. I was going to need some time to think it all over before I told Rachel about the latest mess I made, and before I could even begin to make a plan on what to do about it, I needed sleep.

CHAPTER 7

A ny other day, the knocking on the front door wouldn't have woken me, but I'd tossed and turned all night, so I hadn't been fully asleep, anyway. I waited for the second knock to come before I dragged myself out of my warm bed to the front door. I assumed if Rachel hadn't answered it the first time, then she probably wasn't at home to open it the second time, either.

By the time I pulled the door open, I was ready to throttle whoever was on the other side as a few quick knocks turned into a stream of them, each one louder than the last.

"What in the hell do you need?" I yelled, flinging the door open wide.

"Good afternoon to you, too, Ms. Westfall," Silas drawled as he stood calmly on my front step in his three-piece pinstriped suit. He gave me a bright smile and ran his fingers through his dark, wavy hair while he waited patiently for me to invite him in.

I stared at him as my brain kicked into overdrive. *What is he doing here? Do I invite him in? What the heck is the protocol for this? Where the hell is Rachel when I need her?* As fast as the questions cycled through my head, my emotions cycled faster, moving from shock to fear, before settling on anger. My go to emotion when I didn't know what else to do.

"Silas." I glared, taking a step back. Then with a sweep of my arm, I invited him inside. He strolled into the small living room, taking a seat in the chair that had originally seemed charming, but now looked ratty with him in it.

As I closed the door behind me, I was keenly aware I was standing in the same room as the Devil, dressed in nothing more than a tank top with pajama shorts, and my emotions flipped again, this time to embarrassment, which flushed my skin bright red. I crossed my arms over my chest self-consciously as he gave me a closed-lipped smirk. I darted into my room, grabbed the robe off the hook behind the door, and pulled it tightly around me. I still felt naked under the fluffy fabric when I returned to the living room, but there was nothing to be done about it.

I made my way across the room, plastering on the most convincing mask of nonchalance I could muster as I took a seat on the couch across from him. My heart sped up as anxious pressure built in my chest, but I pushed it away, reaching once again for anger even though I was fully aware of the dangers it posed.

"What are you doing here?" I asked, my voice dripping with disdain, though my misery, in whatever form, meant his pleasure. My reaction only made him smile wider, setting my nerves on edge.

He carefully lay his briefcase across his lap, releasing the two clasps before lifting the lid and removing a heavy cream-colored sheet of paper.

Holy shit! Is that my contract? It has to be my contract. What else would it be? My heart raced wildly, and my head spun. Was he here to release me from my contract—no, I wouldn't allow myself to drown in the shallow pool of hope when there was the ever-present danger of being drowned in the vast ocean of disappointment. I needed to compose myself, ignore the urge to whoop and holler until I heard the words come out of his mouth.

Silas was known for playing mind games, hence the hell on earth sentence. It was clever, if you asked me. Stick me in a place just out of reach of my siblings, knowing I gave up my soul to fulfill a promise to watch over them. Give me immortality, but no way to dull the madness in my mind. But despite all of that, his word was his bond, and all I needed were those sweet little words, and I'd be free. *Please Goddess, let this be over.*

I braced myself, trying not to shake from the anticipation. That crazy witch at the bar the night before was right. I was going to get to go back to my life and forget this nightmare that had been my existence for the past few years. I wondered briefly if I get to go back to the day I died or if I just go back now like nothing ever happened. Either way, I would be happy, so I pushed the thought away to focus on what he had to say instead.

"Imagine my surprise when I found this sitting on my desk this morning," he said coolly, closing the case and returning it to the floor near the chair. He held the sheet gingerly between his fingertips as he looked over the document casually. "It's very old-fashioned to broker a deal over a handshake, but it's valid, nonetheless." He held it out to me, and I accepted it before quickly giving it a once over. My excitement faded as I realized that this wasn't my contract after all— this was the agreement I'd made with the woman from the bar last night.

"What do I do with this?" I held the sheet of paper up in one hand as I pointed to it with the other.

"It's a contract." His tone edged toward bored as he stated the obvious. "The contract for the deal you made last night, to be exact." I sat there holding onto the contract, not sure what to do with it or why he had brought it to me. "I agree, it's sloppy work. You didn't even get her to agree to give up her soul, but she's important in the witch community, and you're obviously new to this. So, I'll let it slide—this time." He emphasized the last two words with the raise of his eyebrow as he stared down his nose at me, lips pursed. "The fact that it showed up on my desk in the first place means that we are obligated to uphold it, and she'll get what she asked for. But when she does, she will owe you whatever it is you wish to receive."

My mind was reeling as he rattled on. It was hard enough to wrap my brain around the fact that I had actually made a binding deal, let alone one that landed Silas in my living room. Maybe this is what the witch had been talking about. If I made a deal like mine, then I could use the favor I requested to get me out of my contract.

"Can I request my freedom?" I asked, immediately cringing when he threw his head back, releasing a deep, hearty laugh that lasted what felt like an eternity before composing himself once again.

"Sorry, you truly are comedic. That will serve you well. Which brings me to the reason I'm here. I want to offer you an internship. You have a gift. Not just anyone could have made that contract happen." He pointed to the paper I still held in my hands. "I want you to consider working for me."

"Are you freaking kidding me? You stole my soul, sentenced me to this place, and all too recently, laughed in my face. There is no way in hell I am going to work for you."

The irony in my choice of wording was not lost on me, but it wasn't like I could take it back. I crossed my arms and sat back on the couch with a huff, feeling stupid for believing the witch in the first place. Silas was off his rocker if he thought he could waltz in here and have me jump at his offer. That was how I ended up in this situation in the first place.

"Anna, be reasonable," he said, losing all formality and calling me by my first name. His deep timbre was soothing, and I wondered for the briefest of moments if he had the ability to compel me the way I had heard a vampire could, because I had the sudden urge to move toward him. My breathing became shallow as I relaxed into the sound of it, and I considered just nodding my head in acceptance. Instead, in a moment of clarity, I grabbed hold of the anger still simmering deep in my core, pulling it to the forefront as I shook off whatever had come over me.

"I want my life back," I seethed.

"I don't make deals for souls I already own." He leveled me with his gaze. His tone, firm but not unkind, caught me off guard, considering who I was speaking to, but it also left me speechless, long enough for him to continue. "I know that you feel wronged, but a deal is a deal, and I'm offering you the opportunity to do something bigger. And, if you prove yourself worthy, I will lift the boundaries of your sentence, and you can freely roam the Earth." He leaned back, putting even more distance between us, and I could breathe again. Placing his elbows on the arms of the chair, he steepled his fingers together while settling in as if to wait patiently for my reply.

My first instinct was to deny his offer again, but the idea of being able to at least leave the city had me giving his proposal a little more thought. It was certainly tempting, considering I complained about that very thing to Matt just a few weeks before, and the idea of being able to leave here already made it feel like less of a prison sentence.

Maybe I don't need to be released from my contract after all... maybe I can still fulfill the promise I made to my mother and take care of them. I could make them understand...

"Will I be able to visit my family?" I brought my hand to my mouth, where I nervously chewed on my thumbnail.

"Only from a distance. They wouldn't recognize you and would go mad if you tried to convince them of who you are." It was like he had anticipated what I might do and squashed my vision before it could even be fully formed.

Damn it! Okay, that plan is out the window. Can I live with that? I tapped my chin with my finger as I chewed my bottom lip. *I guess it would be like I'm their guardian angel.*

"So, I can't interact with them, but I can check in on them?" I hoped desperately that seeing my siblings might be enough to satisfy me.

"Yes, but again, it's a moot point unless you prove yourself first, and it won't be easy."

What if this is just a new way to punish me?

"I need some time to consider."

"You have until I walk out that door," he said with a point of his slender finger toward the front door. He sat back, a sly smile gracing his thin lips, and my heart started racing now that he had put me on the spot.

"Ugh. This is ridiculous. You know that, right?" I said, my voice thick with exasperation.

"I'm the Devil. I've been known to be difficult." He shrugged.

"Answer something first," I said, not expecting him to actually agree, but when he gave a slight nod of his head, I hurried on with my question before he could change his mind. "Has anyone ever gotten out of a contract with you?"

"No." The honesty of that simple word washed over me, and even though I had expected it, it still broke my heart as the last ray of hope I'd held onto for the past few days crumbled to dust. In all honesty, it didn't matter. I knew deep down I was going to take the offer either way.

"Fine. I'll do it," I agreed.

"Fantastic." He gave a sharp clap of his hands that made my heart jump into my throat. "Your training will start soon." He stood with enthusiasm, buttoning his jacket before picking up his briefcase while I sat there, dumbfounded.

"What do you mean, training?"

"Is that a serious question?" he asked, a look of concern coloring his features. "Did you not read that contract? I can't have you running around making deals with people that benefit them and get me nothing in return," he let out a laugh. "So, in the meantime, you need some training."

"Not now?" I demanded.

"Of course not. I believe you have other obligations... right?" I wasn't sure if he was referring to my house arrest or Idir, but it didn't matter because I was ready to get down to business. The sooner I proved myself, the sooner I would be able to leave the city.

"No," I shook my head vehemently. "There's nothing more important I need to be doing."

"Sorry, love. Until I can negotiate you out of your house arrest, you're stuck with it," he shrugged. "It's either that, or you can go to the High Priestess yourself. But we both know how well your last run-in with the witches went." He gestured around the apartment with his free hand. "And once she finds out about your new contract, she's going to want your head," he teased. *What the hell does that mean?*

He stared me down, almost daring me to go to Melinda myself. The crazy thing was that a big part of me wanted to, but an even bigger part wanted to make sure I got my freedom. So, instead of arguing, I bit my tongue and gave him a hard nod. He turned and headed to the front door, letting himself out, while I continued to sit on the couch replaying everything that had just happened.

The whole exchange took less than half an hour, and, once again, everything I knew had changed. This was the third time in less than a month. *I must be going for a record*, I thought, rolling my eyes in frustration.

Spotting the sheet of paper still sitting next to me on the cushion, I picked it up and read it again, this time a little more carefully. I must have somehow skipped over the name inked in heavy black font near the top of the page, but now, it was the only thing I could focus on. According to the contract

I held in my hand, Genevieve Farrington now owed me a debt of my choosing. I'd made a deal with the daughter of the High Chair of the West Coast Coven, who'd shown me leniency. No wonder Silas said she was going to want my head.

Shit, what did I do? I fell back onto the couch, slapping my forehead as I let out a loud groan. *Why had the witch at Idir sent me in Genevieve's direction? She had to have known that both of our asses would be on the line, certainly hers more than mine. Maybe she thought that I would get all the blame? But to find out one of her own coven members betrayed her would be a hundred times worse... I could only imagine she'd be out for blood.*

Either way, I was in deep, but what was done was done.

My lungs expelled a long breath, an image of Melinda holding my severed head on a platter flashed through my mind, fear gripping my chest, followed by relief that I hadn't bartered for Genevieve's soul. Finally, I was overcome with elation of my newfound leverage. The daughter of my jailer owed me a favor, and it wasn't one I was planning on wasting.

Carefully folding the sheet in thirds, I headed to my bedroom, where I put it in the back of my dresser, hoping it would be safe. I wasn't sure if I needed to keep it or if Silas had merely given it to me as proof that my agreement with Genevieve was binding, but I didn't want to leave it lying around.

The click of the front door closing was unmistakable, and I shut the drawer before peeking my head out of my bedroom door. I rushed across the room to help Rachel, who was struggling under the weight of three large paper bags.

"Thanks," she breathed heavily, allowing me to slip one of the bags from under her arm while she smashed the other one to her and readjusted the third that was once again slipping through her fingertips. Together, we hauled them to the kitchen counter, where we unloaded them and began putting things away. I noticed two out of the three bags were stamped with the logo from the local produce store.

Seriously? I can't survive on this rabbit food. I grumbled internally and placed the baby carrots on the counter. Rachel was a stickler for fresh fruits and vegetables, which she restocked the refrigerator with every few days, and while I didn't mind them, what I really wanted were potato chips.

"I grabbed some of these for you," she smiled, pulling a bag of chips out of the bag in front of her. It was like she read my mind, and it was both awesome and startling at the same time.

"Did you just hear my thoughts?" I asked suspiciously, taking it from her hands. Her light, airy laughter filled the room, causing me to let go of the breath I had been holding when she shook her head at me in disbelief.

"Of course not, silly. You went through two bags of these in one week. It normally takes me over a month." She shrugged. "I'm perceptive; what can I say?"

Nodding in agreement, I opened the bag, lazily popping a few of the perfectly crisped pieces into my mouth while she continued moving around the kitchen. The whole thing felt comfortable for the first time since I moved in, and I was suddenly glad to have found a friend outside of work, regardless of the circumstances.

"So, how was your afternoon?" Her eyebrows raised at me with curiosity. "You're up earlier than usual, and you seem preoccupied."

"Fine, I guess," I shrugged.

"You had a visitor." It was a statement, not a question, and I wondered how she could possibly know that. I glanced around for any signs of Silas, self-conscious about his visit, but there was not a thing out of place.

"The wards," she said, answering my inner thoughts. "I always know when someone has come in or out, and they won't let in anyone intending harm, so it must have been a friend. My guess is Matt." She wiggled her eyebrow at me. I knew what she was thinking, but there was no way I was going to do stuff here with him when we had all the privacy we wanted at his place.

"Are you sure they're not broken?" I sighed, resting my elbows on the counter as I leaned forward.

"What's that supposed to mean?" she sniped, taking offense at me questioning her protections.

It means that your wards were supposed to zap him.

"I need to tell you something. But you have to promise not to get mad at me." I bit my lip as I watched emotions cycle across her face, going from surprise to curiosity, then fear, before finally landing on suspicion.

"I'll try." She gave a terse nod, her dark curls bouncing with the movement.

"It was Silas." I grimaced when I said his name, and a shiver ran through me as I tried to physically shake it off like some vile thing I could get rid of.

Her brows shot to her hairline. "The Devil?" She gasped as her hand moved to cover her expression of shock. "The Devil was in this apartment?"

"Yep." My voice sounded almost bored now that the whole thing was over and done with.

Well, she took that better than I expected. At least she's not yelling...yet. I slumped against the counter, the edge digging uncomfortably into my hip.

"Why? Why was he here? How did he get past the wards?" she asked, more to herself than me.

I waited patiently as she paced back and forth from the kitchen to the front door, muttering to herself under her breath. Finally, she looked at me, and I stood up straight under her scrutiny.

"What in the hell did he want?" Her voice was barely more than a whisper, which was scary enough in and of itself.

I looked at the planks of hardwood beneath my feet, not

wanting to meet her gaze. "He offered me a job." I tasted the tang of blood before I realized I was chewing my lip, and it stung as I ran my tongue over the swelling wound.

"Tell me everything. Right now." She grabbed ahold of my elbow to drag me to the same spot I'd occupied a short while before and waited for me to tell her all about what had happened.

Several shocked gasps and a few repeats later, she was still sitting in front of me, hand over mouth, eyes wide with shock, while she let the information sink in.

"Oh. My. Goddess." She settled back into the chair for the first time in our conversation. "How could you do this, Anna? I vouched for you. I took responsibility for you, and now we are both going to end up in the Prism," she whispered, her eyes growing even wider with fear. Getting to her feet, she shook her head in denial, staring at me expectantly.

"What the heck is the Prism? And you weren't a part of this, so you shouldn't worry about it. I made this mess, and I'll get myself out of it," I explained, trying to reassure her while my own mind started a downward spiral.

"The Prism is a magical prison. Where you get to live your worst fears over and over again until you go insane. It's where they send the worst of the worst, and by making a deal with Gen-freaking-Farrington, you basically just guaranteed us a one-way ticket. It doesn't matter that I had nothing to do with it. You're my responsibility," she argued. "Why in the heck would you make a deal with her, anyway?"

"Because the stupid witch at the bar told me it was the only way to get out of my contract!" I yelled, my frustration mirroring hers.

"What witch?"

"I don't know who she was. She came up to me and said she overheard our conversation with Melinda."

She was silent for a moment, and I could tell she was

thinking the same thing I had when the woman approached me. She hadn't seen anyone else there, either.

"And she specifically told you to target Genevieve?" Her eyes begged me to think hard, to be sure, before I answered.

Well fuck, now you have me second guessing myself. But I was sure she had specifically pointed out Genevieve.

"Yes."

"And that didn't raise any alarm bells with you?" Her voice verged on frantic.

"How was I supposed to know who she was?"

"I don't know, maybe take an interest in someone other than yourself for two minutes and ask them their name," she shouted, throwing her hands in the air with frustration. "You're making rash decisions that aren't going to get just you into trouble, but me too!" She rubbed her face as she paced back and forth between the kitchen and living room.

"Well, then you should have stayed out of it in the first place," I shot back angrily, hands on my hips. "You think you did me a favor by stepping in and 'saving' me from jail." I made air quotes with my hands. "Well, I have news for you; I can't be saved. This is hell. Literally. And all you did was make it worse because now, I'm stuck here with you." I gestured at the space around me.

"Then why did you let me?" she asked quietly. "You could have opted for jail time."

"What choice did I have? There was nothing I could have done in that situation that wouldn't have made it worse."

"Well, thanks for the honesty. Now I need to figure out what to do about this mess because you may not care what happens to either of us, but I do. And I don't want to go to prison because you're making dumb decisions," she admitted, the previous anger in her voice replaced with weariness. "You need to turn him down because nothing good can come from this, and you know it."

"I can't."

"Can't or won't? Because you have choices. You may not like them, but you have them," she insisted.

"Then I guess I'll have to figure it out. Because I'm not doing that," I said. "We'll just have to agree to disagree." At the finality of my tone, she headed to her room without another word and slammed the door behind her, and like that, I was left alone with my thoughts once again.

I was fuming mad, and I wasn't sure if it was because of our conversation or the fact that reality had finally smacked me in the face. I'd been so consumed with the idea of getting freedom and justifying myself to Rachel, I hadn't had time to process what it all meant. But now, because of my new contract, I was going to have to figure out how to be okay with stealing people's souls. Either way, this was more than I had bargained for when I opened the door for Silas.

"She doesn't get it." I shook my head, closing my eyes to try to block it all out as I tried to push away the guilt and self-loathing that were gnawing at me.

Rachel didn't get it. I had to work for Silas. It was the only chance I was ever going to get to be free of this place. The shame and anxiety were crushing, weighing my shoulders down with the hatred for myself bubbling inside me every time I thought about condemning another soul—it would be enough to kill me if I wasn't already dead.

She called me selfish, and I was, but I didn't have the luxury of being anything else. If I wanted to see my family again, I was going to have to prove myself, regardless of the circumstances.

I had already accepted Silas's deal, and he wouldn't take too kindly to me changing my mind. He'd be more likely to fry my ass in the deepest pit of hell for an eternity. I made my way back to my room and pulled the sheet of paper out from its hiding place to look it over again before I went to work. Even holding it now, it was still surreal, and my chest tightened with frustration at the thought that I had probably had the ability to broker deals all along and had just now found out about it.

I wasn't sure who I blamed more about that. Matt, who had known a possible way out this entire time; me, who never thought to search out a remedy for my predicament before; or Declan, who was responsible for actually making my deal and dumping me off here in the first place. Honestly, I couldn't be mad at Matt because before a few weeks ago, he hadn't had any reason to think I was unhappy with where I was in the first place. As for Declan, I had not seen his face since the day of my sentencing, and I doubted he had any more information than I did. That meant the responsibility for my situation landed solely on my shoulders, though that didn't sit well with me, either.

"This is just my luck," I muttered as I folded up the sheet once again, placing it back where it was before and slamming the drawer shut. There was no use in worrying about it now. I set my elbows on top of the dresser and stared at my reflection in the mirror, noticing the faint blue shimmer around the edges of my irises. I pushed myself away from the mirror, unable to look at myself another moment.

This truly is hell. He has put you in a place that is going to make your soul so dark; even if you are free, you'll never enjoy it. I stifled a scream, cursing the day I ever met Declan or Silas. Then I grabbed tight onto my anger, strengthening my resolve. Silas was going to see what I was capable of. I was going to prove myself worthy of getting the boundaries of my sentence lifted, and then I would leave this place for good.

CHAPTER 8

A re you fucking kidding me right now? The bourbon from the glass I carried dripped down my shirt, leaving a dark stain across the light blue cotton. Five days had gone by since my new deal with Silas and my fight with Rachel; Idir was stifling, and I was ready to fight. It didn't matter with who.

"What in the hell is wrong with you?" I snapped, turning on Nate. It was the third time we had bumped into each other in the last half an hour.

"Me? What's wrong with you? It's like you're only half here tonight. I've had to replace more wrong drinks than I can count —we might as well be giving them away," he growled as his irises flashed yellow, warning me that the wolf was simmering just under the surface. "Whatever. I'm out of here in five anyway, and then Matt can deal with you."

I grabbed a towel from the bar and dabbed at my chest. He was right. I had been off all night—spilling drinks, breaking glasses, and getting orders wrong. I couldn't help it. I was on edge waiting for Silas to show up and start my training, and every day that passed with no word just had me more and more wound up. I was annoyed as hell, and everything was getting on my nerves. *What if he changed his mind?* He was taking so long, I was beginning to think I had just made it all up, like one of those really lucid dreams where you can swear something happened, but in reality, none of it had.

A hand on my shoulder made me jump, and my throat tightened as I fought my fight or flight instinct. Nate must have called Matt down before he left and told him what had happened because when I looked over my shoulder, Nate was nowhere to be seen, but Matt was there, looking like he wasn't sure whether to stay or run. Apparently, Nate hadn't been the only one on the receiving end of my wrath lately.

"Here's a clean one," He handed me one of my t-shirts from his apartment.

"Thanks," I grimaced, taking it from him as I ducked around him and headed toward the women's bathroom, where I swapped it out, then dropped the wet shirt on the handrail of the stairs to pick it up later. My chest was still sticky from the alcohol, but I couldn't have cared less. I just wanted to finish the night, so I could go upstairs and shower before I crawled into bed next to Matt. At least in his apartment, I could shower and not die a little every time Rachel shot a judging look at me.

I'd been more than willing to face the pain for breaking my house arrest to avoid more confrontation, but, thankfully, that wasn't the case. Because even if I was in the apartment upstairs, I was technically still in my place of employment.

Matt hadn't asked any questions. He knew something was bugging me. But the longer this went on, the more I knew it in my gut that eventually, I was going to have to tell him about everything that had happened with Silas and my new agreement. I was dodging that conversation because he was going to be furious with me, and I couldn't risk losing the one stable thing I had going for me right now.

"Is everything okay?" He placed his hand on the small of my back, his warm brown eyes looking deep into mine. His reassuring touch made the stress release slightly from my shoulders, and I gave him a nod as I turned back to my work.

"Everything is fine. I'm having an off day. It happens." I shook my head. He didn't look convinced, but he let it go anyway, probably because he had enough on his plate. The bar was due for an inspection with the Guard soon, and he had been up until all hours of the morning recently, making sure the books were in order. If he was off by even a dollar, he could be fined, and they could revoke his license. With all the tension lately because of what happened with me and the warlock in the alley, he needed to be extra careful. My heart ached with the undue stress I'd caused him, but I also secretly enjoyed the fact that he could sympathize with the unfair treatment I'd received.

"Why don't you go finish up with the paperwork? It's slow enough out here that I can handle it on my own," I reassured him. A look of relief crossed his face before being replaced by one of concern, and I was worried he was going to turn down my offer since I hadn't exactly been a model citizen recently.

"Are you sure? I know things have been rough lately. I don't want to add more to your plate," he replied, then breathed a sigh of relief when I nodded.

"I'm sure. Go take care of business, boss man, but leave enough energy for me later." I winked as I gave him my sauciest grin. He wiggled his eyebrow at me suggestively before pulling me in for a quick kiss that left me breathless as his hands roamed down my body. Then he pulled away, laying one smaller kiss on my forehead before he turned and disappeared down the short hallway to his office.

I grabbed a tray and a towel and started wiping down booths and tables, collecting empty glasses as I went. Jessica and Nina were both off on Wednesdays, since it was always the slowest night of the week, meaning there were no servers to work the floor. That meant everyone came to the bar to order, and when it wasn't too busy, I would go through and clean up.

"Can I get another Gin and Tonic?"

I turned to the petite pixie in the booth next to me and gave her a nod. Then I picked up my things and headed to the bar, where I filled a glass with ice before grabbing the bottle of Gin from the shelf. *One...two... three...four...* I counted as I poured, then topped it off with tonic water and a lime wedge. *Was she there before?* I asked myself. I could not, for the life of me, remember seeing her before, so I figured Nate must have made the drink the first time, and now I was chastising myself for not checking on her sooner.

"Here you go." I set the drink on the table in front of her.

Red, puffy eyes looked up at me, tears staining her tanned cheeks, and my heart broke for her. "Are you okay?"

"Yeah, sorry," she said with a sniffle, but just as I turned away, she let out a sob that had me turning back to take the seat across from her. "I'm sorry." She brushed the tears away with the back of her hand to no avail.

"Why don't you tell me what's going on?" I encouraged, and while my brain protested, my arm automatically reached across the table to take her soft, delicate hand in mine. It was like I couldn't control it, and, at the same time, my heart beat faster with the excitement of possibly making another deal.

"My mate left me for a fairy," she wailed, pulling a handful of napkins out of the dispenser with her free hand to help staunch the flow of the latest round of tears.

"I gave him everything, and all he had to say was, Lucinda, you're not fun anymore, and I need something more in my life. What the hell does that even mean?" She sobbed again, louder this time. "There's no one more fun than a pixie, especially not a damn fairy." She scowled, her full lips pouting as she dabbed the corners of her eyes with the already wet napkins.

I reached over and plucked out several more, then handed them across the table with one hand while accepting the messy pile with the other. I dropped the wet mess onto my empty tray, then rubbed my hands across my jeans as I tried not to be grossed out. I wasn't sure what to say to her. *Is it even possible for a fairy and a pixie to be 'together'?* I hadn't the foggiest idea, so I said the first thing that came to mind.

"I'm so sorry. He was an idiot to let you go—anyone could see that. You're obviously a catch." I patted the back of her hand gently. It was the honest truth; she had a down-to-earth beauty to her, the kind that needed no make-up or frills. Her long, dark hair flowed in big, loose ringlets framing her face, accentuating her dark brown eyes. "Is there anything I can do?" The magic building between us was palpable, the electric buzz in the air crackled around us, just waiting for her to give me an opportunity, and I leaned forward, licking my lips in anticipation.

"I want someone who's going to love me the way I love them. Someone, I can spend the rest of my life with who will never take advantage of me just to throw me away. Unless you can give me that, then no, there's nothing you can do for me." She sighed, shaking her head and closing her eyes. She pulled her hand from mine, covering her face while she let her sorrowful tears leak through her fingers. "I'm just so tired of falling for the wrong guys."

"I can help you." I glanced around, making sure that no one was paying any attention to us. The few patrons in the room were sipping their drinks, either too focused on their phones or the TV screen to notice us, and the fact that there was a woman crying only made them less tempted to even glance over. Weird how crying women had that effect on people. "What if I could give you exactly what you wanted?"

"How? Are you some kinda fairy godmother or something?" She hiccuped, wincing as her slip of the word fairy brought more fat tears to the corners of her eyes.

"Something like that." I shrugged. Her eyes grew wide, and she tentatively slid forward in the seat before leaning forward, placing her forearms on the table.

"Can you grant me a wish?" she asked eagerly.

"Not a wish, exactly," I hedged, not sure it would even work again. But the magic I felt flowing around us told me I should at least try. "More like a deal."

"Anything you want," she replied, not skipping a beat. The magic around us swelled, pushing in on me, almost as if it were coaxing me on. It pushed me to give her what she wanted in exchange for the one thing she could not afford to give me.

I can't believe I'm going to do this. My stomach turned, and I bit down on my cheek. I wasn't so sure I was cut out for the job, after all. Then I pictured the smug look Silas would give me if I had to tell him I couldn't do it. It was enough to send me over the edge. *This is what you signed up for, now do your job.*

"I want your soul," I said calmly. I reached my hand out across the table as I placed all the levity I could muster into my words. I hoped she would understand the seriousness of what she was doing, but at the same time, deep down, I knew she wouldn't.

Just like most living creatures, she wanted instant gratification, and she was willing to give me whatever I wanted in return without considering the consequences of her actions. I watched as a slight shiver ran down her spine, but she strengthened her resolve and reached out, grasping my hand in hers and giving it one firm shake. The magic condensed, wrapping itself around our clasped hands and pulling almost painfully tight, then sealing our deal before either of us could pull away.

For a moment, I smelled the unmistakable tang of gunpowder, but it was gone so quickly, I chalked it up to a memory of my own deal with Declan. Just like Genevieve, she pulled her hand to her chest, cradling it there as if she had been burned by the magic, but I was sure it was just shock. After all, I wasn't feeling any ill effects from it.

Her cheeks flushed pink as realization washed over her stunned features. "You weren't kidding," she breathed, scooting as far away from me as the booth would allow. Sweat beaded on her forehead, her eyes wide as saucers as she began to grasp what she had just given away. My mouth opened to speak, but the groaning of the heavy front door caught my attention.

You've got to be fucking kidding me, I swore internally as the man who had been featured in my nightmares since the day I died stalked toward me.

CHAPTER 9

What is Declan doing here? Hatred washed through me. He had no business being here unless his goal was to make my afterlife even more miserable. Though the bitter scowl he wore as he stomped across the room suggested that was exactly what he was there to do.

His ice blue eyes glowed around the irises as he walked toward me in his three-piece suit, looking like he'd come straight out of a business meeting.

"What in the hell is this?" he demanded, slamming the paper down on the table in front of me.

"I should go." Lucinda gathered her purse and coat and slid out of the bench. Just then, another young pixie came through the door, and the elated feeling in my chest told me he was meant for her. The golden thread connecting them might have also clued me in, but even without it, I knew he was her soulmate.

"Hey, Lucinda," I called after the woman's quickly retreating form. A big part of me wanted to do a happy dance, but I suppressed the urge.

She turned back to me, her eyes lighting up when I pointed a finger toward the new guy and gave her a wink. Unfortunately, I wouldn't be able to bask in the feeling of success because Declan still stood there staring daggers at me until I acknowledged him.

"Sit down and stop making a scene," I chastised. "I need to get drinks. If you want to stick around, that's your prerogative, but don't make me kick you out." My voice didn't shake despite the mass of butterflies in my stomach, though my legs were a little weak as I exited the booth. I shook off the feeling of his glare before doing a lap around the room to collect any empty glasses I could find, using the time to regain my composure. Unfortunately, it hadn't picked up in the time I spent talking to Lucinda, so I slowly made my way back to the booth before I was ready.

Declan sat there, long legs stretched out, sipping on the gin and tonic Lucinda had left behind untouched. From the look on his face, he would have rather been drinking dishwater, but I wasn't about to try to make him comfortable. Besides, I was sure he was just drinking it to blend in after storming in and making a scene in the first place, but it still unnerved me to see him sitting there.

I picked up the sheet of paper from the table top and read over it, noting the differences from the one still stuffed in the back of my dresser at home. Where the contract for Genevieve said, "Debt unconfirmed," this one had "Soul" written in heavy black script. At the bottom of the page, under both of their names, each of the contracts had a footnote with the words, 'Verbal agreement made official by a handshake between willing participants.' *Interesting.*

"What are you doing here?" I asked Declan as casually as I could, and he cringed as I folded up the sheet and stuck it in my back pocket.

"You do realize that's a legally binding document, right?" he drained the last of the contents from the glass before pushing it toward me across the table.

"What do you want?"

"Well, I'm your new mentor, of course," he laughed wryly.

"No way," I said firmly, anger beginning to bubble within me. *What in the hell was Silas thinking? He was supposed to mentor me, not this asshole.*

"You think I wanted this?" he snarled, pounding his fist on the table hard enough to shake the glass. "You are an incompetent little girl who has no business going around making deals that you know nothing about," he whispered loudly, the alcohol he had just finished still lingering strong and hot on his breath. It wasn't unpleasant, but Juniper had never been my favorite.

"Obviously, I know more than you think, or you wouldn't be sitting here right now, would you? And who are you to come in here and call me incompetent?" I shot back.

"Me having to show up here unannounced only proves my point. Silas told you not to make any more deals until you had a mentor, and it took you less than a week to defy his orders. And if you can't take orders from Satan himself, then you definitely won't take orders from me. You're a stubborn, half-cocked disaster just waiting to happen," he seethed. His eyes shone with anger as he leaned on his right arm over the table, looking more like a chastising father than a mentor.

"Well, if Silas had shown up to mentor me sooner, then maybe none of this would have happened," I said with a snarky sweep of my hand. "It's not my fault the opportunity showed up here in front of me. I just took advantage of it." I sat back; my lips pursed as I stared defiantly at him. I knew I was acting childish, but people had a way of bringing that out of me lately. "Besides, you don't have to worry about it. I'll be calling Silas first thing because there is no way I'm working with you. He obviously wants me to do this, or he wouldn't have made me the offer, so he can train me himself, or I'm out." I jutted my chin out confidently.

He shook his head at me and laughed, his blond hair falling

lazily across his forehead for a moment before he smoothed it back into place with an unconscious brush of his hand. The tingle between my thighs at his gesture was unexpected, causing my heart to speed up as my breaths became shorter and shallower. I bit my tongue at my response to him, trying to stop the annoyingly inappropriate thoughts that were running through my mind.

You are so messed up, I thought as I pushed the thoughts away. I hated him—at least I thought I did, but all I could think of was how hot the sex would be. That is, until he opened his mouth again.

"It's cute that you think you have any say in this situation. You were better off staying under the radar. Now, he has you exactly where he wants you, and this will go one of two ways. Either you'll follow the rules and let me train you, or life as you know it will get considerably worse." He stood, buttoning his jacket before smoothing out any imaginary wrinkles in the expensive fabric, just like Silas had in my apartment before he continued on. "If you think otherwise, you're a fool," he said with a nod. "And don't bother trying to tell anyone about your new... opportunity. It will only complicate things further." He turned away and disappeared through the door as quickly as he appeared, leaving just the lingering scent of leather and juniper. Something about it left a niggling feeling in the back of my mind, and once again, I chastised my body for its response to him. He was attractive, I couldn't deny that. But he had also ruined my life, and I needed to remind myself that he was still the enemy here.

I stared at the closed door, wondering how things could possibly get any worse for me. He obviously didn't remember I was already in hell, so this really was rock bottom for me.

I slid my cell phone out of my apron and typed in the phone number printed neatly across the letterhead of the contract, noticing for the first time that the name written above it was

"Silas A. Tan." Clever. It was written right there in plain script for everyone to see, but I was sure no one would even notice.

"What can I do for you, Anna?" asked the deep voice on the other end of the line. I had been too busy scrutinizing the contract to notice it had stopped ringing.

"What's your game here?" I asked heatedly.

"Ah, I take it Declan finally graced you with his presence. I was wondering how long he would make you wait. My bet was at least a year." He chuckled. "I'm guessing he was unhappy with your newest stunt."

I could practically hear his grin through the line.

"You never told me he would be the one to mentor me. I'm not working with him," I complained.

"Declan is well qualified to mentor you. I have every confidence that he can train you as well as I can. Besides, I have far too many responsibilities to do that kind of thing myself. Hell doesn't run itself."

I scoffed as I twined a piece of my hair around my hand, feeling the strands bite into my flesh when I pulled it taught in an effort not to scream into the phone. I had no leverage. I could feel the last of any control I thought I had over my afterlife slipping away, and there was nothing I could do about it. *Fuck you, Silas.*

I gritted my teeth until my jaw ached, and still, there was nothing I could do. "If you're not training me, then you can forget it because I won't work with the same guy who conned me into giving up my soul." My ultimatum was pathetic even to my own ears, leaving me desperate to cry, but I refused to give him the satisfaction.

"That's very 'pot calling the kettle black', don't you think? Considering you just convinced a very vulnerable pixie to sign over hers just a little while ago, right?" he reminded me. "And I would be very careful about your next move, my dear, because if you decide to go back on your word, I can make things a lot worse for you." His warning sent a shiver down my spine.

"You think that the hell you're experiencing is bad? Well, there are much worse circles. Ones that don't provide a cushy existence with all the luxuries life has to offer, and believe me when I say that I will not hesitate to transfer you to one," he said menacingly.

A knot of fear formed in my stomach as he spoke, and I felt cold sweat beading down my spine. It was terrifying that he could evoke such a powerful response from me without even being in the same room, and this was his way of reminding me he was not someone to be trifled with.

Matt came around the corner grinning from ear to ear, and I knew that meant he was finally finished with his paperwork.

"I understand," I said to Silas as I returned Matt's smile, the knot in my stomach growing even heavier while my brain actively searched for the lie I would tell once I hung up.

"I'm glad you see it my way," Silas said. "Oh, and I'll make sure Declan is more amenable next time."

Then without another word, he hung up the phone before I could respond. I slid the phone back into the pocket of my apron just as Matt slipped into the booth across from me, holding two shots of rum.

"Anything I should be worried about?" He nodded toward my phone. I shook my head, taking Declan's warning to heart after my chat with Silas, and quickly changed the subject.

"I'm guessing you're finished," I tried to put on my most convincing smile.

"Every single penny has been accounted for. Those books are almost too perfect," he said with a shake of his head.

His long, wavy hair brushed the tops of his broad shoulders. His eyes wrinkled at the corners as his smile reached them. But it was his calm, easy going demeanor that helped to settle some of the tension I held as we both tipped back our glasses.

"And just in time to close up shop so we can really relax," I said as I glanced around at the nearly empty room.

"Why don't you head upstairs and shower while I close this place up, and we can celebrate properly."

He didn't have to tell me twice, and in less than five minutes, I was upstairs, stripping out of my clothes. I barely gave the water enough time to be lukewarm before I stepped in to wash the still-sticky alcohol from my skin. I allowed the steam to swirl around me, sending hints of leather, alcohol, and gunpowder through my nose.

Suddenly, my heart was racing, and I felt exactly like I had when I was back in the bank, trapped, as Declan held my hand firmly in his. My brain replayed the scene, and I could only watch while I sealed my fate on that heavy sheet of paper with my own blood. The onslaught of memories caused my stomach to turn at the thought that I had just done the very same thing to Lucinda in the bar.

Before I knew it, I was on all fours. The rough surface of the shower floor bit into the sensitive skin of my palms and knees as I heaved the contents of my stomach into the drain. It ran in rivers down my face, washing away the physical manifestation of my guilt while leaving behind mental scars I would have to carry with me from now on.

"Are you okay?" Matt turned the water off quickly before wrapping me with a fluffy towel and guiding me slowly toward the bed.

"I'm fine now. Probably just something I ate," I lied, my knees shaking as I waited for him to pull back the covers. He crawled in behind me, cradling me to his chest before covering us both up. I shivered in his arms, my teeth clacking together lightly, but we didn't talk anymore. He just held me until I fell into a fitful slumber.

My dreams were haunted by images of Lucinda. She begged me to know why I had done this to her as flashes of Declan in the bank interrupted, and the overwhelming stench of gunpowder threatened to choke me. Tossing and turning, I tried to escape the images, only to find them waiting for me around every corner of my mind until I woke in a panicked sweat.

Matt, who had been awakened by my sudden movement, turned over and pulled me close once again. He held me tightly in his comforting embrace, his fingers running gently through my hair in a soothing gesture until I was able to drift off once again into a peaceful slumber in the black void of my mind.

CHAPTER 10

"Wow." Matt paused with his cup of coffee halfway to his mouth as he stared at the screen of his phone. The color drained from his cheeks, and he looked like he'd seen a ghost.

"What's going on?" I curled up next to him on the couch, my own steaming mug quickly warming my cold hands.

The nights had gotten colder recently, and the old apartment was drafty with all the single-paned windows, leaving me almost permanently chilled. I glanced at the article on his screen, almost dropping the cup at the sight of the girl staring back at me. It was Lucinda, and the headline at the top read, 'Local Pixie Murdered by Vampire Terrorizing the City.' Thankfully, Matt didn't notice my reaction as he continued reading over the article, tossing his phone to the side after one last glance at Lucinda's smiling face.

"How sad. She was such a nice girl." He sighed, shaking his head in disappointment. His wavy locks brushed his shoulders, leaving damp streaks behind from his shower on his dark gray tee.

"You knew her?" I asked curiously, sipping slowly on the steaming hot liquid while I tried to get my heart to stop thudding.

My phone vibrated in my pocket, and I barely registered

Matt's response as I opened the text message from Declan on my screen.

Meet me outside. 5 min. Don't even think of ignoring me, or I will come in and get you.

"Rachel?" Matt asked, pointing to the phone.

"Hmmm? Oh. Yeah, sorry." I slid the phone into my back pocket, feeling crappy lying to him. But Declan was right; I was running around halfcocked thinking I knew what I was doing, and both he and Silas told me not to say anything.

I got up from the couch and made my way to the kitchen, watching out of the corner of my eye as Matt padded down the hall to the bathroom. With a gulp, I set my cup on the counter. I was reluctant to see Declan after our encounter the night before, but I was also wary of blowing him off after the warning from Silas to fall in line. So instead of pushing my luck, I shrugged into my hoodie.

"I'll be right back," I called, sneaking through the door. I didn't wait for a response as I closed it quietly behind me and took the stairs two at a time. My sneakers squeaked over the tile floor in the back hallway, and before I knew it, I was pushing through the door into the back alley. My breath was almost knocked out of me as I barreled into Declan just as I passed through the doorway.

My hands planted firmly on his chest, and his arms went around me, pulling me close as he steadied me after the impact. Something about the way he held me, coupled with the leathery scent, brought a memory of a similar moment to the forefront of my mind...

I waited patiently, glancing up from my phone to see the crossing light blink green. My foot stepped off the curb, landing only momentarily before being pulled back. My body crushed up against Declan's chest as a car horn blared behind me, too close for comfort. His chest heaved a sigh of relief as he pulled away, holding me at arm's length, his blue eyes searching mine. Then he shook me, and I was jolted back, yet somehow still staring into the depths of his eyes. My heart pounded as I tried to compose myself.

"What the hell?" I shook my head, trying to clear away the disoriented feeling that lingered.

"I warned you I would come in after you. You cut it close enough—no doubt pondering whether or not I was serious," he huffed.

My mind reeled as it tried to grapple with the dual images of him, but it was fading too fast, like fog in the early morning sunlight. I scrutinized him for a second longer before he dropped his hands to his sides. *Do I know you?* I searched my brain for something more, only to come up short as confusion washed over me. *What was I doing?*

Declan's eyes searched mine, and I wondered why we were standing in the alley as he took a step back and smoothed his long, thin fingers down the front of his sweater. He seemed frazzled but brushed it off like lint before reapplying his calm, cool demeanor. I wanted to ask him about it, but I couldn't explain why I didn't already know.

"What do you want?" I crossed my arms over my chest.

"We need to collect a soul," he chastised as he headed off down the alley.

"Hey, I can't leave here unless I'm going back to my apartment," I said, not fully registering his words as I placed my hands on my hips and planted myself firmly in place. It was too early to get painfully zapped, and I couldn't go anywhere except the bar and home. Though, calling the apartment, I currently shared with Rachel home was being generous. Especially since I hadn't exactly been staying there for a while. With a groan, he turned around, walking purposefully toward me, and produced a sheet of paper from his inside pocket.

"Read this," he sighed.

I admired the seeds and petals that made up the hefty sheet he handed me before trying to decipher the looping handwritten script scrawled across the page. It looked like Italian or maybe Latin, but either way, I had no idea what it meant, so I took a breath and spoke the words out loud, hoping not to butcher them too badly.

"*Vacat vobis, liberum.*" I read, feeling the magic of my house arrest dissolve along with the sheet of paper which floated toward the ground around my feet like dust.

"What? How?" I stuttered in disbelief.

I pulled up the sleeve of my hoodie and gawked at the unmarked pale flesh of my wrist in awe. The Gebo rune disappeared like Rachel said it would, and I wanted to jump up and down in celebration. But Declan was already at the end of the alley, foot tapping while he waited for me.

I hurried down the alley, and we walked for a block before I could breathe easily. I was still a little shocked it had been so easy to be released from the spell. But I definitely wasn't going to complain about that.

"Where are we going?" My feet sped over the pavement as I struggled to keep up with his break-neck pace.

"Consider this your first lesson. You have a soul to collect, and you're late, so now we need to hurry," he answered grumpily.

I stopped in my tracks as the reality of the situation hit me. My feet felt like they were made from lead.

"Are you kidding me? This is going to take all day if you don't hurry up," he complained through gritted teeth once he realized that I was no longer following him.

"I can't collect a soul... I can't." I shook my head, stepping back.

"What did you think was going to happen when she died?" His brow arched as he looked at me expectantly. When I didn't respond, he took my hand in his, tugging me forward. Finally, my feet took over, carrying me forward on their own. "Her soul is your responsibility, and if you don't collect it, then she stays here until you do. However, the longer you wait, the more difficult it becomes, and the worse her sentence will be because of it."

The feeling of dread sat like something rotten in the pit of my stomach. I had no idea what he meant, but this was going to be bad. The further away we got from Idir, the more I wanted to run, but once again, Silas's warning about backing out had me forcing my feet to continue on our path straight ahead.

It felt like we had been walking forever, but in reality, it was around five blocks. It wasn't until we rounded the corner that I realized we weren't far from Rachel's apartment. Maybe only three blocks southeast behind a slightly older set of units.

Lucinda's ethereal crying reached us before I saw her translucent form kneeling in the dirty alley, and, as if pulled by a string attaching the two of us, I hurried toward her, laying my hand gently on her shoulder. I was surprised by how substantial she felt, despite the fact that I could see through her. But I pushed the thought aside as I focused on the situation at hand.

"Lucinda." I patted her gently on the back. Her head whipped toward me, her once deep brown eyes now red with anger as she registered who I was.

"You," she screamed, pointing her finger at me while silvery tears rolled down her face. I took a step back, not sure whether or not she could actually hurt me in this form and definitely not wanting to test it out.

Death wasn't something I feared anymore, being a soulless and all, but I certainly felt pain. "This is your fault," she moaned, floating toward me, her outstretched finger mere inches from my face.

Declan, who was closer than I realized, placed his hand reassuringly on my back and stepped up beside me.

"Lucinda... can I call you Lucinda?" He politely held his hand out toward her. The smooth baritone of his voice brought my brain hurtling toward the memory of the night he collected my own soul. It was a memory I forgot all about until now, refusing to remember the gentle way in which he comforted me, and instead, I focused on the fact that he was the one to make my deal. He did something similar then, too, though it seemed he had been there the instant my soul had left my body, not hours later.

"Who are you, and what do you want?" Her eyes narrowed until they were barely more than slits of red on her now pale face as she stared at him with distrust.

"Who I am isn't important. The only thing that's important right now is helping you to cross over," he soothed. His words triggered her, prompting her to remember that she was now dead, and it was me she blamed.

Her head whipped toward me once again, her anger manifesting in electric blue lines that coated her form as they amplified. Hands outstretched, her soul rushed toward me, causing me to duck down into a protective stance, my arms shielding my head. After a moment, when nothing happened, I removed my arms slowly from my face, looking up to where Declan now stood, hand wrapped firmly around her throat.

"I had hoped it wouldn't come to this, Lucinda, because now it's going to hurt. I'm sorry Anna was so careless with her job," he apologized.

I was taken aback at the sincerity in his tone, while at the same time annoyed by the fact that he had called me careless. Especially because I couldn't do my job well if I didn't know what my job actually was.

"*Dare nobis transitum,*" he muttered, grasping my shoulder with his free hand.

As Lucinda let out an ear-splitting scream, all the air was sucked from my lungs, the pressure building around us as if I were being sucked into a vacuum hose. *Maybe I can die again.* My head spun as the world around me turned black. Suddenly, I was doubled over on the thick crimson carpet in Silas's office building, my stomach roiling and my brain disoriented. I looked up and met Silas's eyes where he sat smirking in a high-backed leather chair behind his desk.

Declan continued to grasp my shoulder with one hand, while the other one held onto Lucinda, who'd gone from screaming to sobbing during our little trip. I took several deep breaths, my lungs still gasping for air as I noted with a fleeting thought that the room smelled of gardenias before standing on shaky legs. I shrugged Declan's hand off me while I waited for Silas to say something.

"I see you have the situation under control," he said to Declan. "Though, now, this one is going to need more serious confinement. She was clearly left too long without her body," he sighed, shaking his head at Lucinda before turning toward me.

"As for you, I told you not to make any further deals without training, and now you're the reason she will end up in the eighth circle," he explained before returning his attention back to the spectre in the room.

"I sentence you to eternity in the lower reaches," he said to Lucinda, who writhed in Declan's grip. With a wave of his hand, Silas opened up a hole in the floor in front of Declan, who, without reacting, released her, allowing her to fall into the fiery pit below.

The floor closed up seamlessly, leaving me to wonder why I still heard her sobbing now that she was gone. As I reached my hand up to cover my shocked expression, my fingers brushed against the wet trails running down my cheeks. Realization washed over me, horror gripping my chest. The sobs were mine...not Lucinda's.

"Get her out of here. And Declan, make sure you instruct her properly next time," Silas said to him with a dismissive wave of his hand.

Declan nodded, taking hold of my elbow while he muttered

the spell again. The next thing I knew, we were back in the alley behind Idir, where I puked up the bile from my empty stomach. Whatever means he was using to travel made my head spin and left me feeling inside out. At the moment, though, it didn't matter. The only thing that mattered was that I had gotten Lucinda sentenced to the lower pits of hell because I hadn't known that I needed to collect her soul right away.

Declan offered me the handkerchief from his pocket. I took the monogrammed cotton square from him, using it to wipe away the last remains of sickness from my mouth before shoving it in my pocket. He held his hand out to help me stand, but I refused, placing my palm on the rough bricks of the wall behind me to help me balance. I was surprised and confused by the concern on his face when I looked up at him and stopped myself before I took a step toward him.

Why do I have this overwhelming urge to run to him? Am I going insane? I wiped my hands across my face, but I couldn't wipe away the emotions warring inside me.

"I can see you're distraught. We'll continue with this another time." The last thing I wanted from him was pity, so I looked the other direction.

With a pointed nod of his head, I heard the door next to me unlock, then he turned and strode back down the alley, hands stuffed deep into the pockets of his jeans.

CHAPTER 11

I took a deep breath, centering myself before I pulled open the door and made my way down the short hallway. But as I rounded the corner to head upstairs, I caught sight of Matt standing near the front door with two Guard officers. He pointed in my direction while the taller blonde man shook his hand, and the three of them headed straight toward me. Once they were closer, I noted their matching black shirts and leather jackets. These two were Guard detectives, a step above their button-down wearing colleagues like Derek Martin. Closing my eyes briefly, I sighed. *This day just keeps getting better and better.* These guys were high level, the kind the Guard sends out when there's a real problem. Unlike the guys who had taken me into the station before.

"Anna, this is Lukas and Tristan. They want to ask you a few questions about last night," Matt said.

He placed his hand lightly over mine on top of the bar but pulled back after a moment. I wasn't sure if he was distancing himself because I was in trouble yet again, or because he didn't want them to know we were together. Either way, it felt like a betrayal.

"Sure, how can I help?" I forced a smile as the two men sized me up.

I slid my hands nervously into the back pockets of my jeans to keep from fidgeting as I waited for them to question me.

"Was this woman here last night?" Lukas thrust the picture of Lucinda in my face — the same one from the news article I had seen Matt reading earlier.

His white-blonde hair fell across his forehead, and he pushed it back in an unconscious gesture, reminding me a little of Declan. I shook away the thought and took a moment to calm my nerves, hoping for my sake that I seemed to be trying to remember one specific person I had served last night.

"Gin and tonic." I nodded as if struck by recognition. He glanced at his partner Tristan who was jotting down notes, waiting a beat for him to finish before he went on.

"How was she? Did she seem scared or nervous at all?"

"No. She was upset, though. I brought her a second drink. She was crying, so I sat down with her for a few minutes," I admitted. It's not like it's against the law to be friendly with a customer. And as long as I stuck close to the truth, I wouldn't have to commit any lies to memory.

"What was she upset about?" Tristan asked, not taking his eyes off the pad of paper in his hands. He was slightly shorter than his partner, though more muscular. His wavy auburn hair was ruffled from the breeze outside. He appeared disheveled, but it suited him.

"Uh, she said her mate left her for a fairy." I shrugged.

"Did she leave with anyone?" Lukas asked.

"Not that I noticed," I admitted with a sigh. I was glad I could say that honestly.

I leaned forward, placing my elbows on the smooth surface of the bar, and began rubbing my temples as I spoke. My head was starting to pound from the events of the morning, along with the fact that I hadn't eaten anything for at least twenty-four hours and had puked up my guts twice.

"Sorry guys, I'm not really feeling great. Can we continue this later?" I asked.

"Okay, I think that's all we need for now, anyway," Lukas said with a nod to Tristan, who closed his notebook and slid it into the inner pocket of his jacket. Matt reached out, shaking each of their hands again, and the two of them gave me a nod before heading out the door, leaving us there alone to chat.

"Are you okay? You're not looking so great," Matt questioned, raising the back of his hand to my forehead.

In all honesty, I felt awful. My head pounded, my throat burned, and my stomach was sore from all the heaving I'd done. And I would have told him everything if I hadn't been such a chicken. Especially now that I saw firsthand what Silas was capable of. The last thing I needed was to drag Matt into such a dangerous situation, only to have him end up in the pits of hell, too.

"No, I think I might be coming down with something." I looked away, unable to meet his gaze as the lie rolled off my tongue. I hadn't been sick one day since I died. Unfortunately, lying was becoming a habit with him, and as much as I hated it, I knew it was necessary.

"Why don't you go upstairs and lie down? I'll check on you a little later after Nate and Jessica come in." He smiled.

As good as that sounded, I really needed to talk to Rachel. She was the only person I could confide in about any of it.

"Actually, I think I'm going to head home. I don't want to get anyone else sick. I'll see you tomorrow if I'm feeling better."

He pulled me in for a hug, squeezing me tight, and I buried my face in the crook of his neck, breathing in his scent before pulling away. I kissed him on the cheek, and it took everything I had not to look back before I walked out into the sunlight.

Ten minutes later, I walked through the front door of the apartment, unsurprised to see Rachel sitting at the table with her notebook open, scribbling vigorously across the page. I wondered what it was she was always writing down but figured she would have shared if she wanted me to know, so I left it alone.

"Are you here for your stuff?" she didn't bother to look up from her work, and I was surprised by the constricting in my chest. I suddenly felt as if she was tossing me aside, and it hurt my feelings more than I thought it would. Instead of letting it fester, though, I decided to let it go because her closed posture told me she was feeling hurt, too.

"Actually, I need to talk. Do you have a minute?" I sat down hesitantly in the chair across from her. I wasn't sure if we were going to pretend our last altercation never happened, but I really hoped that was the case.

"I guess. What's up?"

My gut twisted, and my knee bounced as I wrung my hands together under the table. *Tell her, that's what you came here for, right? To get this off your chest.*

"I may have done something stupid," I admitted, my voice low from embarrassment. We didn't leave things on good terms the last time we discussed my new agreement with Silas.

"Please tell me you didn't land yourself back on house arrest the same day you got released from your sentence." She groaned, her shoulders slumping forward, and she closed her eyes, waiting for my response.

"You'll have to tell me how you pulled off that little trick later, by the way." She held up her right arm so I could see her rune was gone, too.

"Well, I'm not going back on house arrest," I reassured her, deciding to leave out any mention of Declan or how he had managed to get my sentence waived.

"Then I'm sure it's no big deal." She gave a dismissive wave as she perked right back up. "But if you're going to be staying, you're gonna have to pay rent. This isn't a boarding house, you know." She smirked. My heart skipped at the thought that she even considered me staying at all now that there was no obligation, but I kept my relief under control, instead opting to shrug in agreement.

"Yeah, fine, we'll talk about that later, though. Right now, there's something more important," I insisted.

"Something more important than money? Never," she laughed.

"I made another deal..." I whispered. I felt gross just admitting it, and my face scrunched tightly while I waited for her to lay into me like last time.

"You made *another* deal?"

Shame washed over me, and I sat silently, my eyes downcast in anticipation of her wrath. I peeked up through my lashes when it didn't come.

"Are you going to tell me what happened, or are you gonna leave a girl hanging?" Her dark brows climbed high as she gave me a look that said, 'get on with it.'

"Who are you, and what did you do with Rachel?" My brow furrowed as I looked around the room, then back at her. *Is this the invasion of the body snatchers or what?* She rolled her eyes, her mouth forming a thin line.

"*I'm* still on probation. That should be enough to tell you I'm no miss goody two shoes, you know. But our fates are no longer tied together, so now I'm happy to sit back and fully appreciate the crazy-ass life you lead." She reclined in her seat, placing her hands in her lap.

"Really? You gave me hell about this a week ago, and now you're fine with it?" I wanted to slap her, or cry, or laugh hysterically. Maybe all three. *Damn! Get it together, Anna; your emotions are out of control today.*

"Yep, I no longer have any stake in this. And to be honest, your life is a hot mess."

I nodded in agreement. *The girl has a point.*

I got up from the table and made myself a cup of coffee as I told her all about Lucinda and her guy troubles. By the time I finished my cup and the story, her eyes had grown wide, and her mouth hung open slightly.

I released a sigh and slumped in my chair, feeling as though part of the weight had lifted off my shoulders.

"Declan is your mentor?"

Seriously? I just told you I watched a pixie get thrown into the deepest pit of Hell, and that's what you want to talk about?

I nodded slowly as I let a stream of air through my pursed lips.

"Well, don't look so upset about it. He's..." She let out a whistle, her eyes staring off into space, and I knew she was picturing him naked.

I leaned forward, snapping my fingers in front of her to get her back on track.

"Umm... hello. Dead pixie...deal with the Devil...deepest pit of *Hell*." I raised my eyebrows, emphasizing each point as I ticked them off on my fingers.

"She knew what she was getting herself into." Her mouth quirked, and she shook her head, making her curls bounce.

"That's not what you said about Genevieve," I reminded her.

"That was different. She's next in line to be High Priestess of the Farrington Coven."

"Well, that's not really the point." I sighed as I rubbed my hands across my face. She wasn't going to be any help at all if the only thing she could focus on was the first thing out of my mouth.

"Then what's the point?" she asked as she stared me down.

"The point is that a girl died!" I pounded the palm of my hand against the table to punctuate every word as it came out of my mouth. *How are you not upset by this? Like, not phased at all??*

"That doesn't mean it was your fault," she answered. "You

don't know that she wasn't going to die last night either way." She had a point, but it didn't make me feel any better about the whole situation.

"Well. She ended up in the eighth circle of hell, thanks to me. So even if I'm not responsible for her actually dying, I'm still responsible for that." I slumped back into my chair.

"How do you know that? She had a choice, right? You didn't force her to make that deal, and Declan didn't tell you that you needed to collect her soul," she reasoned as she set her pen down and gave me her full attention. "So... what did she ask for?" She leaned forward onto her forearms while she waited, her eyes gleaming as she licked her lips in anticipation.

"True love," I sighed, releasing all the air from my lungs as I thought about the golden thread that had appeared between her and the guy at Idir after she made her deal. I wondered briefly if maybe it was him who killed her. I shook my head, dismissing that thought just as quickly. *He* hadn't been a vampire, and I was sure there was no way anyone could kill their one true love.

"Did she get it?" She shifted in her seat as she waited with bated breath.

My palms turned slick with sweat, and my heart beat double time as magic started to build around the two of us. An opportunity was about to present itself to me, and even though I was disgusted by the circumstances, I couldn't help but be a little bit excited, too.

"The minute she made the deal," I admitted. I knew Rachel had made up her mind as soon as the words left my mouth. Slowly, I shook my head at her, begging her with my eyes not to ask, but I knew she would, anyway.

"Can I make a deal?" She slid forward in the chair, shortening the distance between us, eager for whatever it was she thought was worth selling her soul for.

"No," I said flatly, surprised I was able to stop myself from acting on the instinct to give her whatever she wanted. "Absolutely not."

"Come on, you didn't even consider it." She all but whined, which only made me push my own chair away from the table. "At least let me tell you what I want," she pleaded, as every cell in my body seemed to scream at me to make the deal.

"I don't care. You have no idea what this is like for me. When I made those deals, I was out of control, like an addict looking for a fix. And when it was done, I couldn't scrub away the self-loathing." I ran my hands over my arms, trying to chase away the slimy feeling, but I knew it was all in my head.

Her eyes flashed red under the fluorescent kitchen light, her face a mask of anger. "You owe me."

"I consider you to be my friend. The *only* one I have. So, I need you to know... there is *nothing* worth selling your soul for. I will never make you a deal. Do you understand me?" My voice was barely more than a shaky whisper as I unclenched my fists at my sides.

"Obviously, there is. Because *you* did it," she shot back.

"I didn't have a choice. I was dying. And if I knew then what I know now, I wouldn't have done it."

"Then make me a deal that doesn't involve my soul, like you did for Genevieve."

"I can't. I know better now, and Silas would banish me in a heartbeat," I argued. "This is not a game."

"So, you'll give anyone else whatever they want, but you won't do the same for the one person who stood up for you?" She scowled.

Stop it...please just stop. I shook my head at her, my lips pursed together in disapproval while I stared her down.

"Fine," she pouted, matching my anger with her own as she picked up her pen and resumed whatever it was she had been doing when I came in. When she didn't look up again, I began to wonder why I had come to her about the whole thing in the first place.

I stomped off to my bedroom without another word and slammed the door behind me with more force than necessary, hearing the clock in the living room shudder before resting peacefully against the other side of the wall again. I looked around the space, feeling both at home and unwelcome, before falling face first onto my bed.

I needed some time to think.

CHAPTER 12

I woke up with my cheek stuck to my comforter, drool dripping down my chin. I sucked it up and wiped my mouth with the back of my hand before blinking my eyes open. *How long have I been asleep?* A quick glance at my phone screen told me it was still too early to go into work, but I figured it would be better to hang out there than the apartment, where Rachel would no doubt corner me until I was forced to give into her demands. I could hear her moving around in her room across the wall, and the dread of seeing her formed like a ball of lead in the pit of my stomach.

That alone made me decide I preferred to take a shower at Matt's then a bath in our tub, even though I longed for a soak with one of Rachel's homemade bath bombs. So, I threw on some clean clothes and pulled my hair up into a messy bun before tiptoeing into the kitchen. I plucked a bright red apple from the bowl on the counter, taking a big bite from it as Rachel came down the hall. Her stockinged feet dragged across the floorboards while she rubbed the sleep from her eyes.

"Sorry about last night," she apologized. "It was a stupid thing to ask."

I almost choked from shock as I chewed the apple, but I recovered with a cough. *Is this a trick? Or is she actually sorry?* My eyes narrowed, and I pursed my lips. Her downcast gaze and slumped posture made me think she was ashamed of her behavior.

I nodded in dismay, but I was grateful she had come to her senses.

"I don't know what came over me." She rubbed her hand across the back of her neck as she shook her head. "Did you mean what you said about me being your only friend?"

Heat crept up my neck to my cheeks. Now it was my turn to be embarrassed. I nodded but didn't say a word as I took another bite of my apple.

"I know I messed things up. I just..." I put my hand up to stop her before she tried to justify her request by telling me what she's wanted. I didn't care.

"I need some time." I tossed the rest of the apple, picked up my bag, slung it over my shoulder, and headed out the door before either of us said something we might regret. Not that asking me to make a deal for her soul hadn't crossed the line already, but there was no going back from that now.

The morning was brisk, causing me to shiver a little as I walked, and I wished I had grabbed something heavier than my hoodie, or at least layered a little more before I left. The days were getting cooler, and the warm steam from my breath curled around me as I shuffled down the sidewalk. However, it wasn't cold enough yet for an actual jacket, especially during the day.

That was the thing about Albuquerque: it was never too hot or too cold, but it was miserable enough for an outsider like me to consider it Hellish. *New Mexico, 'come on vacation, leave on probation.' Maybe that's where the locals got their saying.* I chuckled to myself, but honestly, it wasn't that bad. In fact, I loved this time of year when the leaves changed colors and sunsets painted the sky like watercolor. But...I missed the rain and trees from home even more.

All the brown that surrounded me in my current environment didn't do it for me, which was probably one of the reasons

Silas dumped me here in the first place. I rounded the corner to the bar and came skidding to a halt when I caught sight of Declan standing on the corner.

"Don't look so happy to see me," he drawled. He leaned against the brick wall, hands stuffed into the pockets of his faded denim jeans, his dark grey sweater making his blue eyes even brighter in the sunlight. It was the most casual clothing I'd seen him wear, and he still looked a little overdressed.

"What do you want now?" I was not in the mood for whatever it was he wanted, especially after everything that had happened.

"I thought we could go on a little field trip." He shrugged. "I'll buy you a cup of coffee."

I took a moment to consider it before answering. *I could use a distraction, and damn it if Rachel wasn't right. He is hot!* I looked away from him as I pulled on my hoodie, fanning myself for a moment. *Pull yourself together, Anna.* I gave myself a mental slap and took a deep breath. A cup of coffee did sound good, and at this point, it couldn't make things any worse.

"Only if you throw in something to eat too," I countered.

"Fine," he huffed sarcastically as he gestured for me to join him.

The two of us headed back the way I came, backtracking two blocks before turning left to cross Central to the *Latte of Love*. I passed by the place a few times and considered going in, but I was well aware it was owned by witches, and honestly, the name kind of turned me off. I wasn't keen on businesses that couldn't come up with something more original than a play-on-words for the name of something they were supposed to care about. Though my history with Melinda might've had something to do with it, too.

The bell above the door chimed when we passed over the threshold, and even though I'd dinged them for their name, the giddy feeling that bubbled through me made it clear that this could become a favorite hangout for me. The room, cozy with its wooden tables and chairs, invited me in like a warm hug. Saliva pooled in my mouth as my eyes were drawn to the glass case near the register— lined with row after row of every type of cookie you could imagine. Stacks of chocolate chip, oatmeal raisin, shortbread, and so many others I had never heard of before were lined up neatly along each shelf. But the ones that caught my eye were the iced sugar cookies with their whimsical cutouts topped with a shiny royal icing. They were by far the most abundant in the display.

"Can I help you?" asked the short guy behind the counter. He was Latino and looked vaguely familiar to me, but I couldn't place him. It was possible he had been in Idir a time or two, but I saw so many people, it was hard to know.

"Large Americano and whatever she's having," Declan said as they both turned expectantly toward me.

"Hey, you're my sister's new roommate," the guy said, his smile widening to show two rows of straight, pearly white teeth. "I'm Gabe."

He stuck his hand out over the counter, and I realized now where I had seen him before. There was a picture of him and Rachel hanging on the fridge at the apartment. His hair was different, and he was a little older now, but it was definitely the same guy.

I smiled back as I shook his hand quickly, hoping not to absorb too much magic from him. I was pleasantly surprised at the total lack of the warm tingle of magic transferring between us. He was a human. It intrigued me, and I held onto his hand a little longer than I probably should have, causing both of them to look at me curiously. Once we let go, I shoved my hands into my back pockets, feeling slightly embarrassed about my ignorance. He had the same curly hair and petite nose that she did. "Yeah, I'm Anna. Have we met before?"

"Only through the picture from your bedroom." His face

scrunched, and his eyes looked up at the ceiling. "I was curious when I went to visit Rachel, and it's the only picture of you in the apartment, so she grabbed it just to show me."

I was shocked momentarily, my mouth hanging open as I considered the fact that Rachel had been in my room. *Can you blame her? You're a soulless living in her apartment. You would have snooped too and you know it.* I composed myself again, closing my mouth before giving him a genuine smile.

"Well, it's nice to *formally* meet you." I bent my head in his direction in a sort of pseudo curtsy, feeling ridiculous about my awkward behavior.

"What can I get you? It's on the house," he whispered from behind his hand as he winked at me.

"I'll take one of those awesome sugar cookies," I pointed to the large mustache cookie in the middle of the case. "And a large almond milk latte. But you can get me next time because he's paying today." I smirked, hooking my thumb toward Declan, who rolled his eyes at me as he pulled his thin leather wallet from his back pocket. But he didn't say a word.

Once he paid, we found a table for two in the corner next to the front window where we could watch people walk by while we waited for our coffee.

"You look tired. Are you feeling better about your training from yesterday?" Declan pulled my chair out for me. His hand held it steady as I sat down, his fingers skimming my shoulder as he moved away, leaving tingles behind like an electric shock, and I was struck by a sense of Déjà vu.

"Way to tell a girl she looks like crap," I joked, kicking his foot playfully under the table.

"That wasn't –" I held up my hand to stop him, a giggle escaping as I watched him stumble all over his words.

"It's fine, I was joking—mostly."

He tilted his head to the side, raising his brow at me as his mouth turned down at the corners. *A swing— and a miss.* I shrugged, averting my eyes toward the ceiling, and he let out a deep chortle. I grinned at him and watched his shoulders fall, releasing the tension, and he looked more comfortable.

"How did you end up doing this?" I didn't want to think about everything that had happened the day before. Besides, we had time to talk about Silas and sentencing. And for the first time since I met him, I was curious to know more about him—as a person.

"I made a deal, just like you. Imagine my surprise when I found out that my boss was Satan in disguise," he chuckled.

Just then, Gabe brought a tray with our order, setting everything neatly in front of us before turning and bouncing off in the other direction. He reminded me more and more of his sister with every movement. Declan shook his head, his eyebrows knitted together in puzzled confusion as he watched Gabe go.

"He's not a warlock," he said quietly. His eyes narrowed as he watched Gabe move back and forth behind the counter.

"It appears he isn't," I agreed, taking a tentative sip from my cup.

"But your roommate is a witch, is she not?"

"Yep. Maybe it skipped him." I shrugged.

I was no expert in supernatural genetics, so it seemed like a logical enough explanation to me. He didn't seem convinced, but he shrugged back.

"How did you end up like me?" I gestured to myself in an attempt to change the subject. I wasn't really in the mood to talk about Rachel or her family.

"Oh, reaping," he replied casually. "I guess the same way you did... I found myself in a position to make a deal for a soul, and it just sort of happened."

He picked up his cup and removed the plastic lid, taking a test sip from it before deciding it was acceptable enough.

"How many of us are there?"

"It's you and me as far as I know," he replied.

I coughed, feeling tiny droplets of coffee spray from my nose as I clamped my mouth shut. *Wait...seriously? Silas has to have reaped Millions of souls.*

"In all these years, we're the only two who can do what we do?" I grabbed a napkin from the holder, blowing my nose to rid myself of the burning liquid.

Taking a napkin of his own, he wiped up the coffee I hadn't realized I'd sprayed across the table. "Believe me, I'm as shocked as you are." His frown grew deeper as he wadded up the spent napkin and dropped it on the table between us.

I was reminded of what Matt told me about there being a *soulless* who got out of their contract. But then Silas showed up and crushed that nasty little bit of gossip. "You're the one that got away," I grumbled, breaking my cookie in half before shoving part of it in my mouth. His eyebrows raised, but he didn't say anything. Instead, he sipped his coffee while he waited for me to chew.

The soft cookie melted slowly in my mouth, leaving a thin layer of sugar on my tongue. *Why, oh why does this place have to be owned by witches?* I closed my eyes, a sigh escaping my lips. These were fresh baked, they had real butter in them, and a part of me hated that it made me love the place even more.

"You worked for Silas? Like in the same building he's in now?" I asked, and he gave a nod.

"How long ago was that?"

"It's been a while," he said with a laugh. "Though I guess if you think about it, I never actually left."

He was right. If he had worked in the same building with Silas, he was a lawyer of some sort.

"Were you married? Did you have kids? How did you die?" I threw a barrage of questions in his direction as they popped into my head.

"No, never married. But I was in love... once." The way he

looked at me had my blood rushing straight to my cheeks. The room grew quiet around us, and I closed my eyes, allowing whatever warm, fuzzy feeling he'd evoked to wash over me. It was like we were the only two people in the room, and I felt the tug of something familiar on the edge of my memory. A hand trailing down my cheek, the brush of lips against mine. It was right there...if I could just grab onto it.

"How are you two doing over here?" asked the petite girl wiping down the table next to us, and before I grabbed a hold of whatever had been nagging at me, the world came crashing into focus once again.

Declan's eyes closed, and he inhaled deeply before turning toward her and sizing her up. At the same time, the pressure of magic started to build around me, its electric buzz dancing across my skin, and the knot in my gut said he'd marked her as a target.

"Actually, can I get another coffee?" he said, then proceeded to drink what was left in his cup in one swallow. "And one of those cookies my friend is having?"

With a smile and a nod of her head, she picked up her rag and headed back toward the counter.

"What in the hell do you think you're doing?" There was no way I was going to let this go down in the middle of a crowded coffee shop.

"My job." He grinned. "Now watch and learn."

The girl returned moments later with a cup and a plate, which she set lightly on the table in front of Declan while she glanced back and forth between the two of us.

"Why don't you join us for a minute?" he asked.

He gave her a thin-lipped smile as he stood, his lean body navigating gracefully around the cramped space as he pulled over a chair from a nearby table for her. She hesitated for a bit before sliding into the chair between us, tucking her hands nervously beneath her thighs.

"Is there something you want to ask us?" he inquired as he took a sip from his cup while I sat back, feeling my heart speed up. I silently watched the scene unfold between the two of them with an almost morbid fascination, not sure whether I wanted to intervene or not. Either way, this girl was going to sign over her soul one way or another before she left this table.

"You can make deals, right?" She leaned closer as she looked over at me, but Declan let out a deep chuckle, drawing her attention back to him.

My right brow arched as I looked at her over the top of my cup. "What makes you think that?"

She shrugged her bony shoulders, her mouth quirking on one side, but she didn't respond.

"Yes, we can do that." His long slender finger gestured between the two of us, and his eyes wrinkled at the corners as he smiled at her.

"How does that work?"

"Well, you tell me what it is you want, and as long as you're willing to pay the price, then I'll make it happen," he shrugged.

"I know the price, and I'm willing to pay it." Magic crackled around us, pushing in on us from all sides. I sucked in a breath of anticipation at the anxious excitement I was feeling and watched, mesmerized, as Declan nodded, encouraging her to continue.

"I want the owner of this shop, here, tonight, after closing," she said in a rushed whisper.

My heart skipped a beat. She was being vague on purpose, given where we were, but vagueness requested meant vagueness in response. I opened my mouth to tell her that she needed to be more specific when I felt Declan's warm hand fall gently over my own on the table. A silent warning not to interfere in his deal.

"I can make that happen." He nodded. "I'll need you to sign, saying that you understand the terms of our agreement."

He pulled the crisp sheet of paper from the back pocket of his jeans where it appeared and smoothed it out on the table in front of her.

"You'll need a drop of blood," he instructed, causing me to wonder why he didn't make his deals over a handshake the way I did.

Like Lucinda, she hesitated for a second, and then, using the edge of the sheet, she sliced into the pad of her thumb, waiting for the blood to pool into a bright red drop before pressing it to the paper. The magic in the air rushed down her arm in a blue shock of static electricity, connecting her to the paper where it dried the blood from her print immediately. She pulled her hand away, sticking her thumb into her mouth to ease the sting and staunch the bleeding while Declan swept up the paper and, with a wave of his hand, it vanished.

The zap of electricity from the magic left behind the lingering scent of gunpowder, causing me to sneeze while it triggered the memory of my deal with Lucinda.

"What now?" she asked, her eyes wide with fear now that the deal was done.

"You'll get what you asked for," he smiled sweetly before turning his attention back to me. He cut her out of the conversation as quickly as he had invited her in. I sat, quiet, my mouth hanging open in shocked silence, when she got up and moved the chair back to its original place before returning to the back of the shop without another word.

"Don't look so sullen." Declan's eyebrows furrowed with displeasure as he took a bite of his cookie.

"Are you kidding me? We're in the middle of a crowded room," I admonished as I leaned over the table toward him.

"You felt it. I saw you react to her at the same time I did," he stated.

But I refused to answer. I leaned back in the chair, crossing my arms over my chest. I wasn't sure why it bothered me so much that he knew, but it did.

"The only reason I took this one was to show how a good deal is made. So, tell me, what happens when you know an opportunity has presented itself. Is it a feeling in your gut?"

I gave a terse shake of my head as I let a long breath out through my nose.

"Okay, fine, I'll tell you my secret. Any time a mark is near, I smell lavender," he admitted, closing his eyes as he inhaled deeply. His features relaxed into a mask of pure elation, and his long lashes fluttered at the thought of it. *Lavender...like my shampoo?*

"Why lavender?"

"Probably because that smell was important to me." The tops of his ears turned red with embarrassment, and I was overcome by a wave of jealousy.

"Does it remind you of your girlfriend?" I teased as I tried to brush away the feeling.

"I think I've shared enough for today."

"What, are you afraid things are getting too personal?"

"What's that supposed to mean?"

"Lavender? Really? You're lying. Like I expected." As soon as the words were out of my mouth, I wanted to slap myself. *Ugh, why do you do that? You're going to lash out at him because you're jealous? You have a boyfriend!*

"Oh yeah? Well, how do you spot a soul that's prepared to make a deal?" he challenged.

"Magic." I scowled at him as I hugged my arms around me. "I can feel the magic like static electricity waiting to seal the deal."

"You realize that we have to do this, right? This is our job." He sat back in the chair, stretching his long legs out in front of him before crossing them at the ankle, waiting patiently for my response as his eyes searched mine for understanding.

It's all fun and games til someone loses their soul.

"I'm only here doing this job, thanks to you. And now, who knows where she'll end up." I pointed toward the young witch as a tear rolled down my cheek.

"Well, you won't have to find out because we'll be long done with your training before I ever have to collect that debt."

I scoffed at his statement, wiping away the tear with the back of my hand as I shook my head in frustration. "I can't believe Silas thinks you're good enough to mentor me. You know nothing. I swear, the smell of gunpowder that followed your deal was enough to tell me you just marked her to die soon."

I scowled at him for a minute longer, taking in the expression of shock on his face before I got up from the table and stomped out the door. It took him a minute to follow because he still needed to settle his bill for the extra cup of coffee and cookie that he ordered, so I took advantage of the delay and hurried down the street back to Idir. The heavy wooden door closed behind me a few minutes later, and I was peeling off my hoodie when it opened again.

"Anna, what are you talking about? What do you mean I marked her to die soon? How could you possibly know that?" he asked, firing off one question after another in quick succession as he wrapped his fingers around my bicep, rooting me to the spot. But I was rendered momentarily speechless by the panic in his voice which was mirrored in his eyes.

Matt came swinging around the corner of the bar, his eyes full of rage as he charged toward Declan, who had yet to notice him.

"Let her go, Declan," he warned.

Declan slowly dropped his hand from my arm but refused to move an inch as he stood up straighter, puffing out his chest as he and Matt stared each other down. I stood sandwiched between them, and I could feel the heat of their bodies radiating toward me from either side. The smell of pine and leather mixed together as their anger rose. Out of the corner of my eye, I saw Declan's fists clench at his sides, and I knew this was going to get out of hand if I didn't do something.

Are you fucking kidding me right now? Why do guys have to get so territorial? I knocked out a warlock, for fuck's sake. I wanted to yell at both of them, but I had the feeling it would only make things worse, so I decided on a lighter approach.

"I'm okay," I told Matt, laying my hand on his shoulder to reassure him. His jaw clenched, and he refused to look away from Declan, but the muscles in his shoulders relaxed under my grip. I breathed a sigh of relief. Unfortunately, it didn't have the same calming effect on Declan, and instead of letting it go, he pushed on, baiting Matt back into a confrontation.

"You need to back off, *Fairy*. This doesn't concern you," Declan said firmly.

"It does when you're harassing my girlfriend, *soul snatcher*. Now get out of my bar." Matt leaned forward onto the balls of his feet, bringing his face mere inches from Declan's.

Well, that was a new one. All the air left my lungs as I brought my hand to my face, pinching the bridge of my nose to stop the oncoming headache. I felt deflated. *For fuck's sake, you two. You're acting like five year olds.*

I looked over at Declan to find his eyes wide with surprise as he looked from Matt to me and back again, before nodding and turning away. He shot a fleeting glance over his shoulder at me as he stormed through the front door, and I swore I could almost see disappointment in his eyes as the door swung shut behind him.

"What was he doing here?" Matt examined my arm for any damage, but I was at a loss for words. I wasn't supposed to tell him anything about my new job, and honestly, after what happened between him and Declan, I didn't want to. He would be pissed if I told him Declan was my new mentor.

"I don't know. He wanted to talk," I lied.

"Declan deals in souls. He doesn't just show up to chat. What's going on?" He widened his stance, his hands moving to his hips as he assessed me.

"I can't talk about it," I mimicked his posture as I dared him to push the issue.

"Can't or won't?" He shook his head at me, his mouth pursed in disappointment. "You've been acting weird for days. Rachel came by looking for you earlier. She told me you were released from your house arrest. Why didn't you tell me?"

"Because it only happened yesterday, and it didn't concern you," I argued.

"Melinda doesn't release people from their sentences early. So how did you get out of it? Did Declan have something to do with it?"

"No. I just did, okay?" I huffed. Tears stung my eyes, threatening to fall as I blinked them back. I wanted to tell him everything, but the rock in the pit of my stomach told me it would cause more trouble than it was worth for both of us.

"You know, I think maybe it's time for us to take a break. You should take the night off. Maybe when you've had some time, you'll be ready to tell me what's going on. If not, then it might be better for us to call it quits." His green eyes glistened with sadness when he turned away, leaving me standing there as everyone within earshot stared openly at me.

I stuffed my arms back into the sleeves of my hoodie and exited the bar, swiping the back of my hand across my eyes to catch the tears that left trails down my cheeks. *This is so messed up. How could things have gone from awful to even worse? Because this is Hell, dummy. What did you expect?*

Thunder rumbled overhead, mirroring my already sour mood, and the sky opened up, allowing a sheet of rain to pour down on me. It wouldn't last—it never did here. But I welcomed the downpour to help hide the tears, even if it did wreak havoc on my hair. Slowly, I meandered the streets until I found myself standing at the heavy wooden doors of the San Felipe De Neri, the place I used to call home before everything had changed for the worse. I took a deep breath and braced myself before going in, hoping to find some sort of solace, even though I had already been condemned.

The wood creaked as I pulled the door open, and I tried to be silent when I pulled it closed again behind me. There were a few people scattered across the long wooden pews whispering prayers while they clutched their rosary beads tightly in their hands, and when I passed by each of them, I wondered if they knew that I did not belong.

Making my way over the worn brick floor, I knelt down on a damp knee next to the first bench, making the sign of the cross before muttering quietly to myself. It was too late for me, but something about following the motions was comforting either way. My clothes left behind a trail of condensation as I slid onto the smooth bench. But unlike the smut I was accumulating from these deals I was making, the rain from my clothes would be easily wiped away. Leaning back against the hard wood, I waited patiently for something to happen.

I stared up at the statues set into their alcoves. *Are you supposed to be comforting? Because I'm not feeling it.* If anything, my insides were twisted up even more. Sadly, it was my choices making me feel that way, not the solid pieces of plaster sitting high on the shelves.

"Anna, it's good to see you back." Father Miguel's voice cut through my thoughts as he slid onto the bench next to me. His dark hair was starting to gray at the temples, but his face held the same friendly, welcoming smile it had that day he had approached me in the park across the street.

"Hi, Father Miguel." I smiled as genuinely as I could, but the weight of everything that had happened over the past few weeks was preventing it from reaching my eyes.

"You're troubled." His eyebrows furrowed with concern as he leaned in closer. "Would you like to make a confession?"

I laughed bitterly to myself. *Confession? Yeah, I think not. There's not absolving the sin of working for the Devil.*

"No," I shook my head.

"Is there anything I can do to help?" he asked encouragingly. I admired his persistence, but nothing he did would change my situation now.

"No." I blinked away the tears that were starting to form at the corners of my eyes. "There are some things not even you can help me with."

"Not me." He smiled. It was his turn to chuckle, and it made me happy to hear the light sound as it floated gently toward the high ceiling. "I can only listen, Anna. It's God who has to do the heavy lifting." His words reminded me of the first time we met.

"No amount of Hail Mary's and Our Father's would help me now," I admitted. My soul was the property of one, Silas A. Tan. "There are some things that can't be forgiven, but I appreciate you trying."

"I think you would be surprised." He lay his hand on my shoulder. "Just remember that you are never alone. I am always here if you ever need help with your burden."

He stood, making the sign of the cross over me and leaving me with a blessing before he made his way over to the gruff man who came through the door. I sat for a few more minutes, feeling even more guilty and defeated, before deciding to head back to the apartment. I just hoped Rachel would be so engrossed in her journal, I wouldn't have to face yet another judging glare. Between Declan, Matt, and the Saints, I'd had enough.

The darkened living room was a welcome sight, and I wasted no time heading straight to the bathroom, where I filled the tub with steaming hot water. Dropping in a peppermint bath bomb, I watched as it began fizzing in the water, filling the surface with a layer of tiny bubbles. I climbed inside to soak away the disappointments of the day and ponder what I needed to do now that Matt had broken up with me. But my mind kept wandering to the wide-eyed surprise on Declan's face after Matt called me his girlfriend.

He was almost jealous, but we barely knew each other, and every moment we spent together so far was forced upon us. The muscles in my shoulders knotted even thinking about it.

I lathered my hair, the scent of lavender filling my nostrils. *I smell lavender...that smell was important to me.*

There was something about the way he had opened up to me in the coffee shop. And the look he had given me when he told me about having been in love had me replaying the way the world around us ceased to exist in that moment. *It's a coincidence, right?* In my gut, I knew I was missing something. He'd been almost vulnerable. Especially the way he came after me when I bolted on him, following me all the way back to Idir.

I inhaled, filling my lungs again with the spicy scent of mint, along with the soothing scent of lavender, before slipping down below the water to rinse my hair. As I released bubbles slowly through my nose, I scolded myself for even thinking about him after everything he had done to me. But I couldn't deny that I now understood the pull of the magic. Declan and I had been thrown together once again, our paths not just crossing this time, but converging. All thanks to my own selfish need to get out of this place, and who knew how long he and I would end up working together.

It wasn't until the water had gone cold and my skin was pruny that I climbed out and padded down the hall to my room. I forgot how nice it was to have time to myself, and I was glad Rachel was still out.

It was a bad couple of weeks, that was for sure. Now I needed to decide if I was going to continue to wallow or soak up everything Declan had to teach me so I could get out of this place once and for all. I wanted to say it would be the former, but the latter option was more sensible.

As I waited for Rachel to return home, one thing kept coming back to the forefront of my mind, plaguing my thoughts. *There's something about Declan I just can't put my finger on. There's something he's not telling me.*

CHAPTER 13

A whole day went by without a word from Rachel or Declan, and I was starting to worry a little by the time I left the apartment for work. It was weird enough that I hadn't seen her at all the night before, but when I walked into Idir to start my shift, I understood why.

I watched from the door as Rachel sashayed across the floor, her hips swaying as her heels clicked across the laminate floor. She carried a tray full of drinks, balanced on one hand, and she leaned forward, expertly placing each glass on the table in front of her as she winked at the warlock beside her. My stomach knotted, my insides twisting with jealousy at how flawlessly she fit in. *Seriously? She went behind my back and got a job in my bar.* I couldn't believe it. She purposely waited until we were in a place she thought I couldn't be outwardly upset with her. Little did she know, work was the place I tended to lose my temper the most, and I was seething at the sight of her as she invaded what I'd come to think of as my sanctuary.

"What is Rachel doing here?" I asked Nate, my forced smile stretching wide while I wrapped the strings of my apron around my waist. I tied them tightly behind my back before slipping my phone into the pocket and taking up my place beside him.

"Matt hired her yesterday." He shrugged as he weaved his

way around me with two highballs for the warlock at the end of the bar. I recognized Officer Martin immediately, even in the dimly lit room, and I was surprised he was back after our encounter in the alley.

I wiggled my fingers at him, giving him my best F-you grin while he shot daggers at me. He grabbed his drinks roughly from Nate before he turned and stormed off in the other direction.

"Make me a Jagerbomb?"

I nodded as Nate passed by me, handing me a glass and a Red Bull before filling a shaker with ice for a Margarita.

My eyes scanned the room as I finished the drink, searching from the colorful neon jukebox to the door before glancing toward the office. Matt was nowhere to be seen. I was sure he would still be mad at me about the whole Declan incident, and a part of me hoped he would be too busy to discuss it. Plus, I was less than ready to rehash our previous conversation since I figured the two of us would be over when I refused to tell him anything more than I already had. He wanted answers I couldn't give him, and I needed space he wasn't willing to give me.

"I didn't realize we were shorthanded." I handed Nate the Jagerbomb, then shot a look toward Rachel.

"Your guess is as good as mine." He cocked his head, his bushy eyebrows climbing as his mouth quirked to one side.

"Don't tell me you drove one of the other girls away," I joked when he passed by again, but he didn't answer. Instead, he gave me a shake of his head accompanied by a thin lipped lopsided grin that said everything I needed to know. "Which one? I hope it wasn't Jessica— I finally decided to learn her name." He shrugged, the tops of his shoulders almost reaching his ear lobes as he scrunched his face, nodding in admission.

"At least you already know Rachel's name, and you can be sure she's not going to leave because of me," he laughed. "If it hasn't happened with her by now, it's never going to. But you, on the other hand, only time will tell." He winked, then wiggled his right eyebrow as he looked me over.

I groaned loudly, rolling my eyes at him, and I handed him a shot of vodka for the satyr two stools down from him, then poured one of my own.

"It will be a cold day in hell," I told him for the umpteenth time, but like every time before, my words were going to go in one ear and out the other.

"Hey, roomie." Rachel broke through my train of thought as she came sauntering up to the bar, her empty tray dangling at her side. Annoyance flared in me, and when I didn't acknowledge her, she sat down on the stool in front of me, staring as I dried glasses before placing them on the shelf next to me.

"You're still not talking to me?" she whined. "I said I was sorry."

"Did you seriously think it was a good idea to get yourself a job where I work?" I asked, giving her a sideways glance.

"I needed something to do until my probation is over. I can't exactly make money if I can't do the thing I normally do." She pouted her lips, letting a loud breath escape her nostrils as she twirled a corkscrew curl around her forefinger. "And you haven't exactly been paying rent." Her brown eyes sparkled as she teased me, trying to lighten the mood.

I ignored her jab, circling back around to the fact that she was there in the first place.

"There are a million other places in this city you could have gone to, Rachel, but you chose here. Convenient, considering two days ago, you asked me to make you a deal for your soul. I need a little space," I whispered as I leaned in as close as I could get across the surface of the bar. She leaned back on the stool, her eyes wide as she realized this might not have been her best idea. Caught, she slid down from the stool, and instead of getting angry or even apologizing, she simply walked away, leaving me to groan with frustration.

"Let me guess. You don't like the new girl." I turned to see Matt standing not two feet away, hands on his hips as he shook his head at me with disappointment, and it dawned on me why Rachel hadn't reacted to me. She'd seen him coming.

"We should talk." He turned away from me and strode toward the office in the back. I rarely went in there anymore, and the fact that we were going there instead of upstairs told me he was already prepared for what was coming.

"Close the door behind you," he said, squeezing himself past the pile of boxes to the other side of the desk, where he settled himself into the old swivel chair that had seen better days.

"Look, I know you're angry at me," I started, my back falling up against the closed door. The previously intimate size of the room was now too claustrophobic and much too warm with nowhere to go.

"I'm not mad at you." He rubbed his hands down his face as he set his elbows on the top of the desk with a thud. "I'm worried that you don't know what you're getting yourself into."

"I'm fine, I just need some time to sort things out."

"Why don't you just tell me what's going on. Maybe I can help," he pleaded.

"I can't without putting you in danger," I admitted, the words slipping past my lips before I could catch them.

"Danger from what? Does this have to do with why Declan was here yesterday? Did Melinda tell you how to get out of your contract?" he asked, his eyes wide as he leaned forward on his forearms.

"No," I shook my head. *I didn't get out of my contract. Quite the opposite, but I can't tell you that. Or anything, really.* "Declan..." *made a deal, and now a girl is going to die*, I tried to say. But before the words could leave my lips, I doubled over at the waist. The acid in my stomach churned, fighting to make its way up my throat while rendering me unable to speak.

"Are you okay?" He was on his feet in an instant, his palms planted firmly on the desktop. The wheels of the chair were muffled as they slid over the carpet, but I held out my palm to stop him from rushing to my aid as my stomach stopped churning. However, the minute I considered trying to tell him again, waves of nausea rolled through me, causing my head to pound as a thin sheen of sweat formed across the back of my neck. A warning not to even think about talking about a contract. Returning myself slowly to an upright position, I shook off the feeling, angry at the fact that even if I wanted to, I physically could not tell Matt a thing.

Damn you, Silas! I cursed him silently, my blood boiling because he had thought of everything, including my inability to keep a secret from Matt.

"What about Declan?" He leaned forward, the tips of his fingers braced on the surface of his desk as he tried to decide whether to come to me or not.

Finally, he sat back down, letting me know he wasn't going to let this whole thing go, no matter how much he cared about me.

"There is no way out of my contract," I rasped. "And this isn't about you, okay? I have to figure things out on my own."

"Fine, I guess that's it, then. I can't be with someone who refuses to tell me the truth," he said with a resigned shake of his head. He took a deep breath, plucking a pen from the metal cup at the corner of the desk, and began scribbling on the invoice at the top of the stack, dismissing me.

My heart squeezed in response to the sudden loss of his caring, friendly demeanor, and I wasn't sure whether to yell at him or retreat and nurse my wounded heart in private. After a few moments of deliberation, common sense won, and I left the room, pulling the door closed behind me. For the moment, I was thankful he hadn't fired me, too. My body sagged against the wall just outside the door as I breathed in the stale air from the bar while I counted down from ten, trying hard to get my emotions in check. My heart hurt knowing he shut me out so easily, and I wanted to cry, but I wouldn't, at least not there and not when there were so many people around to witness it.

I was so focused on breathing, my heart leapt into my throat when Rachel came crashing around the corner. She carried a large black trash bag over her shoulder, staggering a little as she struggled under the weight.

"I'll take it," I said with a sigh, reaching for the bag as she got closer. But instead of handing it over, she angled it away from me, setting her mouth into a firm line while she readjusted it.

"It's fine, I don't want to inconvenience you," she retorted.

Ugh! Really? You came into my space, and you're the one who's angry at me? I breathed in deeply through my nose and held the breath for a moment before releasing it through my lips. "You know that's not your job, right?"

"Yes, *Anna*, I know. But it won't kill me to take it out," she huffed.

Let it go, this isn't a battle worth fighting. I shook my head as I gestured for her to go ahead before skirting my way past her in the opposite direction. *Goddess, just get me through this night.* I sent out a silent prayer as I bit my lip. I couldn't help but be frustrated, but I didn't know if it was because she had tried to make a deal with me, or because it felt like she'd already taken over the only space we had to get some space from one another. Especially now that Matt and I were done.

I wouldn't be staying over at his place anymore. I let out a groan, pressing my fingertips to my forehead between my eyes, hoping to relieve my oncoming headache before facing the crowd. Nate needed my help, so I would have to deal with the Rachel situation later.

Every seat in the bar had been taken by the time I took up my spot next to Nate. Even the crappy bar table in the far corner that was balanced only by a bottle cap and a piece of gum was occupied. Before I knew it, Nate was calling out drinks for me to fill while he hustled them back and forth—a good thing because after the night I was having, I was bound to be throwing punches with any warlock who dared to even look at me the wrong way.

A short while later, I glanced around the room, searching for Rachel's mess of curls, realizing I had not seen her again since I passed her near the office, but she was nowhere to be seen. Thank goodness Nina was good at her job, and there wasn't an empty glass in the room. As soon as it slowed down, I headed down the short hall, pushing through the back door into the alley to get onto Rachel for shirking her responsibilities the first day on the job.

When I didn't see her right away, I walked slowly toward the dumpster, where a scream escaped my lips, piercing the chilly night air as soon as her slumped body came into view. Her back was propped up against the side of the grimy green dumpster, her hands pressed weakly against her abdomen as blood oozed through her fingers.

"What happened?" My legs, like my voice, were shaky as I rushed to her. Dropping to my knees, I pressed my palms down hard against her side. The feeling of her warm, thick blood oozing through my fingers made my stomach turn as I tried to help stop the bleeding.

"He came out of nowhere...," she whispered.

Her voice was raspy as she struggled to breathe, her tan complexion ashy. But it was the light blue tinge of her lips under the fluorescent light that had me concerned because she was losing blood...fast.

"I don't want to die." Her eyes were wide with fear as she stared up at me.

"Hang on, let me get Matt." I moved to get my phone from my apron, but she grabbed my hand to stop me as she shook her head at me. My fingers were already sticky with her blood as I struggled to stay calm and not lose the contents of my stomach all over the pavement.

"There's no time. I've lost too much blood." Blood rattled through her lungs with each labored breath, and I knew that whatever her injuries were, she was not going to last much longer.

"We have to try. Let me get Matt, Nate, someone..." I tried to stand, but she gripped my hand weakly in hers, giving me a slight shake of her head.

"Make me a deal," she begged, causing me to retreat away from her, landing with a thud on my own butt as I shook my head.

"No... I told you I won't do that." A small sob escaped my lips as warm tears slid down my cheeks.

"Please?"

"No. I can't take your soul, Rachel. You can't get that back. I don't want to be responsible for you ending up like me, or worse. I won't do that to you," I said shakily.

When Silas showed up at our door, it never even crossed my mind that I might be faced with a situation like this. And as much as I wanted to give in, I refused. I would not be the reason my friend ended up in Hell. *Any* version of it. Especially if I might be able to save her without a contract. *There has to be another way.* Though I had a sinking feeling in the pit of my stomach that she was beyond being saved without some serious intervention.

"Help!" I screamed before she could ask again, hoping someone would hear me over the din of music on the other side of the door I had come from.

Images of Declan raced through my mind as thoughts of myself cowering in the corner at the bank surfaced. I'd been bleeding out just like Rachel. *Where are you when I need you, damn it.* I lacked his calm, cool demeanor in this kind of situation. An image of his face floated through my mind while I pushed my hands against her wound once again.

Then from the shadows at the end of the alley, a tall figure approached. The casual way he strolled, hands stuffed into the pockets of his dark jeans, told me it was none other than Declan.

"No." My voice was hoarse from screaming, and I put my hand out to stop him in his tracks, but he kept on walking. "No — I didn't mean for you to come."

I pointed my shaking finger at him as if it were his fault that I had somehow summoned him from my imagination. Instead of engaging me, he ignored me, almost as if he were subconsciously drawn to Rachel's limp form.

"Don't you dare touch her!"

"Or what?" His eyes flashed as he turned to me.

My brain blanked. There was nothing I could do.

"Rachel, darling," he soothed as he knelt down beside her, taking her hands in his, exactly the same way he had done with me. My breath hitched at the similarity. I scooted back, settling myself onto the dirty pavement, grateful for the stinging pain from the loose asphalt as I pressed my palms more firmly into the ground and tried with everything I had not to let my own trauma overwhelm me.

I stared at them, knowing what he would tell her to get what he wanted. Though no matter how hard I listened, there were no words, only the sound of blood pounding in my ears while I watched him take out that stupid contract.

Rachel nodded, light fading from her once lively, sparkling eyes, and the coppery smell of blood permeated the air as a sudden wind whipped through the alley. Loose napkins and receipts swirled around before being whisked off into the inky darkness. The magic in the air pressed down on us, and I could swear the night had grown even blacker. It threatened to engulf the light from the streetlamp, and I wondered fleetingly, *am I seeing things?*

I continued watching, unable to protest as she struggled to lift her arm and pressed her bloody thumb against the stark white of the paper. The crackling magic continued to build, swirling itself into a frenzy. Until finally, it culminated into a streak of power that sealed her print to the page and promised her soul to the Devil.

I hope it was worth it.

CHAPTER 14

The smell of gunpowder was beginning to seem normal, but I knew deep down what it meant. Declan may have saved her life for the moment, but she was going to die regardless, and soon. All she had done was delay the inevitable.

"Guard dispatch, what's your emergency," the melodic voice on the other end of the line asked with a sense of urgency. It jarred me back to the present as I realized that, somewhere in the chaos of what was happening, I had pulled out my phone and called for help without even thinking about it. The small, slim phone shook in my hand as I pressed it against my ear, answering her questions without thinking. Before I knew it, the flashing lights of the ambulance were pulling to a stop in front of us, and we were pushed back while they loaded Rachel onto the gurney, starting an IV right away to help replenish some of what she had lost.

I realized she wasn't in any more danger, but the reality of the situation was that she had almost died in my arms, and I was going to let her. Declan stood silently beside me while we watched them load her inside, slamming the door closed and disappearing into the night as if nothing had happened.

"You have to tear up the contract," I said as I turned to face him. It annoyed me that there didn't seem to be even a drop of blood on him, yet I was covered in it.

"I can't," he scoffed. "And even if I could, I wouldn't."

"Please, Declan, don't take her soul," I pleaded as a fresh set of tears rolled down my cheeks. Instead of responding, he shook his head, his eyes weary as he muttered under his breath before disappearing, and not a moment too soon. The black sedan rounding the corner meant one thing: Guard Officers were there to take my statement about what had happened. They obviously would have been dispatched along with the ambulance, but I was shocked it had taken so long for them to show up.

"Anna Westfall?" asked the short warlock who stepped out of the car, his partner joining him a second later when I nodded in the affirmative.

"I'm Officer Bryant, and this is my partner Officer Thompson." He extended his hand to me. When I didn't reciprocate, he dropped it back down to his side, shifting his weight to his other foot in a nervous gesture. "We understand you found the victim. Can you tell us what happened?"

"She took out the trash, and when she didn't come back, I came to check on her. That's when I found her." My voice cracked as I pointed a shaky finger to where she had been sitting.

"You have a lot of blood on you. Were you hurt as well?" His question took me by surprise as he showed more concern for me than any other warlock I had met.

He obviously doesn't know who or what I am, or he wouldn't be so nice. I shook my head at him.

"Did you see anyone else? Did she say anything about who attacked her?"

"She said he came out of nowhere," I repeated what little information she had given me.

"Is it normal for one of the waitresses to be out here alone?"

"No, it's the cook's job to take out the trash. I offered to help her, but she refused, and we were pretty busy, so I didn't push the issue," I said.

"Okay, well, I think that's all we need from you. We'll get a statement from her, but make sure to stick around in case we have any other questions for you." He lay his hand gently on my shoulder for just a moment.

The two of them turned in unison, but before they reached the car, Officer Bryant turned back to me. "Are you sure you're not hurt? Is there anywhere we can take you?"

"I'm fine. I need to talk to my boss." My answer was clipped as I tried to hold back the tears that were threatening to fall once again, and with a nod, they climbed back into their car and left.

My first instinct was to get away from there, but I decided to turn myself around and go tell Matt what had happened. Grabbing the door handle, I noticed once again that my hands were sticky with Rachel's blood. The realization caused my hands to tremble now that the adrenaline seemed to be wearing off, and I wiped them on the thighs of my jeans before wrenching the door open. I didn't want to spend one second longer in the alley than I needed to.

I entered the hall as Matt came out of his office, his eyes wide with concern as he ran toward me.

"It's not mine," I said, my whole body starting to shake while he searched me for the source of the blood. "It's Rachel's. She was attacked in the alley when she took out the trash. She's on her way to the hospital." My voice sounded almost robotic, even to my own ears.

His hands gripped my shoulders firmly as his brown eyes looked deep into mine. His voice, full of concern as he fired off questions. "Is she okay? Why didn't you come get me? What happened?"

"I think she's going to be okay. Everything happened so fast...I just need to go. I need to get out of here."

"It's okay. Come on. Let's get you upstairs and cleaned up," he said as he guided me a few steps down the hall.

"No, I need to go home," I said with a shake of my head. "I can't be here right now."

"Okay, let me just tell Nate, and I'll walk you home—"

"I'll be fine." My legs moved me forward on autopilot, and I headed straight for the door without another thought.

I was aware of the steady thud of his steps behind me as his Doc Martens hit the pavement, and I was comforted by his presence. But he made no attempt to catch up with me, allowing me some space. Everything else around me was a blur as I walked down the darkened street, and before I knew it, I was standing in the living room, back pressed against the door, staring down at my blood-stained hands.

"Declan," I screamed, releasing all of my fear, anger, and sadness in that one word as I sank to the floor. I knew it in my gut that he had heard me, and in less than five minutes, he stepped out of the ether, appearing in front of me. I sobbed openly, tears streaming down my cheeks, snot starting to run from my nose. I didn't care about the smears of dark crimson I was leaving all over his soft slate gray sweater when he pulled me into his arms. He held me tightly against his chest as his fingers stroked my hair.

A flash of memory shot through me, *Declan holding me while I cried, sobbing inconsolably.* But the more I fought to hold onto that piece, the faster it disappeared, like spun sugar in water.

"How could you?" I sniffled, finally able to think clearly again. "How could you make her a deal?"

"You called me there. What was I supposed to do?" he asked sincerely, reminding me that I was the reason he had been in the alley in the first place.

"You were supposed to let her die."

"You don't mean that, and you know it," he whispered as he reached out and tucked my hair behind my ear. Like so many times recently, there was something pulling at the edges of my memory, but no matter how hard I tried, I couldn't grab onto it, and it was making me crazy.

"I do," I yelled, putting all of my frustration into that statement. "She's going to die, anyway. The only difference is that you extended it for her, and maybe only by a few days."

"How do you know that? You said the same thing yesterday, like you know when they're going to die," he pushed, his eyes drilling into me for the information he was seeking.

"I don't know when they're going to die. But I know in my gut that it will be soon."

"But how?" he pleaded.

"Because I can smell it," I spat. "I can smell the gunpowder from the same shot that would have killed me that day if you hadn't shown up with your fucking deal. I smelled it right after I made my deal with Lucinda. She died that night. Then, I smelled it again after your deal with the girl in the coffee shop, and then again with Rachel. You might have saved her tonight, but I guarantee you, her days are numbered."

"That's absurd, Anna. It's a coincidence," he reasoned. "One death doesn't make a trend." His long, thin fingers continued stroking my hair as he tried to convince me. But I knew I was right. I needed a way to get Rachel out of her contract before she died, and I would give him whatever he wanted to make that happen. Even if it meant being sentenced to the deepest pits of Hell for telling Silas, I no longer wanted to be his intern.

"Declan, please, you have to void her contract." I turned my face up toward his, pleading as I grasped him by the forearms with my dirty hands. Rachel's blood had dried long ago. and it formed a cracked mosaic over my own skin, flaking off in places when I moved, but none of that was important at the moment. *I need to save her from this fate, or worse.* My stomach knotted as I clutched the soft fabric from his sleeves.

"I can't," he emphasized as he shook off my hands. He slid me from his lap and stood to pace the room, the leather soles of his shoes silent as he glided over the hardwood floor.

"You mean you won't." I balled my hands into fists, my fingernails digging into the flesh of my palms as I tried to get my emotions in check.

"Once a deal is made, it's binding. Silas is owed a soul. That doesn't just go away. And even if I wanted to, I wouldn't. I didn't force her to make a deal." He sighed as he ran his hand over his face before pushing his fingers through his hair.

"Then leave. I don't want you here." I pointed toward the door. I would find a way to save Rachel's soul even if I had to do it myself.

His features grew hard as he took in the seriousness of my tone, but he didn't argue with me. He didn't say one word to me. Instead, he muttered his incantation once again, then disappeared the same way he had come, leaving me in the deafening silence of my now empty apartment, grieving my friend who wasn't even dead yet.

I curled up on the floor, allowing the sobs to wrack my body until I couldn't cry anymore. Then I dragged myself down the hallway to the bathroom, where I finally washed the blood from my hands. My skin was tender and red by the time I finished, but no matter how hard I scrubbed, I would never be able to get rid of the invisible stains it left behind.

CHAPTER 15

Every part of me, body and soul, was raw by the time I climbed in between my sheets. I wanted to smother myself in darkness. To hide away from the world, if only to avoid having to face my new reality. I was alone, and the silence was deafening. I'd succeeded in isolating myself from the few people I cared about in the past few years, and I had no one to blame but myself.

I lay in the dark, staring up at the ceiling, feeling the crippling fear overtake me as my chest constricted. *What am I going to do? How am I going to save her soul when I couldn't save my own? There's got to be a way. I make deals for the Devil, for fuck's sake.* My thoughts swirled, but I was so overwhelmed by what I couldn't do, I was unable to see past it.

"Anna, wake up. We need to go," Declan said as he shook me gently. I rolled away from him, pulling the covers firmly over my head in an attempt to escape once again. I must have fallen asleep at some point, and I wasn't ready to leave the refuge of my bed.

"Don't make me drag you out of here," he growled.

"What do you want?" I yelled as I sat upright, pushing the covers off in the process. He grabbed a hold of my forearm, and before I knew it, we were outside of the barn at Melinda's house, listening to an argument inside. I was starting to hate that little trick of his, though the lack of nausea told me I might be getting used to it.

I could see the faintest blue line pulsing on the ground from where we stood, extending to somewhere inside. Within a few moments, the line vanished. Someone had died.

"What happened?" A confused voice asked from behind me, causing me to turn just in time to see Abigail, the girl from the coffee shop, suddenly standing in front of Declan.

"I'm here to collect on your end of our deal," he said brusquely, and I was surprised to see him deviate from his typically gentle demeanor when addressing a soul.

"But that can't be possible."

"I'm afraid so. That's what happens when you make a deal with the Devil and your body dies."

"I can't be dead; that wasn't the deal. Gen was supposed to die, not me," she whined as her fists balled up at her sides. Her petite stature and her trembling bottom lip made me wonder if she was on the verge of a tantrum.

"No, the deal was to get your boss to the coffee shop last night, and I did."

"Then I can't be dead."

"Your body is on the other side of that door if you want to see for yourself. Either way, I will be taking you for judgment tonight," he said dryly.

Her jaw dropped, her already translucent features becoming even more pale in the dim light of the moon as she realized he was telling her the truth.

For a moment, I thought she might fight back, but then she resigned herself to her fate, shaking her head before taking his outstretched hand in hers. He turned toward me, his tired blue eyes meeting mine as he held out his other hand, and in less than a minute, the three of us were standing in front of Silas's desk waiting for her to be judged. The trip this time wasn't as bad as the one to deliver Lucinda's soul. My stomach was thankful for that.

Silas sat stiffly behind his desk, his elbows propped up on the surface, his fingers steepled while he considered what to do with the soul of the witch in front of him. "Abigail Bishop, after reading your file, I see that you made a deal to betray your cousin for personal gain. For that reason, I am banishing you to the deepest pit of hell for a term of no less than one thousand years, after which time you will be eligible for transfer," he said somberly.

"Why?" she demanded, her eyes darting between the three of us. "She gets to serve her sentence here; why am I being punished so harshly?" She pointed an accusing finger at me.

"Because Anna didn't make a deal for her own personal gain. She didn't betray those who were close to her. *She* almost died taking a bullet for someone. And *she* only made a deal so she could live to protect family..." he said, and for the first time since getting involved in this whole mess, I had garnered information about what made me different. Before she could ask any more questions, he opened the pit with a wave of his hand, sending her hurtling into it to start her sentence.

The gaping hole in the floor knit itself back together, leaving nothing behind but the seamless red carpet. I stared at the spot, my brain reeling from the swiftness of the interaction, yet somehow satisfied in knowing she'd tried to betray family. Declan took me by the elbow, but I shook free before he could travel us back to my apartment.

"Why did you sentence Lucinda so harshly?" I asked Silas.

"You left her soul without its body for too long, making her soul malevolent. Nothing else could have been done. But... even if you had brought her to me right away, she acted selfishly and lied about her situation. Things aren't always as they seem, Anna, and you *never* have all the information. Opportunities present themselves to you for a reason."

He sighed deeply before turning his chair to face the giant wall of glass behind him that looked out onto the city.

"You two can see yourselves out," he said, ending the conversation.

Once again, Declan took my elbow, and the next thing I knew, we were back in my apartment. My first instinct was to kick him out again because anger was simmering just below the surface anytime I thought about Rachel. But my curiosity over recent events had me holding my tongue for the time being.

"Why didn't I get sick when you brought me to reap that soul and then to Silas this time?" I meandered over to the sofa, dropping wearily onto it before gesturing for him to take a seat on the chair nearby.

"You didn't fight me this time," he explained as he sat down hesitantly.

"I guess that makes sense." I chewed my bottom lip while I considered it. "Can you teach me how to do that myself?"

"You won't be able to tear reality unless you're an Apprentice," he said with a shake of his head. His dark blonde hair fell across his forehead, and he pushed it back with one hand as he settled himself into the chair. I harrumphed while I stared daggers at him.

"Well, then what good is having you as a mentor? You need to teach me something," I demanded.

"I'm here to make sure you know how to make a good deal and reap a soul, that's it. Remember, you answer to me, not the other way around." He scowled, and then he disappeared right before my eyes as if to prove his point.

"Ugh! Are you kidding me?" I groaned, throwing my hands up in the air.

I was no closer to getting my freedom or releasing Rachel from her contract now than I was before, and things only seemed to be getting worse by the day. I needed a plan, and fast, because people were dropping dead around me quickly. *Well, aren't I just a little ray of sunshine? Maybe I'll start calling myself the harbinger of Death.* I rolled my eyes at myself, but it stood to reason that since the witch from the coffee shop was reaped, Rachel would be next.

CHAPTER 16

I looked at my watch for the fifth time in seven minutes, which was how long I had been pacing across the street from Idir. The anxiety that decided to dig its claws in before wasn't going anywhere, no matter how much I tried to shake it off, and if I didn't go through that door soon, I was going to be late. *I should have called in. What was I thinking coming back here so soon? I haven't even heard anything from Rachel. What if she's in worse shape than I thought?*

Another glance at my watch told me I was officially late, and even though my stomach was churning, I took a deep breath, crossed the street, and pushed through the front door before I could talk myself out of it. *You need a distraction. Just get behind the bar. You'll hear something soon enough.*

No sooner had I thought the words did my breath catch in my chest, my feet refusing to move as I caught sight of my roommate, smiling as she dropped off a round of shots for a table full of warlocks. The fact that she was there looking like nothing had ever happened made my head rock back as if I had been hit by the shock. I wasn't sure whether I wanted to cry in relief or scream, but before I knew it, I was grabbing her by the elbow as she passed by, almost as if she hadn't seen me.

"Seriously? Why are you back here already?" I snapped. She nearly dropped the empty glass she was carrying as she spun from the force of it. Her brown eyes widened, and she handed it off to Nina before addressing me.

"What the hell?"

"Exactly. What in the hell are you doing? You were in the hospital last night," I whispered.

"Yeah, it's amazing what a deal with the Devil can do. I woke up this morning ready to take on the world. I don't even have a scar," she bragged in a conspiratorial whisper.

"Hey, Rachel, this one's for the pixie in the back," Nate called, interrupting our conversation, and Rachel bounded away quickly, leaving me standing next to the bar alone and fuming.

"Anna, I need you in the office," Matt called from the hallway as he gestured me over with a wave. I was annoyed he'd let Rachel come back so soon, and I was starting to wonder if I'd even talked to him afterward. With one last glance over my shoulder at Rachel, I shook my head in dismay and followed after Matt.

"Can you watch the bar tonight?" He was gathering things from around the room, placing them into a second black duffel bag that sat in the middle of his desk.

"What is Rachel doing back so soon? Is everything okay?"

"Not really. I've been summoned to a Convocation meeting to discuss the recent issue with the vampires in the city. I'll be back tomorrow, but I need someone to watch over the bar and close up. You can stay here for the night," his eyes pleaded. His request caught me off guard, considering how we had left things the night before.

"Why didn't you ask Nate?" I asked, and he gave me a look that said, *seriously?*

"Fine," I said with a sigh, knowing I owed him at least that for everything he had done for me over the past few years. He smiled, picking up a bag in each hand before giving me a habitual peck on the forehead as he breezed past me.

My heart skipped a beat, and I wondered if he even realized he'd done it. I shook it off, squaring my shoulders as I prepared myself to play boss. It was going to be a long night, that was for sure.

Thankfully, there was no downtime, and the night seemed to fly by with no time to worry about Rachel, who seemed to be lighter on her feet than ever before. She weaved her way expertly around the tables, laughing and flirting with customers while she delivered one drink after the next.

Once it was time for last call, we were still busy enough that I had to shout over the music and conversation to be heard. I gave a sigh of relief when Nate rounded up the last few stragglers fifteen minutes after closing. My eyes scanned the room, noticing every stray napkin, water stain, and leftover cocktail pick, and my heart sped up when I didn't immediately see Rachel.

"Hey, where's —" I gasped as she popped up from one of the benches of a booth, holding a twenty-dollar bill clutched in her fist.

"Think you could stay and give me a hand finishing things up?" I asked, and she gave me a thumbs up before I waved Nate out the front door.

"Does this mean we're good?" She dropped her tray on the bar top, her brown eyes looking at me through thick dark lashes as she quirked her mouth to one side.

How am I the only one still upset about this whole thing? How are you not freaking out right now? I bit my bottom lip and shook my head.

"Don't get me wrong. I'm not happy about any of this. But I am glad you're okay." *For now.* My throat constricted even thinking the words, so I knew there was no way they'd pass my lips. She nodded, then turned back to her work while I continued putting glasses on the shelf. At one-thirty, we were both practically dead on our feet, and I was looking forward to some sleep as I turned off the lights, but I wasn't going to let her out of my sight. At least until I could figure out a way to break her contract.

"Hey, I'll walk home with you. Let me just lock up." I turned toward the office, where I knew I could find an extra set of keys in the safe.

"No, don't worry about it. I'll just have to walk you back here out of obligation, and it will be a whole vicious cycle." Rachel laughed, and it took me a second to see her logic before I rolled my eyes at her.

"There's no way I'm letting you walk home alone. Not after what happened. Why don't you just stay here with me? There's a pull-out sofa."

"It's fine. I signed a contract, remember? I'm not going anywhere anytime soon."

"How could I forget..." I crossed my arms over my chest, letting my breath out in a loud huff. "But having a contract doesn't mean you can't die."

"You're not dead." She countered, her right brow climbing toward her hairline in challenge.

"I am according to the U.S. government and everyone I ever knew before this."

"Yeah, but look at you. You're immortal; you can never die."

"That's only one of the reasons why this is Hell for me. Even if you got to stay in Hell on Earth, you would never be able to come back here. You would never see Gabe or anyone you love again because you would be dead to them."

"I can live with that," she insisted with a shrug.

"Could you live with being stuck wherever Silas decides to drop you? Even if that's the deepest pit of Hell? Can you live with being hated by the warlocks or shunned by the coven? What about never being able to do magic again?"

"I saw you do magic that night you knocked out Derek in the alley—"

"No, you saw me manipulate *his* magic." My shoulders slumped, and I leaned against the counter, dropping my head into my hands. "I'm stuck here in this city. Forever. Knowing that the only family I had left will die, and I won't be there for them in any way." A tear rolled down my cheek, but I wiped it away before I lifted my head to look her in the eyes.

"Then make me another deal so that I can live forever. Then I won't be able to give my soul to Silas."

A bitter laugh escaped my lips. "Silas doesn't make deals for souls he already owns." I parroted the phrase he'd used on me that day in the apartment.

"I don't buy that," she argued. Her eyes grew wide, her hands covering her mouth as the reality of what she had done sank in, but I just gave a sad shrug. I was tired and defeated, and I had no idea how to comfort her when I couldn't comfort myself.

"We'll figure it out tomorrow, okay? Let's just get you home for now."

She nodded, her expression blank as she pulled on her jacket, slipping the strap of her purse over her shoulder as we headed out into the cold night.

Our footsteps tapping over the cracked cement sidewalk was the only sound as we walked. My brain barely had time to notice the searing pain in my neck as my head was wrenched to the side, and I was forced to focus on the crushing pressure of the arm around my ribcage as a shape blurred in front of me. A second later, I heard Rachel's muffled scream, but there was no time to figure out what was happening before my vision blackened around the edges until darkness consumed me.

CHAPTER 17

What in hell? Where am I? My head pounded, and I massaged my temples with my thumbs in an attempt to clear away the pain and lingering fogginess from whatever rendered me unconscious as I sat up in the darkness. I wasn't sure how I'd ended up in the alley, but one thing was for sure: someone tried to kill me.

My heart thudded against my ribcage as Declan appeared less than two feet away from me.

"Are you okay?" He knelt down in front of me, his warm hand settling on my shoulder as his blue eyes searched mine, and I gave a nod. "What happened?"

"I'm not sure. But how in the heck can you just show up wherever I am?" I grumbled.

"You're tethered to me," he said with a sigh. "I can come through wherever you are. It doesn't matter the location." He stood holding out his hand, and I took it, allowing him to help me to my feet as my stomach lurched.

"What in the hell do you mean you're tethered to me?" I demanded, placing my hands on my hips as I glared at him.

His shoulders slumped as his eyes averted to look at anything but me. "Silas thought it would be a good idea."

"And you couldn't say no?"

"Have you tried saying no to Silas?" He cocked a blonde

eyebrow and pursed his lips as he leaned toward me. It reminded me that I had, in fact, told Silas no, and he'd threatened to make my existence even more miserable. I refused to acknowledge the fact that he was right once again before remembering that it was after three in the morning, and we were standing in the middle of a dirty alley.

"What are you doing here now?"

"I'm here to collect her soul," he said, reminding me of why I was there in the first place. *Rachel.* The fluorescent light flickered at the end of the alley, and I almost missed the silvery form of her soul as she paced back and forth across the space between one building and the other, muttering to herself. I choked back a sob when I caught sight of her slumped body leaning against the wall. *No! This can't be. How did this happen?* My hands covered my mouth in an effort to stifle a scream, but they couldn't hold back the tears that streamed down my cheeks.

"Anna!"

She rushed toward me, her hands outstretched. But instead of being able to embrace me, her translucent figure went right through me, and I shivered violently, feeling as if I had just immersed myself in a tub full of ice water. "What the..." she trailed off as she looked down at her corporeal form. "Oh, my goddess."

It was then that she realized she was no longer in her body, and she hurried back down the alley with Declan and me close on her heels.

"Oh my goddess, oh my goddess, oh my goddess, what happened?" she turned toward us, her hands covering her mouth, her eyes bugging out. "Please tell me this is a bad dream." But all I could do was shake my head.

"I'm sorry, Rachel," Declan said, and unlike his demeanor with the young witch the previous morning, he was back to his normal, caring self.

"I told you." I turned toward him, my tone accusing as I pointed a finger in his direction. "I told you this was going to happen. Declan, please, you have to let her go."

"I told you. I can't," he said his deep voice heavy with remorse.

"Anna, you have to do something," Rachel begged, her eyes wide with fear, but there was nothing I could do. Her contract was not mine.

Shit! Shit, shit, shit! What do I do? My hands rubbed the back of my neck as I paced, and when I pulled them away, I noticed the palm of my right hand was coated in blood. *No wonder I can't think straight, I'm bleeding...*I pushed the thought aside. I would have to deal with that later. Right now, I needed to buy some time.

"I'll give you anything, just please don't take her to Silas."

"There's nothing you can give me that would be enough to void her contract."

"You said Silas is owed a soul," I said, grasping at straws. "But that doesn't mean it has to be her soul." I pointed to Rachel's still-shocked form, which was now floating back and forth between us and her lifeless body. Declan sighed loudly, but he didn't deny what I was saying, giving me the steam to keep going because maybe, I was onto something. "What if I can find you a better soul? Someone more valuable?"

"Like who? The only thing that would be valuable enough to make Silas forget that it wasn't the original contract would be a selfless soul, and it could take a millennium to find one of those."

"Give me a chance."

"It's impossible."

"Let me try. I know things you don't," I lied. "I knew that the witch from the coffee shop and Rachel were both going to die soon," I reminded him, and he nodded reluctantly. Just then,

Rachel rushed back to me, causing my heart to skip a beat at how fast she moved.

"What do you mean you knew I was going to die soon?" she asked. "When did you know this, and why didn't you tell me?"

"I only knew after you made your deal with Declan, and, apparently, I can't talk to anyone about any of the deals we make. It literally makes me so sick, I can't speak," I spat. It was harsher than I intended, but at the moment, I was less concerned about hurting her feelings than I was about saving her from an eternity in the depths of hell.

"One week... that's all I can give you. I can put her in limbo, but it can't be any longer than that," Declan said, interrupting our conversation.

Fuck, Anna! You seriously aren't thinking straight, are you? Now you have to go out and make a deal for a soul that really doesn't belong in hell. Could you make things any worse? I smacked my forehead with the palm of my hand. Not only that but a week was not nearly enough time to find a selfless soul when I didn't even know what I was looking for.

"I thought a soul couldn't be left outside of its body for that long without becoming malevolent," I protested. I thought that if he agreed, she would be able to at least live as a void until I could find someone better.

"If a soul is taken to limbo, it will be fine for seven days. I'm giving you five. If you can't find a selfless soul by then, she'll have to go to Silas for judgment," he warned.

"Well, how will I know if I find a selfless soul?" I asked, my voice rising as I started to panic.

"You tell me, you're the one who knows things I don't," he taunted.

"Fine," I said through gritted teeth and hoped beyond hope that I would be able to come through. Without another word, he held out his hand to Rachel, and she hesitated a moment before placing her hand in his. They disappeared, leaving me with her empty shell of a body in the dimly lit alley.

I wasn't sure whether to leave her there or not, so after about ten minutes of debating with myself, I decided it was probably best not to leave her body to be discovered in the gutter. I would want her to move me, after all.

"Declan," I called out quietly, and within seconds, he appeared.

"What are you still doing here?" he hissed as he scanned the area to make sure no one was watching.

"We can't just leave her body here." I gestured around the disgusting space.

"Ugh," he groaned, then grabbed hold of my hand before leaning down and taking hers, too. The next thing I knew, we were in my apartment, Rachel's body lying atop her bed, as if she were sleeping.

"Will she last here like this?" I whispered before realizing that I could yell and it would still not disturb her.

"Her body will be fine until your time is up, and then we'll return her to where she was to be found." He sighed. It annoyed me that he assumed I would fail, but I was too worn out to argue with him about it now.

"What happened to her?"

"She was drained by the vampire that's been hunting in the city. It's unfortunate, really. She just happens to look enough like the intended victim that she ended up in the crosshairs," he admitted, and I was taken aback.

"You know about the vampire attacks?" My hand moved to my neck, but there was nothing there but dried blood. Not even a raised patch of skin where I assumed the vampire had bitten me, too.

"I know about a lot of things."

"Well, who is it? Who are they hunting?" I thought of Matt at the Convocation, and in the back of my mind, I wanted a little tidbit of information to give him so that maybe I could get back in his good graces.

"It's not our matter to interfere in." He leveled me with a look that said, *we are not going there*, and I rolled my eyes at him as I looked down at my only friend's dead body once again.

"That vampire tried to kill me, too." I sat on the edge of her bed, feeling her weight shift behind me.

"I'm sure they viewed you as collateral damage. But it doesn't matter because you can't be killed."

"The vampire obviously didn't know that."

"Well, either way, we can't get involved. Silas and Melinda have an agreement. This is a witch problem, so let it go." His eyebrows crept toward his hairline as he inclined his head toward me to say, 'got it?'

"Fine, but it seems like this is getting out of hand. She's the third person to be killed by this vampire so far, and every single one of them has made a deal with us. That's going to look suspicious, don't you think?" I asked. He shrugged, stuffing his hands deep into the pockets of his jeans without saying a word. "The Guard already questioned me about Lucinda," I reminded him.

I fumed at his lack of response, but I could tell by his casual posture he was not going to budge.

I closed my eyes as I raised my face to the ceiling while I shook my head in dismay, releasing a groan from deep in my chest. "Fine, just take me back to Idir."

The only thing that alerted me to the fact that we had moved was the slight change in temperature, and when I opened my eyes, I stood next to the foot of the stairs leading up to the apartment. Declan was nowhere to be seen. After checking the locks on the doors once more, I stomped up the stairs. I needed some caffeine and a plan if I was going to have any hope of finding a selfless soul in five days.

CHAPTER 18

"**A**nna, wake up. It was just a dream," Matt roused me from my sleep, stroking my red waves as I opened my eyes to see him leaning over me. The notebook I'd been using to jot down ideas was on the floor, and half a cup of cold tea sat on the nightstand with a spoon still in it.

"You're back early," I breathed, turning my cheek into the palm of his hand. I couldn't remember whatever it was I had been running from in my dream, but my heart hammered a staccato beat against my ribs regardless.

"That must have been some nightmare," he said, his face etched with worry. "You were really thrashing around."

"Well, it's gone now." I smiled, happy to have him there with me even though I knew he wasn't really mine any longer. "How did things go with the Convocation?"

He sighed as he rubbed the back of his neck, and I could feel his frustration roll off him in waves. "To be honest, it was a waste of time. No one knows anything, and all Melinda talked about was finding the vampire responsible for the attacks before she loses any of her family." He gave an annoyed shake of his head. "If you ask me, the witches have been in power long enough, or at least the Farrington witches."

"What do you mean?" I sat up facing him, our noses mere

inches apart, and I had to stop myself from leaning in and kissing him.

"Well, the only reason there are vampires in the city in the first place is because they're hunting Melinda's daughter, who had to have done something really stupid to end up on the docket."

"The docket?" I asked. In the two years, I had been working at Idir, it was the first time Matt had ever mentioned it.

"You know, the hit list for supernaturals," he said, furrowing his brows at me like this was something everyone knew.

"I've never heard of it," I shrugged. No wonder Genevieve was willing to make a deal with me; she was on a hit list. She knew vampires were after her. But that didn't make sense, considering Declan told me the night before that the girls who'd been drained by the vampires, including Rachel, looked like the girl they were hunting. If I remembered correctly, Genevieve had blonde hair and fair skin.

"You literally made a deal with the Devil, and you don't know about the docket?" he asked incredulously.

"I had no idea supernatural beings even existed until that day." I slid to the end of the bed, put the notebook into my back pocket, and slipped on my sneakers while he watched silently from his perch. "I have to go, and I'm taking a few days off if that's all right," I said as I crossed the room and pulled open the front door.

"Yeah, that's fine." He nodded. He got up and moved toward me, but I was already walking through the door by the time he had crossed the room. I wanted to gather more insight from him, but as curious as I was, I had other things to do, like saving Rachel. I also didn't want to end up arguing with him when he inevitably brought up Declan again.

"Thanks for covering last night," he called after me, and I waved him off as I headed down the short flight of stairs. I almost turned around and backtracked when I realized I hadn't told him Rachel had been drained by the Vampire the night before, but that would have meant explaining how I knew that. Besides, I still had five days to get it figured out, so there was no reason to bring it up now if there was a chance I could be successful.

By the time I reached the front door of my apartment, I had a knot in my stomach the size of a golf ball. I didn't want to see Rachel's empty shell of a body, but I couldn't stop myself as I moved down the hall, past my bedroom door, until I was standing at the foot of her bed.

If I tried hard enough, I could almost pretend she was sleeping, but the longer I stood there, the more I focused on how pale her lips were and the lack of movement in her chest. And the more I looked at her, the angrier I became. "What were you even doing taking out the garbage in the first place. That's not part of your job. You were just being stubborn going out there on your own." *And I was too caught up in my own shit to go with you.* I blamed myself as much as I blamed her for the predicament we found ourselves in.

Ugh! I should have just kept walking that night and minded my own damn business. "I wish you had never spoken up for me with Melinda," I told her still form. *Because now I have to figure out how to return the favor and save your eternal soul.* Besides, she was the only person I could confide in about any of this and the only witch I had met so far who didn't seem to loathe me. And as much as I hated to admit it at the moment, I considered her my friend.

"I hate you right now," I growled at her, feeling the weight of the words as I directed them inwardly as well.

I spun away, leaving her corpse alone once again, and headed back down the hall to my room. It was pointless yelling at either of us now. She couldn't hear me anyway, and I refused to stay there and feel sorry for myself a minute longer.

I sat down on the edge of my bed, taking in my surroundings, and I couldn't help but be bitter. I didn't feel like I could stay any longer. Not after everything that had happened in the past few days, and especially now that my house arrest was over.

Rachel and I had never really finished discussing it, but I assumed she would want her apartment to herself again. I let out a heavy sigh, resigning myself to the idea that it would be better this way before I got to my feet and started to work.

Once I had taped up the box from the back of my closet, it took very little time to pack up everything I owned, and as I stood at the front door, I was surprised at the twinge of sadness in my chest about leaving the place that had been my home for such a short time. Part of me even felt bad for leaving Rachel's body alone. Though I knew that no one, aside from me and Declan, would be able to get in. Even then, Declan needed me to be inside before he could cross the wards, so as far as I was concerned, she was as safe as she could be.

The cold breeze chilled me right to my bones, and I wondered briefly if it were an omen before brushing the thought aside completely. After all, how could things get any worse than they already were? I had ticked off my mentor, lost my boyfriend, my friend was a corpse, and I was basically homeless.

While I walked down the street carrying the cardboard box in my arms, I prayed to whoever would listen that Father Miguel would not turn me away. Thankfully, the trek back to the church was a short one, and the minute Father Miguel saw me, he made his way to me from the front of the sanctuary.

"I see you've decided you need that help, after all." He smiled, and I nodded solemnly in agreement.

I was grateful for the comfortable silence we shared while he walked me back to the rectory, opening up the little room I had occupied in the not-so-distant past before handing me the key once again.

"I'll see you tomorrow for weekly cleaning?" he asked, to which I gave another silent nod, and he left me to be alone, a genuine grin gracing his aging features as he closed the door gently behind him.

I looked around the meager room with its single bed, sturdy desk, and small wooden chair. I contemplated whether or not I should unpack my things before deciding to just leave the box in the bottom of the closet. It seemed pointless to call any place home, especially with everything so out of control.

When I sat down at the desk, I remembered the notebook in my back pocket and pulled it out to go over the notes I'd written the night before. But it was a moot point because the only thing there was the list of things I already knew. It was hard to come up with a plan if I had no idea where to start.

Step one... figure out what's different about souls. Talk to Matt, see if he knows anything. I crossed out Matt's name, replacing it with Nate's, only to cross it out again. *Great, you have no friends. No one to talk to about this.* But as I thought about it, one name kept popping up.

I wrote down Declan next to the other two names. *Now I just need to figure out how to approach him...*

CHAPTER 19

A loud clap of thunder had me jumping in my seat, and I was surprised to see that, according to my phone, I was due to meet Father Miguel in the sanctuary soon. I stretched my arms above my head, working out the stiffness in my muscles from sitting at the desk all night.

The dark wood surface was covered with sheets of paper scrawled with notes about anything Declan or Silas had said recently that might be important. At some point, I'd decided to pore over the contracts I had made with Genevieve and Lucinda, passing the time scrutinizing every word in each document before dismissing it all as irrelevant to what I needed.

I rolled my neck and stretched my legs out under the desk as I listened to the rain tap against the glass of my window before deciding it was time to get to work. I had a sanctuary to clean, and the sooner I got it done, the sooner I would feel less awful about needing Father Miguel's help again. *And some distance from all of this might help with some insight.*

I gave my underarms the sniff test before swiping on some deodorant, then pulled on a clean tee and a pair of faded jeans before running my fingers through my hair. I pulled it back, securing it in a messy bun with the rubber band I kept around my wrist. Taking the stairs two at a time, I made my way down to the first level and across the quaint little courtyard through the rain in search of Father Miguel.

He wasn't in the sanctuary where I thought he would be. Instead, a young man stood at the front of the church, his long, sandy blonde hair partially obscuring his thin, pale features as he tried to break the lock off the old wooden donation box. I tiptoed behind him, laying my hand on his shoulder as he grunted in an effort to rip it open.

"What the hell?" he shouted, whirling around with his fist raised, ready to attack.

His light brown irises had a glowing yellow ring around them that I might have missed had he not been standing directly in the shaft of sunlight that had broken through the thick blanket of clouds outside. I was taken aback at the sight of it because it reminded me of the way Nate's eyes had looked when his wolf surfaced, but I was pretty sure the guy in front of me was not a werewolf.

"Don't worry. I'm not going to call the cops on you." I smiled as I took a step back, raising my hands in an attempt to show him I was not a threat.

"What do you want, lady?" The glint in his eyes told me he felt cornered, and I took another step back but didn't exactly clear a path for him. There was something about him that intrigued me, and, even though I was loath to do it, I knew by the stifling push of magic around me that he was in desperate need and would be more than willing to make a deal.

"Look, I don't care what you were trying to do, but I get the sense that you're in trouble, and you could use some help," I said. He angled his head at me curiously, looking at me out of the corner of his eye before relaxing his shoulders slightly.

"Are you one of those 'come to Jesus' people?" His assessment caused me to scoff. The irony of his words was not lost on me.

"I am as far from that as you could possibly get," I replied with a shake of my head. He relaxed a little, his fists unclenching as I turned and walked over to the pew closest to us.

Is he gonna bolt? It would be the smart thing to do. But when I turned back around and sat down, he was still standing there, except now he had his hands pushed deep into his pockets. The way he stood reminded me of Declan, and I got a sudden glimpse of what he might have looked like at that age.

"Do you need help or not?" I challenged.

"Why would you want to help me?"

"Because I'm in a unique position to be able to do that," I shrugged. The magic grew thicker around us, and I wondered if he could feel it, too. He shivered as if a chill had passed over him, the fine hairs on his forearms standing up for a moment, and he ran his hands over his skin to brush it off.

"Unless you can give me a lot of money, right now, then there's nothing you can do for me," he stared down at his shoes as he scuffed the dingy toe across the floor.

"I can do that." I smiled. His head shot upward, and his eyes grew wide as he searched my face for any tell that I was lying.

"Sure you can." The way he rolled his eyes could have rivaled any teenage girl, and I laughed in spite of myself.

"Do you really think you're going to get a lot of money from that?" I asked with a raised brow as I pointed to the donation box.

His mouth turned down while he considered what I had asked him, and the bright yellow ring around his irises dimmed as he realized I was right.

"What's the catch?" he asked.

"You have to promise me your soul."

You are such an asshole, Anna. You're no better than Declan. My hands shook despite the calm tone of my voice, so I wrapped my fingertips around the edge of the pew tightly and tried to look unaffected while the magic in the room threatened to

163

overwhelm me. It was stronger than any of the previous times I had made a deal, but I had no idea what was so different about this one, other than the fact that we were on hallowed ground.

"You're joking, right?" He laughed, more at ease now that he thought I was just messing with him.

"Do I look like I'm joking?" I deadpanned. He took in the seriousness of my face and turned away from me, walking a few steps back toward the box he had tried to open a few minutes earlier before he turned back to me.

"How much money are we talking about here?"

"How much do you want?" I asked. I could have thrown out a number, but I was curious to know how much he would ask for—*how much does he feel his soul is worth.*

"Ten million," he smirked, showing me that, even in his early twenties, he lacked the age and maturity to fathom something more than that. Little did he know, I could give him a hundred times that amount without batting an eye.

"Done."

I smiled sweetly as I reached toward my back pocket with confidence, the same way I had seen Declan do it. I could feel it in my gut that there would be a contract waiting there for me, and as soon as my fingertips met the heavy paper, I felt a zing of satisfaction deep inside. I smoothed it out on the bench next to me before I gestured for him to come forward. He took a few tentative steps toward me, stopping just a few inches from where the paper sat.

"You'll need to use a drop of your blood to leave your fingerprint at the bottom," I instructed. "It works well to just slice your finger with the edge of the paper, unless you have a pin handy."

I chuckled, and his eyes widened again once he registered the seriousness of the situation. He stepped back, and, for a split second, I thought he was going to run as fast as his legs could carry him in the opposite direction. To be honest, I wouldn't have blamed him. Instead, he began pacing again as he mulled it over.

"Are you the Devil?" He turned sharply on his heel to face me once again. His eyes roamed over me, assessing me while I laughed hard enough to make my eyes water. *This guy is smart, I'll give him that.* He was the first person I had come across so far who didn't just jump at the chance to give me his soul in exchange for what he wanted. I respected that, and I liked him already. *Though he was trying to rob the church. That's not very good guy of him.* If I'd personally had the kind of money he was asking for, I might have considered giving it to him. *At least he has the common sense to question what he's about to do.*

I wiped the tears from my eyes with a crooked finger. "Do I look like the Devil?" I asked, sounding more than a little offended.

"How should I know? I've never seen the Devil before. It could be a woman. In fact, I wouldn't be surprised if it was," he reasoned. It made sense, but I still bristled at his comment.

"No, I'm not the Devil. I'm pretty sure I wouldn't be sitting here with you if I was," I replied, my eyebrow raised in challenge.

"Then why do you want my soul?"

"Why do you want ten million dollars?" I countered.

"Touché." He nodded.

I folded my arms across my chest as I sat back against the hard wood of the pew, waiting while he mulled it over some more. I was all too confident, thanks to the still present electric feeling of the magic in the air that, no matter how long it took, he was going to agree. *Whatever he needs that money for, it was good enough to contemplate stealing from the church in the first place. Now it has him considering selling me his soul. I wish this wasn't necessary.*

My knee bounced, and I chewed my lip as I wrung my hands together while I waited. *This is wrong.* But it was too late.

The flash of yellow around his irises told me the second he made up his mind, but instead of slicing his finger on the edge of the paper, he pulled the small flag shaped pin from the front of his jacket, sticking the meaty flesh of his thumb before pressing it firmly to the paper.

This time, instead of the blue zing of electricity, there was a silver streak, and I waited for the familiar smell of the gunpowder sealing his fate. Instead, I breathed a heavy sigh of relief when after a minute, it never came.

"So..." He kicked at the carpet, shoving his hands into his pockets once again, the sign of a nervous habit. I glanced over the contract, still warm with magic. *Seth, son of Adam and Eve... fitting. Even if it is just a story humans tell themselves.* I knew what he was waiting for, so I folded the contract and slipped it back into my pocket before pulling a business card out from the other pocket. I glanced at it briefly, noting a list of instructions along with three separate numbers at the bottom of the card. On the other side was Silas's business information.

"I should have seen that coming," I said under my breath before handing it over to him. "Here's the information for your new account. I hope it brings everything you've ever wanted."

A part of me was shocked that I genuinely hoped it would. He took it from my outstretched hand, turning it over and scanning both sides before giving a nod.

Without another word, he moved with purpose toward the big wooden doors at the back of the church, leaving me sitting there alone in the sanctuary. My hands shook from the adrenaline still coursing through me, and the guilt of what I'd just done smashed into me. It was less than a minute after he passed over the threshold when my stomach lurched. *Shit...this can't be good.*

I bolted off of the bench, my sneakers slapping against the worn brick floor as I ran as fast as my legs would carry me straight through the side door. I made it as far as the row of rose bushes along the side of the building before I emptied the contents of my stomach. Thankfully, the granola bar I'd eaten on my way down from my room earlier was not the worst thing I had ever expelled, but I still felt sick even after it was gone.

My knees trembled as I sat down carefully on the one little concrete step next to the door, and I was pretty sure my reaction had been due to the fact that I had just made a deal for someone's soul in a sacred place. But I had no way of knowing for sure because I wasn't about to ask Declan or Silas.

Before I knew it, tears were streaming down my cheeks as I thought about Seth. His contract was tucked into my back pocket, and I hated myself for making a deal with him, even though I had refused to make one with Rachel. *How am I going to keep doing this?*

"What is wrong with you?" I banged the back of my head lightly against the stuccoed wall behind me. Everything around me was spiraling out of control. I clenched my fists, pushing my nails into my palms until a drop of blood slicked the skin of one hand. I had no idea how to stop any of it, and no one I could even talk to about it now that Rachel was gone. Even worse yet, I had just made a deal I was sure wasn't for the selfless soul I had promised to trade Declan. My only comfort was that I wasn't going to be collecting his soul any time soon.

Making my way back into the sanctuary, I pulled the wood polish and a clean rag out from under the cabinet in the back bathroom and spent the next few hours polishing everything around me until I could practically see my own reflection. Father Miguel had yet to show up by the time I had put everything back, and I was glad because it meant that I wouldn't have to look him in the eyes, knowing what I'd done. Though that was the least of my worries since time was running out for Rachel.

What did worry me, however, was the text message from

Matt that popped up on my phone screen a little while later that had my stomach doing backflips again.

Any idea if Rachel will be coming in for her shift today? She's not answering for me or Nate. -Matt

My thumbs slid quickly across my screen as I rushed out of the church and back down the street toward Rachel's apartment.

Yeah, she told me. Sorry. She's not feeling great. She's gonna need a few days. I hit send, hoping to buy us both some time. He sent back a thumbs up emoji, but I figured I should probably at least grab Rachel's phone and text him and Nate back so they didn't get too suspicious later.

I took off through the door, jogging down the street the few blocks to Rachel's apartment. *I am not a runner. Why am I running?* I bent at the waist, placing my hands on my thighs as I sucked in a lung full of chilly air that burned my nose and throat. *I really need to exercise more often.*

The door opened easily under my touch, telling me that even though I had moved my things out, I was still allowed inside. I let out the breath I had been holding as I made my way down the hall because I hadn't been sure I would be able to come in after I had left, so it was a comforting revelation.

I stood over Rachel's body, looking down on her peaceful face for a moment as I steeled myself for what I was about to do. *This isn't a big deal, don't be a baby. It's not like she's really Dead, dead,* I chastised myself. But no matter how hard I tried, I was never going to feel okay about frisking her dead body. So, I slid my hand into the back pocket of her jeans, feeling a little creeped out as I struggled a little with her dead weight. I tried my best to be careful not to roll her over or off the bed. The screen was locked, and I let out a long sigh when I realized I would need her fingerprint to unlock it.

A shiver went down my spine, and I shook myself, rolling my neck and shoulders as I bounced on my toes. *You can do this.*

You just need to hold her hand long enough to unlock the phone. You're halfway there. My pep talk wasn't working, so I paced a few circles and shook out my hands. Finally, I took a deep breath and lifted her cold, stiff hand, pressing the screen to the pad of her thumb until the phone screen lit up. My skin crawled at the feeling of the coolness of hers, and I retched, barely managing to contain myself, then immediately went into the settings and changed the security feature. I didn't want to have to do that again every time I opened her text messages.

I sat down on the edge of her bed after seeing she had three missed calls and fifteen unopened messages. Not just from Nate and Matt, but from her brother Gabe as well. I sent a generic reply to all of them, getting some quick 'feel better soon' replies from Nate and Matt. Unfortunately, from the looks of it, Gabe wasn't going to be as easily convinced. He sent back a snarky reply about missing lunch with him and insisted that he come by the apartment after his shift to bring some coffee and cookies from work.

After mulling it over for a bit, I looked over their previous messages to get a better feel for her tone and phrasing before I decided on what to say. *I appreciate it, but I need sleep. I'll send Anna to you k.* Then I quickly hit send before I had an opportunity to chicken out, and I paced back and forth across her bedroom. I held my breath while I waited for what seemed like an eternity before the phone dinged and breathed yet another sigh of relief when he agreed to let me pick things up for her later. Now, all I needed to do was convince him face to face that his sister was okay...

CHAPTER 20

The bell above the door tinkled when I crossed the threshold into the warm, cozy seating area of Latte of Love twenty minutes later. The smell of fresh baked sugar cookies hung in the air, reminding me of Christmas when I was a child. I inhaled the scent, savoring the comforting warmth from the lingering memory before the sound of the bell signaling an exiting customer brought me crashing back to reality.

Gabe was nowhere to be seen. Instead, a girl with long, black hair worked behind the counter, filling empty spaces with big red and orange leaf shaped sugar cookies. They were easily the size of my hand, and I marveled at the sugar that had been sprinkled over them. It glittered in the overhead light, making them look as if they had frost coating their edges, and I wondered if there was magic baked into them or if the decorator was just that gifted.

"Can I help you?" The girl smiled sweetly at me as she wiped her hands on the front of her apron, leaving behind light streaks of flour and sparkling sugar.

"I'm looking for Gabe." I returned her smile while I tried to keep my nerves out of my voice.

"Oh, he's baking today. Give me just a second, and I'll get him."

When she turned into the light, I noticed her big brown irises had the same bright ocher ring around them as Seth's had. No magic built around me in the air, so I breathed a sigh of relief, but still felt anxiety clawing at my chest. The shock of it made me take a slight step back as my heart began to race. I bumped into the chair behind me, causing it to scrape across the floor with a loud squeak. She turned back to me to investigate the sound. "You good?"

I needed some time to compose myself and give me something to do with my now shaking hands. "Actually, can I get an almond milk latte and one of those cookies first?"

"Sure, no problem. Anything else?" she asked brightly. I shook my head. I needed to get away from her, so I spun toward the dining room, careful not to hit the chair again in my attempt to put some distance between us. Unfortunately, my awkward escape brought me face to face with Tristan, the Guard Officer who had questioned me at Idir about Lucinda the day after she was found in the alley.

I bumped right into his broad chest, and I closed my eyes as his strong hands caught me before I fell on my ass. I felt blood rush to my cheeks. *What is your deal? Are you trying to bring attention to yourself?* I normally was not that clumsy, so the fact that I had bumped into two things in under a minute only served to remind me how off-kilter I was.

I opened my eyes, tilting my face up slightly to make eye contact with him, and I couldn't help but gasp at the sight of the bright silver ring circling his irises.

"What is wrong with me today?" I whispered to myself. *I must be seeing things.*

"Are you okay?" He took a step back from me as he held onto my shoulders to steady me.

"I'm fine," I stammered. "I'm so sorry."

"It was my fault. I wasn't paying attention. My mind is somewhere else today," he admitted, but I couldn't bring myself to do anything more than nod lamely at him while I continued to stare at that ring of silver.

"Here's your order," the barista called from behind me, and I turned away from him, thankful for the chance to escape yet another awkward encounter.

I took the cup and the cookie she held out to me, forcing a smile onto my face before turning my eyes to look down at the floor while I made my way past him to a nearby table. I made sure to step far to one side of him to avoid bumping him again. The barista took Tristan's order, making quick work of his two americanos before handing him the cups over the counter. He made a quick exit as she headed into the kitchen area behind her to get Gabe.

A few minutes later, they both emerged, and, now that I knew who he was, I could see the resemblance between him and Rachel much more clearly. He wiped his hands on a towel before pouring himself a cup of drip coffee and joining me at the table I had chosen in the corner.

"So, what did she get herself into this time?" He smiled, as he slid smoothly into the seat across from me. His dark curls were disheveled, but a quick swipe of his fingers through his hair set them neatly back in place. If things were different, I might have flirted with him a little. He was attractive after all, and I was recently single.

"Excuse me?" I looked him directly in the eyes.

My brows raised with surprise, and I tried not to be too freaked out by the fact that he, too, had a distinct ring around his irises. His were unlike the ocher color of Seth and the barista. They were a direct contrast to the silver I had seen in Tristan's eyes. A shocking yellow color—practically gold glittered around his irises, giving his eyes an almost cat like quality.

"There's no way Rachel would pass up free coffee and

cookies unless she was either maimed, in prison, or on her deathbed." He laughed, checking off the options on his fingers as he spoke, while I tried not to cringe at just how close to the truth he was.

"Has anyone ever told you that you have the most amazing eyes? They're almost... gold around the edge," I said, changing the subject. I wasn't sure it was a safer topic, but anything was better than talking about Rachel's current situation.

A grin spread across his lips as he gave me an appreciative nod. "You see auras." His eyes wandered over me in assessment, and I felt naked under his gaze.

"Excuse me?" I asked, feeling like a broken record. My eyebrows knit together, the corners of my mouth drooping in a frown as I tried to work out what it was he was talking about.

"You know, auras. Rachel's abuelita could see them, too." He nodded as he picked up his mug and took a tentative sip.

"Rachel's abuelita? Not yours?"

"No, Rachel is my half-sister. We have the same dad, different moms, which is why she's a bruja, and I'm a *human*," he whispered from behind his hand.

"So, you're not a warlock?" I mimicked his secretive demeanor before remembering that I already knew that. I had realized it when Declan and I had visited before, but it had slipped my mind.

"Oh, no," he said, shaking his head vehemently. "And as far as you and everyone around here is concerned, I know nothing about witches, warlocks, or any of the other things that go bump in the night."

He leveled me with a serious gaze, and I nodded in understanding as I made a show of zipping my lips shut and locking them before tossing the imaginary key over my right shoulder.

I knew it was against the law for humans to know about the supernatural community, but I'd never met a human who actually knew about it, so I understood his need for secrecy. The witches Council made sure to snuff out anything other than typical superstition because the last thing the supernatural community wanted was a repeat of Salem.

"Can you tell me more about auras?" I asked curiously.

"Sure," he said with a bright smile. "Though you should probably ask your parents or Rachel, they would be able to tell you more than I can."

"Why would you say that?"

"Because they're witches. I'm not. All of my knowledge is second hand," he admitted, holding the mug to his lips once again. *What are you talking about?*

"My parents weren't witches," I said, frowning at the thought.

"Then how do you have the ability to see auras?" he asked skeptically.

"I have no idea." My family was as human as human could be. There wasn't even a whisper of superstition from either of my parents or any of my grandparents, as far as I knew.

"Maybe it skipped a generation," he offered before brushing it off with another shrug.

"Tell me what you see." He made a sweeping motion with his hand that encompassed the room. Relaxing further back into his chair, he continued sipping his coffee while he waited patiently for me to survey our surroundings.

I looked around the room, stopping on everyone that gave me a clear view of their eyes. There weren't many people this late in the afternoon, so it didn't take long, and I tried not to linger too long on any one person.

My palms started to sweat, and I rubbed them across my thighs while I studied people's eyes. My heart sped up, fluttering in my chest with excitement. It was exhilarating to be talking about this with someone, figuring it out, and getting some answers before I convinced myself that I was a crazy person. At the same time, it made me feel a little bit like a creeper.

"Well, your eyes have a gold ring around the iris, but the barista," I said as I pointed my finger sneakily at the girl behind the counter, "hers are a deeper yellow. That girl," I pointed to the girl sitting behind him, "hers are... brown." I frowned. It was a strange contrast to her light blue irises, and I wondered if I had been able to see it had her eyes been brown. I figured I would because the color almost glowed, but it definitely would have been easier to miss.

"Hmmm, interesting," he took a minute to consider, tapping his finger against his chin before answering. "The Gold, of course, indicates beauty, extravagance, and artistic flair. Yellow is indicative of intelligence, caution, and logic. Brown..." he said, trailing off for a moment. "Brown shows a lack of confidence, fear, and even sometimes selfishness. Though I know her, and I can tell you, she's not selfish. So, my guess would be that she's probably struggling in some way."

He gave a sharp nod, happy with his own assessment before regarding me once again. *You mean to tell me that people's eyes have built in personality detectors?* I cocked my head, my eyebrow arching as I looked at him like he'd sprouted another head.

"So, auras show someone's personality?"

"Sort of, I guess. I always thought of them like a mood ring because they can change, but the deeper or brighter the color, the steadier that trait is," he said. "Though, like I said, I'm no expert."

I let his words sink in, allowing the silence to settle between us for a few minutes until I remembered Tristan's strikingly silver aura. "Are there other colors?"

"Of course, but you should know that. Seeing as how you're the one who can see them," he chuckled.

"This is all new to me," I admitted. Though in all honesty, I really couldn't recall when it had started, only that it had been so much more noticeable as of this morning. "In fact, I didn't even know this was a thing until just now."

"What kind of witch are you?" he whispered.

"I'm not. I'm what witches call a soulless." I considered telling him I was a reaper, but my stomach told me it wasn't a good idea.

"You're a void," he gasped, his hand coming up to cover his open mouth as he stared wide eyed at me.

"That's a really derogatory term, just so you know," I scowled. He blushed and looked down at his mug while he apologized under his breath.

"I didn't realize," he said, louder this time as he rubbed his hand across the back of his neck. "It's just that you're like a unicorn in the magical world," he explained.

My face screwed up in confusion. *That's a new one.* "What do you mean?"

"I've overheard talk here, and there's not many of you guys."

Declan did say that we were the only two reapers he knew of... I would have to ask Matt or Nate about that.

"What about silver, or blue, or red, or purple, or even black?" I asked, changing the subject back to what I really wanted to know.

He quirked his mouth to one side again. "Pretty sure there's no such thing as a silver or black aura, but blue is what abuelita called un alma virtuosa, and red, well red is un alma impulsiva," he frowned, shaking his head sadly.

"English please," I huffed as I rolled my eyes at his dramatic demeanor.

"You know, virtuosa, like virtuous, they have a good heart, and impulsiva, impulsive yes, but also selfish and typically mean." He gestured with his hand as his face scrunched in concentration. It was as if he were trying to pick the right words from the air around us. "Purple is impulsado, driven, they know what they want, but they're also insightful."

"Hmmm..." My lips pursed as I rested my chin on my fist. Now it was my turn to think. "Are you sure there's no such thing as silver or black? I mean, it would stand to reason that if there's a gold, there would be a silver."

"Not that I've ever heard of, but remember, my information is second hand. If you want more, you'll have to ask Rachel." His mouth turned down at the corners.

"Well, what about her abuelita?" I asked, trying to sound casual. Rachel was obviously out of the question, and I was sure there was no way Declan was going to allow me to talk to her soul, especially if it meant helping me out in any way. He might want a selfless soul, but he was also pretty confident I wouldn't be able to find one.

"Psh, good luck with that, Chica. She's been dead for six years," he replied. "Unless you can raise the dead, you're out of luck."

His dark eyes narrowed as he scrutinized me for a second, but I just shook my head at him. Maybe it was possible, but it definitely wasn't something I could do at the moment.

I filed it away in the back of my mind. It might be worth asking Declan about, if the two of us ever got on good terms with each other.

I tried not to be too annoyed as I rubbed my hands across the back of my neck before draining the last of my latte from the cup. "Yeah, I guess I'll have to ask Rachel, then," I agreed. "Was there something you wanted to send with me?"

"Yes," he said, jumping up from his chair and rushing back to the kitchen. A few minutes later, he came bustling back, holding a brown paper bag in one hand and a to-go cup in the other.

"New cookies, and, of course, a coffee. Cream and sugar, just the way she likes it. Tell her to feel better because I'm not letting her off the hook for lunch next week. It's her turn to buy." He smiled, wiggling his eyebrow conspiratorially. I laughed, giving him a firm nod before turning on my heel and hurrying out the door, feeling just a little bad for having lied to him.

As soon as I got to my room, I set the bag on the desk, opening it a crack to peek inside. There were four beautifully frosted light blue and white snowflake cookies settled on the bottom. They had been sprinkled lightly with sparkling sugar, and as much as I wanted to groan at the fact that they were rushing into Christmas before we had even celebrated Thanksgiving, I could not help the upturn of my lips as they formed a reluctant smile.

My pocket buzzed against my thigh, and I reached inside, fishing out two phones instead of the one I had been expecting. But it was Rachel's phone that lit up, and I sank onto the bed, trying to decide whether or not to even open it.

Selene. The notification bubble on the screen flashed at me. The name seemed familiar, but I couldn't put a face to it, so I tossed it onto the desk next to the bag without bothering to read the one line of text under the name.

A few minutes later, it buzzed again, so I picked it up, noting it was still the same message, only this time, I read the four words underneath. *We need to talk.* That was it.

I hastily typed *Busy* into the message bar and sent it before I powered off the phone. My foot tapped against the wood floor as I massaged my forehead, where the oncoming headache was pulsing between my eyes. *Lies, so many lies. How am I going to keep this up?*

I slid the phone beneath the thin mattress on the bed and picked up my own phone. It was still early enough that I could take a bus to Melinda's house and back if I hurried. She was the only person I could think of who might be able to tell me more about my newfound ability and if I could use it to help me find the type of soul I was searching for.

Gabe had been a plethora of information, so now I just needed a way to fill in any gaps he hadn't been able to. Like the fact that silver auras existed. Because Tristan's was clearly silver, and the nagging feeling in my gut said that maybe he was what I was looking for. I just hoped Melinda wouldn't turn me away this time.

Hopefully, she doesn't know about Genevieve's contract yet... I stood and paced the room. *She would have sent someone after me by now if she knew.* I sucked in my bottom lip as the memory of being bitten by the vampire flooded my mind. *Maybe she did.*

I shook my head, trying to dismiss the idea, as I grabbed a hoodie. Declan said we were attacked because Rachel looked like whoever was being targeted.

The clock is ticking, Anna, you don't have time to be paranoid. I took a deep, cleansing breath as I forced myself to move, making sure to lock the door behind me before heading to the bus stop on the corner where the long red bus was pulling to a stop.

As the bus rolled down the street, stopping every so often to let someone off or on, I considered what I would ask her. But I dismissed every idea before it was even fully formed because it all seemed too ludicrous. I wasn't sure how much she knew about my new contract with Silas, but he had to have told her something to get me out of house arrest, and though I didn't want to jeopardize my new situation, I also knew I physically wouldn't be able to tell her anything I wasn't supposed to. And, as awful as it was, I actually took some comfort in that thought.

The bus pulled into my stop, and I started the trek up the road toward her property, realizing too late that something was clearly happening. There were witches and warlocks milling around, too caught up in their own stuff to even notice me. *Crap. I need to ask her questions, but this is clearly not a good time.*

I stalled for a second, considering my options. I could crash whatever was going on, or I could go to Matt and see if he might be able to point me in the right direction. I made up my mind and started back down the street but only made it a few steps before a familiar voice behind me had me turning back around.

"What are you doing here?"

My heart jumped, and I spun in my tracks, coming face to face with the witch from the bar. *It's you.* Her hair was down, falling over her shoulders, and her swollen eyes were ringed red from crying, but I recognized her without a doubt. *You started this whole mess.*

My mouth opened and closed like a fish out of water as I struggled with what to say to her. "I was looking for Melinda," I stammered, feeling as if I had been caught in the middle of doing something awful instead of walking down the street. "I didn't realize there was something going on, so I decided to come back another time."

"Don't bother. There's no one here who would help a Devil like you. My daughter is dead because of you," she snarled.

"Excuse me?" I replied, my brain grasping for any reason she might think something so crazy. "I don't have any idea who your daughter is, so I'm not sure why you would think that," I responded defensively as I pushed aside the fact that she had just called me the Devil.

"You had one simple job, and you couldn't even get it right. I handed her to you on a silver platter, and instead of taking her soul, you took my daughter Abigail's," she accused. Her anger made the red ring around her brown irises almost glow.

"I don't know what you're talking about. You're the one who came into the place I work and made me think I could get out of my contract with Silas. You sent me to make a deal with the daughter of the most powerful witch in the city and didn't even tell me what I was supposed to be doing," I spat, my own anger rising to meet hers.

"Get out," she seethed, pointing a long, thin finger down the road in the direction I had been headed in the first place. *Gladly.* My jaw clenched as anger burned in my chest and unshed tears stung the corners of my eyes. Who was she to judge me when all I did was follow her vague instructions?

"Don't you ever come back here again, or I'll tell Melinda what you've done, and she will put you in a prison so vile that it will make this hell you're in look like heaven." The venom in her voice sent a shiver down my spine as I considered her threat. A mere heartbeat passed before I decided there was nothing I could do about it. So, without another word, I turned and marched myself back toward the bus stop, fighting back tears of helplessness the entire way.

"What in the hell just happened?" I asked myself as I flopped down on the bench to wait. It would be at least five minutes before the next bus came by, and I couldn't stop the helpless feeling that overtook me.

I bent at the waist, holding my head between my hands as I struggled not to hyperventilate. *How is this my fault?* I didn't even know who she was talking about. While I sat, I thought about the girl from the Latte of Love. Silas said her name was Abigail. But that hadn't been my deal—that was Declan.

I'd wanted to warn that girl not to make a deal, but Declan had stopped me. Then, when Silas sentenced her, she was punished harshly for betraying her cousin. That could only mean that Selene was Melinda's sister. The more I thought about it, the more I could see the resemblance between the two women, but it didn't explain why she wanted me to make a deal for Genevieve's soul in the first place, or why Abigail wanted to betray her. It also didn't explain how I ended up involved in the whole crazy mess, unless I was just a means to an end—a pawn in the crazy game they were all playing for power.

Either way, it didn't matter. I had more pressing concerns. I needed to figure out why I could see auras, and I needed to do it without the help of witches. Even more importantly, I needed to find a selfless soul to give Declan, and I only had four more days to do it.

The more I turned it over in my mind, the more I circled back to one thought. *Fuck! I'm screwed.*

CHAPTER 21

I dir was busy when I walked in, so I decided to wait until things slowed down before approaching Matt. Especially since I had requested time off, yet here I was during prime drinking time. I ducked behind the bar and made an amaretto sour for myself, making eye contact with Matt before settling into the farthest empty booth I could find in his line of sight.

My drink was long gone by the time he made his way over with another, setting it down in front of me before he slid onto the bench on the other side of the table.

"You here to see me?" He leaned back, stretching his legs out underneath the table. I nodded and took a drink as I considered the best way to broach the subject without having him ask me a million questions I wouldn't be able to answer.

"Thanks again for covering for me while I was gone," he said casually, running his fingers through his long, sandy hair.

"It was no problem."

"How's Rachel?" he asked.

"Fine, as far as I know," I shrugged. "I moved back to the rectory, so we won't be seeing much of each other anymore, I suppose."

"Ah. Well, I guess there's no reason to stay there since you were released from your house arrest."

I nodded, but didn't want to discuss that with him, seeing how he was already curious about how that'd happened, and I wanted to avoid any more conversation about Rachel.

"Do you know anything about auras?" I stared at the deep yellow ring surrounding the iris of each of his eyes.

"Auras? You mean like the colors around people that psychics can see?" he scoffed, making air quotes around the word psychics as he rolled his eyes.

"Yep," I nodded, pursing my lips in a way that suggested I might be as skeptical as he was. In some ways, I was, which was why I'd hoped he'd have some answers. He would also never steer me wrong. "And what's up with the discrimination towards psychics?"

"Seriously? Those people are all a bunch of phonies," he said with a laugh.

"You're a fairy, I'm soulless, and Nate..." I said, pointing at him across the room. "Well, you know. You realize that everyone who comes through those doors technically doesn't exist in the human world, right?" I asked. "And you want to say that there's no such thing as a psychic?"

I placed my forearms on the table, intertwining my fingers as I cocked my head to the side and raised my eyebrows at him.

"What is going on with you lately, Anna?" He furrowed his brows in concern.

"I don't know what you mean," My eyes averted to the dark liquid in my glass as I picked it up and swirled it around, watching the ice cubes clink together before taking another drink from it.

"Ever since I told you there might be a way out of your contract with Silas, you've been acting strange," he said with a sad shake of his head. "You disappear on me all the time, and you've been hanging out with Declan..."

I tried to interject, but he held up his hand, letting me know he wasn't finished, so I mirrored his pose and sat back in the bench, folding my arms across my chest like a petulant child who had been reprimanded.

"Don't try to tell me you haven't been hanging around with him," he continued. He narrowed his eyes at me, daring me to deny it, but when I didn't, he went on. "You've gotten sick more times in the last month than the entire two years I've known you, and even worse than that, you won't tell me anything about what's going on."

I didn't come here for a lecture. My knee bounced under the table as I looked at him, my eyes pleading. "I can't," I said through gritted teeth as I tried to convey to him everything I couldn't say.

"Can't or won't?"

"Can't," I spat. He watched me for a minute as he considered what to do next. I finished off my drink, opting to down the rest of the contents instead of sipping it like I had done before while I waited for him to respond.

"Spell?" He raised his right brow with curiosity. I shrugged, giving him a shake of my head. *I have no idea.*

"Is there anything you *can* tell me?" he asked.

I dunno. Is there anything I can tell him that won't make me puke up my guts? I looked around the room, taking in the groups of people laughing and talking around us. *What can I tell him?* Then it hit me like a slap to the face. *Duh.* "I get sick." I leveled him with a stare.

"That's literally what I just said." His brown eyes roamed my face, as I encouraged him with my eyes to think about what I said. *Come on Matt, connect the dots.* "Ah... I see," his fingers tapped on the table as he nodded, his lips pursing in a thin line.

"Though, to be completely honest, I don't know that I would share even if I could," I admitted.

As soon as the words left my mouth, blood crept up my neck to my cheeks. His eyes widened, his shoulders drooping as he set his elbows on the table, placing his mouth against his closed fist as if to stop whatever words he might want to say. I had never seen him look so deflated, and my heart hurt knowing I had done that. *You and your stupid, big mouth.*

"I just don't want to involve anyone who doesn't need to be involved," I said, backtracking as much as I could without actually taking it back. I had meant it after all, and he knew it.

He let out a sarcastic laugh as he shook his head at me. "Well, then why did you come here?" His voice deepened, and he licked his lip as he leaned forward.

I could feel the line being drawn in the sand between us. It had been there, after we broke up, but not quite so solid. This was definitely a turning point for us, and I found myself standing at a crossroads. Either I could apologize profusely and try to soothe his wounded ego, or I could be indifferent and hope we could still walk away from this as friends. Either way, our relationship would never be the same, and it hurt me more than I wanted to admit.

"Because you're the only person in this whole damn place who didn't treat me like a leper when I showed up. I value your opinion, and more than anything, I trust you."

The tense set of his jaw began to relax a little as he released some of the angry breath he had been holding. I knew this was a minor patch, he wasn't over it by any means, but at least he hadn't fired me and kicked me out. I would count that as a win.

"I don't know anything about auras. Why don't you ask the witches? Or Declan..." he grumbled quietly.

"Because, as you know, I am persona non Grata in the witch community," I huffed, disregarding his jealous comment about Declan.

"Then ask Rachel for help. She's your friend."

"Yeah, she is, but like I said, I don't want to involve more people than I need to."

"Fine. Let me make a call," he sighed, pulling his phone from the pocket of his jeans as he stood and strode toward the steps to his apartment. He hadn't invited me, so I continued to sit there, rolling the glass back and forth between my hands while I waited.

"Need another one?" Nate asked, dropping a third glass on the table in front of me a few minutes later.

"Thanks." I smiled, picking it up and tipping it toward him in salute before sipping just a little from the glass.

"Everything good?" He glanced from me to the stairs where Matt had disappeared a few minutes before, then back to me again.

"Yep, everything's peachy." I was sure he thought maybe I'd been fired or something. Hence the drink. "Just had some things I wanted to discuss."

"Does this have anything to do with Rachel skipping out on her shift today?" he asked as he rested his weight on his forearms across the table. I shook my head, trying not to let on that there was anything out of the ordinary.

"I wanted to know if Matt knows anything about auras," I changed the subject as I noted that Nate's aura was a much lighter shade of yellow, like midday sunlight. It seemed to be a pretty common color, or at least one that I'd noticed most often. And I suddenly wondered if it was his aura I had seen every time I thought his wolf was showing through.

"Like colors? Around people? The kind of stuff that psychics talk about on TV?"

Are you fucking kidding me right now? Not you, too. "Yes, colors, around people. And what is it with you guys and psychics? *We* all exist, so why is it so far-fetched to think that maybe psychics exist too?" I grumbled and took another, longer drink from my glass, unsure why their reactions were bugging me so much.

"You're serious?"

"Yes, I'm serious," I huffed.

"Well, in that case..." he trailed off as he leaned sideways across the table, resting his weight on his outstretched forearm. "What do you want to know?"

Wait, what? His reaction caught me off guard, and it took me a second to recover. "Really?" My forehead scrunched tightly as I stared at him.

"Really. I know things." He grinned.

"Then, I guess, give me everything you've got," I said, folding my arms over the table as I got comfortable.

"First, why do you want to know?"

"Call it research." My shoulders relaxed now that I felt more in control of the situation.

"It's uncommon to see them. In fact, it's a pretty sought-after trait in the witch community." He pressed his lips together as if to say, *I know what I am talking about.*

"Why is that?" I asked skeptically.

"Because the ability to see auras is basically the ability to read a person's true intentions," his aura sparkled as his dark gaze bore into mine. "It would give anyone with that ability an edge over everyone else to be able to amass some serious power. Or it would allow whoever controls that person the ability to maintain power."

I chewed on my bottom lip, bringing my hand to my chin while I let his words sink in. Maybe it was really lucky for me that I hadn't been able to talk to Melinda, after all. Especially if what Nate said was true. It would mean being trapped on a whole other level, and I refused to allow that to happen.

I sat up straighter in my seat, putting some distance between us. "How do you know about this?" I narrowed my eyes at him.

"Are you kidding me?" he scoffed. "This is a bar, Anna. People get drunk and want to talk. Usually about things they're not supposed to." He raised his eyebrows as he turned his head slightly, giving me a quick knowing. "And because if there's the slightest bit of suspicion," he said with a gesture to himself, "I'm outta here."

"Why? What's the deal with that?" My knees bounced up and down under the table as I glanced around the room to make sure no one was paying attention to us. It was far too quiet, in my opinion, and my level of paranoia had reached an all-time high.

"Bad blood. There haven't been vamps or shifters of any kind in this city in over twenty years, and the witches would like to keep it that way. In their eyes, this is their territory, so if you're not a part of their group, then you don't belong as far as they're concerned," he said gruffly.

"No wonder they hate me."

I sighed heavily, my chin dropping further toward my chest as I recalled one bad encounter after another with the witches and warlocks.

"Oh no, that's not why they hate you. They hate you because they don't know enough about you to know whether or not you're a threat," he said with a nod, raising his eyebrows knowingly. "As far as I know, there aren't many people who are allowed to serve their sentence here on Earth, making you a rarity. Something that hasn't been studied. You're like a unicorn in the supernatural community. Frankly, I'm surprised the witches didn't just swipe you off the street and lock you away somewhere until they had all the answers," he admitted, causing me to take a sharp breath. I hadn't thought about that before, and now I was curious about it, too.

"Why do you think that is?"

"My guess is that no one wants to scuffle with the Devil. You're his property, and as such, it provides you a level of protection."

"Then why were they willing to throw me in jail or put me on house arrest?"

"Because you broke the law. Even the Devil can't argue with

that. There's a reason he hides in plain sight as a lawyer. But just snatching you off the street would have been seen as an act of war," he said, bobbing his head lightly.

"Then why not take that opportunity to study me instead of putting me on house arrest with Rachel?"

"Melinda probably figured it wasn't worth the trouble. Things are tenuous around here as it is, with the vampires popping up after being gone so long. And how do you know they didn't? You live with a witch."

He shrugged again, and his words hit me like a freight train. He was right. The whole thing could have been a setup. They could have been watching me the entire time.

My heart beat rapidly, thudding against my ribcage as I considered it, but after a minute, I realized it didn't add up. If they were watching me, then surely they would have known about my ability to make deals and about Rachel, and since they weren't breaking down my door, I had to assume Rachel had kept my secrets.

Movement in my peripheral caught my attention, and I turned to see Matt come bounding down the last two stairs, causing Nate to get up from the table. "We can talk more later if you want," he said with a reserved smile. "And um, tell Rachel I won't say anything to anyone," he added before turning and heading back to his post behind the bar.

"What was that all about?" Matt asked, taking up the space Nate had vacated.

"Nothing, just checking in on me. Wanted to make sure you hadn't fired me," I joked, trying to lighten the mood a little.

"Well, I'm not going to fire you. The only way you won't be employed here anymore is if you quit," he said. My chest squeezed at his statement, and I had to fight back tears. It was good to know he wasn't going to abandon me. Because if Matt said it, he meant it. Fairies could skirt the truth after all, but they could not tell an outright lie. That was one thing he made sure I knew when we first started spending time together outside of work hours.

"Thanks Matt. That means a lot." I took a deep breath, getting control of the sudden rush of emotions before I embarrassed myself.

"I called someone I know, but there's not a lot to know about auras. Most people, including those in the supernatural community, think it's just a gimmick used by fake psychics because it's easy to convince naive, unsuspecting humans that they can see colors around people." He quirked his mouth to one side.

I nodded in understanding, pursing my lips in what I hoped seemed like disappointment and not constipation before deciding it was probably better to sip my drink instead. Besides, it didn't matter. Nate had given me more information than I had bargained for, and I was sure I didn't want to discuss auras where there might be an eavesdropping witch or warlock in the vicinity.

"But he did tell me that there's something you can try, to see if it's a spell that's responsible for your sudden... illness," he said, leaning forward as he folded his arms on the table. That information, I was interested in, so I copied him, leaning forward until I had closed as much space between us as I could.

"We should probably go upstairs." He took my hand in his as he slid off the bench. My cheeks heated at his touch. I followed behind him, allowing him to lead me up the narrow stairway I'd used at least a hundred times before.

When we got to the top, he dropped my hand before pushing the door open. "Sorry, I figured it was easier if people just continue to think what they will," he explained.

I nodded in understanding and took a seat on one of the stools next to the kitchen island while he rummaged around in his cabinets. He filled his silver kettle with water and set it on the stove to heat while he gathered the rest of the ingredients.

"Anise, for removing any jinxes." He dropped in a few of the star shaped seeds before closing the small jar and setting it to the side. "Burdock root for uncrossing, and ginger for protection."

The sharp scent of the spices filled the air, and he collected the steaming kettle after placing the jars back into the cabinet.

Setting it between us, he opened the lid and dumped in the contents of the bowl before closing it again and allowing it to steep. After five minutes of whispering over the pot with his eyes closed, he poured me a cup of the still steaming liquid.

"You need to focus your energy on the tea. Think about clearing away any spells that might be present on or in your body," he said, his eyes staring intently into mine.

"Really, it's that easy to break a spell? Why didn't you just do that for me when I was on house arrest?" I asked.

"Because that's against the law," he scolded. "And this tea won't break the spell so much as it will tell us whether or not there is one."

I scowled at him for a moment before adjusting myself on the stool to focus on the tea. I closed my eyes, holding the warm cup between my hands, and took a deep breath. I allowed the spicy scent of the steeping herbs to fill my lungs while I concentrated my energy on finding anything that might be making me unable to talk about my deal. Though I really had no idea what I was doing, so I found myself repeating over and over in my head, *Let me know if there's a spell on me, let me know if there's a spell on me,* until I felt like a suitable amount of time had passed.

"You can drink it now," he encouraged. I lifted the cup to my lips, letting the liquid coat my tongue before deciding it was cool enough to drink it down. It didn't taste bad, but tea had never really been my thing, so I finished it in one big gulp, setting the cup gently on the counter while I waited.

"How will we know if it worked?"

"Try to tell me something you couldn't tell me before."

I thought about it, considering what would be the least incriminating or awful thing I could tell him about everything that had happened over the last few weeks before deciding on something generic.

"I made a new..." *deal with Silas.* The words caught in my throat. There was no immediate pain or illness the way there had been before, but no matter how many times I tried, I couldn't say the words.

"Does that mean there's a spell on me?"

"I don't think so; otherwise, you would have glowed when you tried to get the words out. The tea would have interacted with the spell that was blocking you. This just tells us that there's something else going on, though you don't look sick, so maybe the tea is helping to temper that." He stroked his chin with his fingertips as he thought.

Just then, he darted around the island toward the coffee table, where he rummaged around for a second in the drawer. I watched with surprise when he brought back a pen and piece of paper.

"Write it down." He slapped the sheet of paper on the counter in front of me as he thrust the pen in my hand. I nodded and began to write, but as soon as I got to the same part, the pen stopped working. He took it from me, using it to draw a quick squiggle across the bottom of the page before handing it to me once again, but no matter how many times we tried, it wouldn't work for me.

"Write it down anyway," he said with a shake of his head. He was not going to give up, especially now that he knew it was because of outside forces. Pressing the pen to the paper, I wrote down what I wanted to say before pushing it toward him and handing him the pen once again.

He pulled it to him, leaning in close to the sheet of paper as he focused on moving the pen back and forth lightly across the surface until it revealed the letters pressed into it.

"You what?" he exclaimed, throwing his hands up in the air in frustration. "How could you do that, Anna?" Leaning against the counter, he dropped his face into his hands with a loud sigh.

"It was stupid, I know. But I have my reasons," I explained, the words pouring out in a rush. Suddenly, there was a roiling in my stomach, and I made it as far as the trash can beside the counter before throwing up until my head ached and my stomach was sore from contracting so hard.

His warm brown eyes were sad when I looked up at him. *Is that silver?* It struck me as strange that there was a very thin band of silver just inside the yellow one around his irises. Maybe I hadn't paid that much attention before. Either way, there it was, like molten metal shining brightly at me while we stared at one another across the countertop.

"What could be worth that?" he gestured toward the trash can.

"It doesn't matter. The important thing is that I did it, and there's no turning back now." I sat down on the floor, my back against the counter as I dropped my head into my hands.

"Then, I guess there's nothing else to say. I can't get involved in anything to do with Silas. It's no wonder you can't talk about it." He shook his head. "This is contract magic, not a spell. You physically cannot speak about the terms of your contract, and you would have known that if you bothered to read it before signing it. Which, I'm guessing by that violent reaction, you didn't."

He was right, I hadn't, but it still hurt to hear his words of blame, even though I knew it was my fault. *How was I supposed to know that you could write something like that into a contract? And I wouldn't be in this mess if you hadn't told me there was a way to get out of my contract in the first place.* Either way, I was in too deep now for it to matter.

"Well, I didn't want to tell you about it, anyway. I knew how you would feel, and now I know I was right." I looked down at the black and white design on the linoleum floor. My eyes stung as I struggled to suppress the tears that were fighting to fall, but I took a deep breath and blinked them away until I knew it was safe to look at him again. *I never should have come here. Why did I think that this was a good idea?* I climbed to my feet, feeling the weight of the silence fall between us. Neither of us was sure what to do next, so I picked up my bag and slung it over my shoulder as I headed for the door.

"I'll be back to work tomorrow," I said as I pulled the door open.

I didn't wait for a response. We needed some space, and I needed a new plan, so it was back to the drawing board. But after twenty-four hours of no sleep, I wasn't sure my body and mind were going to cooperate much longer.

CHAPTER 22

I'd barely slept a wink after pacing, my brain going around and around in circles but always coming back to the same thing. *Why did I offer him a selfless soul? I don't want to take any souls, and now I'm going to have to condemn a good person to save Rachel.* I had three days until she had to be sentenced, and I grudgingly concluded I was gonna have to get good with taking some souls. My approach so far had been to search for a selfless soul, but without knowing how to find one, I was stuck. I needed more time that I didn't have, so it was time to put my big girl pants on and do what I needed to do. *Yeah, you just keep telling yourself that.*

My insides felt all jumbled, but I forced myself to eat a cup of ramen. The salty noodles made my stomach rumble, but my belly felt satisfied by the time I slurped up the last of them. I looked at my watch and grabbed a granola bar before heading out the door. It was almost time for my shift, and I was anxious about getting to work because I knew Nate would be there. And as much as I wanted to continue our conversation from the night before, I also wanted to avoid it at all costs. Now that I knew seeing auras might be a valuable commodity worth kidnapping and imprisonment, I wanted anyone I'd mentioned it to forget about it as quickly as possible. In fact, once I got back to my room the night before, I turned on

Rachel's phone just to make sure Nate hadn't texted her about it.

Thankfully, her phone remained silent. A part of me wondered if that might be a bad thing or if I was just being paranoid. I hoped it was the latter, seeing how I had enough on my plate to worry about without having to deal with managing her personal relationships, too.

The moment I rounded the corner near the bar, I knew something was amiss. There was a short, thin woman with long, stringy brown hair standing next to the door. When she caught sight of me, she stepped off the curb and headed my way. My stomach knotted, but I continued walking, my eyes straight ahead until she was no more than three feet away from me. Her clothes were clean, but by the looks of it, she hadn't had a shower in a few days, and the hairs on the back of my neck raised in alert.

I came to a halt, frustrated by the fact that she was obviously on a mission and had been waiting for me when I had no idea who she was.

"Can I help you?" I tried to keep the annoyance from my voice, but it was there, nonetheless.

"I heard you're the person to talk to about getting something I need." Her gravelly voice was barely more than a whisper as her eyes darted around the nearly empty street. *Seriously? Do I have some kind of mark that says, 'talk to me about making a deal with the devil'?* Maybe I did because the magic I was becoming all too familiar with lately made its presence known. I closed my eyes tightly and sighed as it wrapped itself around me, cocooning me like a comfortable blanket while I considered what to do about her.

"I'm not sure what you mean," I hedged. I was pretty sure she was a sprite, considering her petite stature and delicate features.

"My friend Seth said you made him a deal at the church

over in the plaza yesterday," she explained. *Well, you're the one who decided you need to make more deals. Here's your chance.* Her green eyes begged me to give her what she wanted, and I wasn't surprised to see the red ring around them, which only prompted me to say no at first. It was like Rachel all over again; this girl was almost too desperate. Not at all in the right state of mind to make any kind of informed decision. But that didn't matter; the magic around me shoved me to get on with it. My shoulders tensed, and my jaw clenched at the insistence of it. *You can do this. Just think about Rachel. Do you want her to spend eternity in Hell?* I didn't, of course. *But I don't want this person to go there, either.*

I glanced at the door to Idir and shook my head as I side-stepped, bringing myself even with her on the sidewalk. "Sorry, I don't know what you're talking about. You must have the wrong person," I said.

"Please. I know the cost." she insisted.

Walk away. But my feet refused to move. *She knows what she's getting herself into.* I repeated the words Rachel said to me when I told her about Lucinda. *Yeah, and so do you.* I needed to stop lying to myself. I wasn't a good guy. Not if I was trading one soul for another. I was just as bad as Declan or Silas.

"What do you want?" I asked through clenched teeth.

"I want my husband's mistress dead. She ruined my marriage." Her aura turned an inky black.

Holy shit! You want me to kill someone?? My fingers locked behind my neck as I shook my head, in denial of the fact that someone could be so cruel. *Will I be the one who has to do that?? I won't be responsible for that, right?? No...Silas would figure that out...I think.* I paced circles as I dragged my fingers through my thick hair. *Oh my Goddess, I can't believe I'm even considering this!*

I looked her over, my skin crawling at her request, and refused to even indulge her any further, instead opting to ignore her as I turned to enter Idir. Her mouth dropped in surprise as she watched me walk away. And I was thankful that she didn't try to follow me in because I had no idea what I would have done, and it would have meant I had, even more, to explain to Matt.

I took a second to physically shake off her energy as the door closed behind me, feeling the vile energy of her words as if it were clinging to me, and it sent a chill down my spine. Gabe had mentioned that a red aura was selfish, and I would have felt that even if I hadn't noticed the red ring.

"You good?" Nate asked as I took up my place beside him, pulling the strings of my apron around me tightly before tying them into an expert knot at my waist.

"Yep, all good here," I smiled, taking the tray of glasses from the cook as he came through the swinging door of the kitchen. "I'll take those." I spun away from them both, happy for the distraction so I could avoid any further conversation.

My hands still trembled, but I breathed easier with every passing minute that went by without further incident. It was nice to get into a rhythm of drying each glass before putting it up on the shelf, and I felt a sense of accomplishment seeing them all lined up and spotless.

"Can I get a drink?" asked a deep voice to my left as I reached up to put one of the last of the glasses on the shelf. Picking up the rag from the counter, I dried my hands before I turned to face him. It was Lukas, Tristan's partner, and I made an effort not to stare too much as I crossed the space between us.

"Sure, what can I get you?"

"Jack Daniels, neat."

I grabbed the bottle from the shelf and poured his drink, appreciating the fact that he didn't seem to feel the need to drink something pretentious.

I handed it across the counter to him, noticing the bright blue ring around his irises. His slight tug on the glass reminded me that I needed to let go, and my cheeks flamed red from embarrassment. But despite my heart pounding in my chest, I waited for just a second to see if he was going to down the whole drink in one gulp or sip it before forcing myself to walk away from him.

"What did Gabe say about blue?" I thought aloud while I swiped my towel across the top of the bar a few feet away from him.

Gold is artsy. Yellow is... cautious, logical and intelligent. Red is impulsiva, mean, conniving...no kidding. I thought about the sprite from earlier, and another shiver ran down my spine. My conversation with Gabe ran circles around my mind. It took a while for me to remember, but I was almost certain, by the time Lukas signaled me over for another, that Gabe had said blue was un alma virtuosa, a virtuous soul. Which I was pretty sure meant that he was exactly the soul I'd been looking for.

I poured him another drink and set it gently on the counter in front of him, making sure not to linger too long before I busied myself with menial tasks nearby. I didn't want to creep him out if I wanted any kind of shot at making a deal with him. *But can you bring yourself to do it? Because you wouldn't even take the soul of that monster, who wanted someone dead.* I bounced up and down on the balls of my toes, trying to burn some of the nervous energy while I waffled back and forth with my conscience.

There weren't very many people around, so I could stay at this end of the bar without rousing suspicion, especially since Nate was at the other end. But to my dismay, it didn't matter how long I hovered near him; the magic that usually surrounded me in situations where a deal might present itself refused to manifest.

Soon, I found myself willing the magic to come in hopes that it would be like ripping off a band-aid. *Cut it out.* I couldn't believe I was hoping to make a deal with him, but truth be told, time was running out, and Rachel's soul wasn't going to save itself.

"This is going to be harder than I thought," I whispered under my breath, not realizing that Nate had sauntered up behind me.

"What's that?" he asked, causing me to jump slightly.

"What's what?" I managed to control my fight or flight response and didn't smack him for scaring me.

"What's going to be harder than you thought?"

"Oh, uh, getting these water spots off the glasses," I lied as I raised a glass up to the light where I inspected it for nonexistent marks. He frowned at me but shrugged it off because he had something he wanted to talk about, or he wouldn't have come my way.

"So, did you talk to Rachel about our conversation last night?" he inquired, causing my heart to jump into my throat. *Damn it.* My hope of him forgetting our conversation died a violent death as I bit back a groan and sighed.

"Yeah, she said thanks for keeping it on the down low." I nodded, grateful for the ability to think on my feet.

"Yeah, no problem. And just a reminder to you," he said, leaning in close, "for Rachel's sake, you might not want to be asking questions if you don't want someone asking them back." His expression was serious, and his aura changed from its glittering sunshine yellow to a shocking sky blue and back again so quickly, I wondered if I had imagined it.

"Yeah, I got that after what you told me last night," I admitted. "Thanks, by the way."

"No problem. Anyway, I came to talk to you because it's pretty dead tonight, and I have some stuff I wanted to take care of. Matt says he's cool with me leaving early if you're good with it. So, are you good here by yourself?" he asked.

I rolled my eyes at him and shook my head in dismay because I figured the stuff he wanted to 'take care of' had something to do with whatever new girl he was hanging out with.

"Yeah, I'm good. Go ahead." I smirked, shooing him toward the door, and without a backward glance, he turned and walked away. He balled up his apron and tossed it into the basket near the kitchen door as he passed, then shrugged into his jacket before practically sprinting out the door. *She must be something to have him almost running. I just hope she knows what she was getting herself into.*

I turned back toward Lukas and noticed his glass was empty once again, so I grabbed the bottle of Jack and made my way to him.

"You want another?" I held up the bottle in question.

He nodded, and I poured him a double, setting the bottle off to the side before leaning my weight onto my forearms over the bar.

"You doin' okay?" I asked. I figured the only way of making this happen was going to be if I initiated a conversation. After all, if an opportunity wasn't going to present itself, then maybe I could make it happen on my own.

"Yeah, I'm good, thanks," he nodded, but instead of taking the bait, he returned his attention to his phone screen.

"Well, I'm here if you wanna talk," I offered, disappointment biting at me because he was not going to make it easy for me. I picked up the bottle and turned around to check on the patrons at the other end of the bar, but I only made it a few steps before he stopped me once again.

"Wait," he called out, causing me to turn back around. "I'm sorry, I know you're just trying to be friendly, but it's been a crappy few days."

"I figured." I placed a hand on my hip and quirked my lips, waving the bottle at him.

"Well, I guess maybe it's been a crappy week," he let out a hollow laugh. "Hell, it's been a crappy few months."

His blue eyes reminded me of Declan's, though his leaned a little more to the grey side of the spectrum, and before I knew it, I was staring into them. I couldn't help but be mesmerized by the almost electric blue ring around each iris.

"So, what's so bad that you're here drinking alone?" I asked, trying to get him comfortable enough to open up to me.

"Vampires," he admitted with a tired shake of his head.

"Yeah? I heard we've had a bit of a problem with them here lately."

"That's an understatement."

His shoulders drooped as he slid further down on the stool, and I noted the dark circles starting to form under his eyes as he looked down into his glass. He swirled the amber liquid around a few times before taking a sip.

"Well, it sounds like you have a really tough job. Makes me glad I only have to pour drinks and put up with the occasional jerk." I grinned, trying to lighten the mood again, and he gave me a shy smile that tugged at my heartstrings a little.

That was when I felt the warm embrace of the magic in the air roar to life. *Shit. Really? Now you show up??* The hairs on my arms stood up, and I brushed my hands down them without thinking. Part of me wished I hadn't been so dead set on making him a mark, but the magic flowing around me said I had accomplished my goal. The only thing I had to do now was get him to tell me what he wanted, and then the deal would practically seal itself.

"So, what can I do to help?" I raised my eyebrow in question.

He looked at me, his blue-grey eyes sparkling with curiosity, and I was pretty sure he didn't know if I was coming on to him or being serious. Honestly, neither did I, though I doubted he'd be interested after I asked him to sell his soul to the Devil.

"Hey, Lukas," Matt's deep voice resonated behind me, catching me by surprise as he made his way closer to the two of us. "Sorry I kept you waiting. I had more to do than I initially thought."

"No problem. I had good company." Lukas grinned before draining the last of the whiskey from his glass. "Thanks for getting me out of my own head for a while, and I'll let you know if I think of anything."

He smiled, and his eyes creased at the corners, making his aura sparkle even brighter.

I gave him a nod and collected his empty glass, awash in relief and annoyance as I watched them disappear up the stairs to Matt's apartment. I thought about Matt as I wiped down the bar top. *He walked right up to me and acted like I wasn't even here.* Disappointment grew in my chest. He hadn't said even one word to me, but it was understandable after the way we had left things between us. It was going to take him some time to let go of the fact that I was in so deep, I couldn't talk to him about it. And like he had said, he could not get involved.

I pounded the side of my fist against the counter as frustration built in my core. *Everyone I know and trust is either angry at me, against me, or dead.* It made me realize, not for the first time since I had started my sentence, that I was truly alone. I grabbed a shot glass from the shelf, filling it with the whiskey that still sat nearby. I drank it down without a chaser, knowing I hated the bitter aftertaste. The burn of the alcohol as it traveled down my throat was a welcome pain, and I chased it with another shot before I put the bottle back on the shelf.

Laying my head down on the top of the bar for a moment, I relished in the feel of the cool resin surface against my burning skin. And I resolved then and there that when all of this was over, I needed to start making some friends. Because being alone for eternity was not going to work out for me. I stood there a little while longer while I contemplated what to do, only to come up empty. I still had no plan, which meant that I had no backup plan, either.

With a huff, I rinsed out my towel and went out onto the floor to start collecting empty glasses and wiping things down before I headed home empty handed once again. While I made my way around the room, wiping down the round tables and pushing in empty wooden chairs, I made sure to stop and make friendly conversation with everyone that was left. I eyed the stairs for any sign of Lukas as I checked all of their eyes for the blue tint I was sure I needed, but not one of them showed even a hint of promise. Unfortunately, the place was near empty, and the colors of the auras in the room were strikingly similar in their tones from blazing red to murky brown, telling me exactly the kind of people in the city that closed down the bar. *Conniving and insecure.*

By the time I made last call, I still had not seen Matt or Lukas again, which wasn't alarming but still unfortunate. At last, I finished up for the night, saying a quick goodbye to the cook before I locked the front door behind me and headed back to my room through the darkened streets.

CHAPTER 23

y brain was functioning at half capacity after tossing and turning the entire night, and though I probably slept, it was definitely not restful. So instead of eating the last sugar cookie that Gabe had sent for Rachel, which was likely stale by now, I convinced myself to walk over to the Latte of Love. Besides, the caffeine wouldn't only help wake me up; it would help chase away the chill from my drafty room. Fall had definitely sunk its claws in, meaning the mornings and evenings were cold enough for a sweater, but the afternoons still felt sweltering.

Thankfully, it was only a few blocks, and I was walking through the door before I knew it. The tinkle of the bell hanging overhead triggered a hello from the same dark-haired barista I had spoken to a few days before. I knew Rachel was not scheduled to meet Gabe for lunch until next week, and he hadn't texted her anymore after I had thanked him for the cookies for her, so I wasn't too worried about running into him.

However, the slight tap on my shoulder as I perused the cookies made me jump, and I twirled around quickly to find Lukas standing well inside my personal bubble.

"Well, fancy seeing you here. If I were a paranoid sort of guy, I might think you were stalking me." He smiled, but unlike the night before, it didn't quite reach his eyes.

"Interesting, because I was about to say the same about you. Though I *am* paranoid, so, are you following me?" I feigned seriousness, plastering on the most deadpan expression I could muster onto my face. His eyes widened with surprise at the quick turn of events, and that was all it took to break me.

My snort of laughter filled the space, and every eye in the room turned toward us for just a second to see what in the world had been so funny. My neck and cheeks heated, and I covered my face with my hands for a moment while I composed myself enough to look at him through the spaces between my fingers.

"I am so sorry," I chuckled. "I was joking. But the look on your face was priceless."

"You really had me there for a minute," he admitted as he pushed his fingers through his light blonde hair.

"Well, sorry." I smiled. There was a comfortable silence that fell between us while I went back to staring at the bakery case for a few minutes before I finally placed my order at the register. To my happy surprise, Lukas was still standing there when I turned around, and I had to make a conscious effort not to be too excited about it.

"Would you like to join me?" he asked, still looking a bit nervous, and I hoped it wasn't because he was still freaked out by what I had said.

I nodded, turning to grab my order before following him to the same table Declan and I had occupied when he made his deal with Abigail; I hoped that it wasn't a bad omen.

"It's Anna, right?" he asked hesitantly.

"Yeah. Lukas, right?"

"Yep, how did you know?"

"How did *you* know?" I countered.

"Matt told me last night," he admitted his own cheeks and neck coloring slightly pink at the admission.

"Ah," I nodded. That actually made a lot of sense. "I'm just good at names," I admitted, picking up my mug to take a sip of the hot liquid.

"Right, we met before. Sorry, I'm awful at names. Part of the job, I think," he said with a shrug. "Look, I wanted to say thanks again for last night."

"It was no problem," I started to say, but he held up his hand to cut me off.

"Thank you again for last night, but..." he continued, trailing off as he got to the point. "I had an ulterior motive for bumping into you today."

My brow furrowed while I waited for him to tell me what was going on. I hadn't expected him to say he really had been following me after our interaction earlier, but now his reaction to my teasing made more sense.

"So, you were following me?" I asked.

"Guilty as charged. In my defense though, I've heard that you might be able to help me solve a problem," he said, triggering my brain to acknowledge the magic I had been ignoring swirling around us.

"I don't think so," I replied with a shake of my head. *Every deal so far has been easy, but this has been too much effort. Maybe it means I'm not supposed to.* I was taking last night's failure at making him a deal as a sign that it wasn't meant to happen, after all.

"You haven't even heard me out." He frowned. "At least let me tell you what it is I want."

"What makes you think there's anything I can do for you?" I asked.

"The fact that you offered last night. It just caught me off guard. I wasn't expecting it, but now that I've had some time to think about it, I'm ready to make a deal with you," he said, his words low and rushed.

"You don't know what you're asking for," I said with a decisive shake of my head. "The price..." I continued, but he cut me off, silencing me once again with his palm facing me.

"I know the price, and I'm willing to pay it. I will sign over my soul to you right here and now if you can guarantee me that someone I care about will not be killed by any vampire that may be hunting her," he explained.

The crackling electric magic circled us, crushing in on me until I could barely breathe. He was so desperate, so willing, it couldn't understand why I wasn't jumping at the chance. I licked my lips. It was so easy. Frankly, I couldn't understand my hesitation, either; he was the ticket to freeing Rachel.

The weight of the contract appearing in my pocket was back breaking, and my fingers itched to reach for it, but the desperation in his voice gave me pause. It was a noble wish, so selfless—he didn't deserve to burn in hell. But the same could be said for any selfless soul I would encounter.

It wouldn't get any better or easier than this, but I was suddenly loath to use my newfound ability, knowing that the fate of his soul, a selfless soul, rested in my hands.

"I know you're asking out of the goodness of your heart, and I'll give you what you're asking for. But before you sign away your soul, you need to be absolutely sure. Eternity is a hell of a long time and trust me when I say there are no do-overs, no loopholes, and no take-backs. A contract with Silas is ironclad," I reasoned.

My voice cracked from the guilt I felt because as much as I needed a selfless soul, I hated myself. As far as I was concerned, I was the scum of the Earth. *This truly is hell on Earth. You should burn for this.*

He reached his hand across the surface of the table, laying it gently over mine before looking deep into my eyes once again.

"I understand that, but I really need to do this. There's some-thing special about her. I don't know what, but I know that she's worth saving if I can," he pleaded with me, with those blue eyes of his that once again reminded me of Declan. It made me wonder if he had looked this desperate when he made his own deal.

I took a deep breath and reached for the contract in my back pocket, smoothing out the creases on the table. I could feel the warmth of the magic beneath my fingertips, and I settled my hand flat on top of the paper, giving myself a moment to come to terms with what was about to happen before sliding it over to him.

"You need to leave your fingerprint with your blood," I instructed, expecting him to mull it over the way the guy in the church had. But without a second thought, he slid the edge of the paper across the pad of his thumb, allowing a thin red line of blood to appear before squeezing more to the surface.

The swirl of lines on the paper dried clearly once the magic had accepted what I now thought of as an offering, leaving the lingering smell of gunpowder floating lightly in the air around us.

I wanted to cry, or scream, or throw up because I was so overwhelmed by the emotional impact the moment had on me. But instead of losing it in the middle of the coffee shop, I pulled myself together and silently sipped my coffee while I died all over again on the inside.

My heart squeezed, knowing his fate was sealed. He would die soon. I was certain of that, though I had no way of knowing whether it was the contracts that were responsible for it or if it was just happenstance. Either way, I was responsible for what had just happened, and I quietly acknowledged how much this particular contract was going to weigh on my conscience. His expression was somber when he handed the sheet back to me, but there was no regret I could distinguish in his features, and his aura glowed an even brighter electric blue now than it had before.

I set down my mug and picked my bag up from where I set

it on the floor next to me. "Well, if that's all, then I guess I'll go." As far as I was concerned, our business was over, and I wanted to get as far away from him as quickly as I could.

But before I could get up, he placed his warm hand over mine again, and I settled back into the chair. "I didn't mean to upset you."

"How did you know I would be able to do that?" I asked. Now that the magic had dispersed, my brain had a moment to reflect on the fact that he wasn't the first person to approach me.

"Word has a way of traveling in this place. It's no secret to the Guard that you have the ability to make a deal for the Devil," he said with a tilt of his head.

"Then why hasn't Melinda come after me?" I asked.

"For what? She can't stop you from giving people what they ask for. Plus, I'm not sure she believes it yet. And she's got enough on her plate to worry about without tangling with Silas, too," he admitted.

I considered that for a moment before bringing my fingers up to massage my aching temples. Now I would have to deal with every Joe schmo off the street who wanted to make a deal. *As if my afterlife wasn't complicated enough.*

"Does Matt know?" I asked, my head snapping up to look him in the eyes.

"I have no idea. If he does, he didn't say anything to me." He shook his head. I glared at him, but instead of intimidating him, it just made him laugh. "Anyway, I hate to make a deal and run, but I have some things to take care of. Hopefully, I'll see you again soon. Maybe we can have a conversation that doesn't involve me following you, or all of the formalities," he winked at me, then he turned and left.

I nodded at him lamely, not sure whether it was my imagination or if he was flirting with me. Either way, it did not matter as my heart sank at the fact that his days were numbered, and he had no idea. I hated knowing that, and as much as I wanted to warn him, I couldn't because I had no idea how or when it would happen, only that it would.

Once he was gone, I just sat there, drinking my coffee and eating my cookie like I hadn't just brokered a deal for his soul. I tried so hard to just be normal for a little while, but the entire time, I was fighting an internal battle about what I was going to do. On the one hand, I was relieved that I would be able to give Rachel her soul and probably her life back. On the other hand, I was torn because Lukas didn't deserve to lose his in exchange for hers. I'd gotten what I wanted, but at what cost? And at the end of the day, it left nothing but a bad taste in my mouth.

CHAPTER 24

Before I knew it, I was sitting at the small desk in my room in the rectory, unsure about how I managed to get there except maybe on autopilot. Once I had stripped off my hoodie, I pulled the contract from my pocket, suddenly eager to find out if I would be able to void a contract for a deal that I had made or if Declan was just making that up so he wouldn't have to void Rachel's.

I turned it over in my hands, examining the thick sheet as I noted the weight and texture of the expensive paper, but I didn't feel as if there was anything different about it. Before I could lose my nerve, I pulled on the paper, ripping it cleanly in two almost directly down the center, my stomach feeling queasy, knowing I might have just destroyed Rachel's ticket to freedom. But before I could celebrate, the damn thing put itself back together. *Okay, well, that didn't work.*

I knew it would never be that easy, but I had another idea. Emboldened by my first failed attempt, I jumped from the chair and headed to the closet, where I rifled through my box of belongings until I found a lighter. After a few strokes of my thumb across the wheel, it ignited in a strong flame, and I watched it flicker for a moment before holding the paper over the trashcan. I held the flame under the corner of the paper, but no matter how long I kept it there, the paper refused to burn. Instead, the lighter just got hotter and hotter until I burned my finger and ended up dropping the whole thing into the can below.

I opened the top drawer on the desk and pulled out a pen, scrawling "VOID" in fat capital letters across the page. Feeling satisfied with myself, I held it up to the light, only to watch the letters fade directly into the paper itself. I threw the pen into the trashcan with force alongside the lighter, as if it were the pen's fault it hadn't been able to void the magic of the deal.

So, apparently, it would soak up ink, it could be torn but not burned, and I was sure cutting it would just result in the same outcome as tearing it. So that answered my question. I could not physically break a contract. Of course, Declan was right. I almost wanted to be angry at him about it, but I couldn't exactly be mad at him for telling me the truth. Which I should have known would be the case, seeing how he had not lied to me as of yet.

I was frustrated as I lay in bed, and I was ready to ball the thing up and throw it away, when I noticed the ink glimmering as I turned it in the light. Upon closer inspection, I realized that the ink used for Lukas's name was a beautiful shimmering shade of blue within the black. Grabbing my bag, I dug through it until I found the contract for Seth, but instead of shimmering blue, it held tiny flecks of yellow within the dark black of the ink. It was a perfect match for his aura, just like Lukas's.

I read through both contracts, and they appeared to be identical except for the color of the ink and what each of them had requested. I decided to compare it to all of the contracts I had stuffed in the bottom of my box, and every single one had a different color sheen to it, except for the last one I checked.

I sucked in a shocked breath and held it until my lungs burned as I considered the ramifications of what it might mean. My hands shook as I held Lukas's contract in my left hand and the copy of my own contract in my right. After scrutinizing them again just to be sure, I couldn't deny that my name held the very same blue sheen in the ink.

Dropping the two papers onto the bed, I made my way to the mirror, where I stared at my reflection, wondering how on earth I could have dismissed the blue ring around my own green irises for so long.

I was a selfless soul.

The earth spun beneath my feet, and I plopped down onto the sturdy wooden chair next to the desk with a thud, bracing my hands against the edge of the desk to steady myself until the world around me stopped spinning.

I'd found the soul I was looking for. *I should call for Declan immediately, right?* I mean, I wanted to, but I just couldn't bring myself to do it. Lukas was the real deal, the kind of person who would give up everything, including his afterlife, for something other than his own personal gain.

Suddenly, I understood what Silas had been talking about when he had sentenced Abigail, and I was overwhelmed by the thought of it. My head dropped into my hands, my fingers tangling in my hair as I grappled with this new revelation. *Find a selfless soul, save Rachel from the fiery pits of hell,* I thought sarcastically. *Well, check and fucking check.* I had set out to free my friend, and I was so close to accomplishing my goal, I could practically taste it.

I thought that was supposed to be the easy part—you know, find the soul, make the deal, save Rachel. Instead, I had found the soul, made the deal, and gotten some answers I didn't even know I was looking for, along with a whole lot more questions and a heap load of guilt.

So, instead of calling out for Declan right away, I sat on the bed, hugging the contracts to my chest as I chewed my bottom lip to shreds.

CHAPTER 25

Rachel's apartment was warm compared to the cold outside when I crossed over the threshold into the quiet darkness of the living room, and even though I hadn't been there in days, the place still felt lived in. Almost like I had never left. And as much as I wanted to get things over with, I still wasn't ready to give up a selfless soul the way I thought I would be, even if he was already doomed. So instead, I made myself a cup of coffee in the single cup machine in the kitchen to warm myself up before sitting down at the dining table.

The wind had been blowing enough on the walk over to have chilled me to the bone, right through my light sweater and hoodie. It made me wish I had pulled on something a little heavier, but thanks to the coffee, I was finally starting to thaw a little inside.

I braced myself for my inevitable chat with Declan and cringed at the sudden knot in my stomach. I wasn't sure whether it was self-doubt or feelings of guilt about my deal with Lukas, but either way, I wasn't so sure that the whole thing was such a good idea, after all.

You're saving her soul. No matter what happens to Lukas, you did this for Rachel. I took a deep breath and held it for a moment as I repeated the words over again in my mind. If I lost my nerve now, then time would be up, so I needed to get on with it if I wanted to save my friend.

"Declan," I called out into the empty room. I was more aware of Rachel's lifeless body down the hall than ever. Especially because I was almost one hundred percent positive that Lukas's soul was a selfless soul, and it would mean her freedom.

I had spent the past half an hour sitting at the desk in my bedroom at the rectory scrutinizing the contract I held in my hands once again before I had worked up the courage to walk to the apartment to summon Declan.

"I have what I promised you," I said as he seemingly stepped into the room out of thin air and took a seat in the chair across from me. I was slightly intrigued. I hadn't considered before now what it might look like to someone else when we traveled somewhere, and it was interesting to see. Though not interesting enough at the moment to stop and have a conversation about it.

I held out the thick sheet of paper containing the contract for Lukas's soul and watched silently as he read it over.

"I can't believe you did it," he said, his eyes wide.

A mixture of awe and appreciation painted his features as he looked at the contract he held up in his hands. There was no question from the look on his face that it was indeed for what I had promised him: a selfless soul. I watched him inspect it while I kept one eye on the lettering of the name. It was deep blue at the top of the paper, glittering softly under the overhead light. It was a perfect match for Lukas's aura, and I was sure if I looked at Declan's contract, I would find the same thing.

"How?" he asked, his brows furrowed as he looked up at me. The bright blue of his aura ringing his irises was more apparent to me now that I knew what I was looking at, and I almost wanted to laugh at the fact that it had been staring me in the face the whole time. But instead of laughing, I shrugged. I couldn't have anyone knowing I could identify a selfless soul so easily. Especially because it seemed like it might actually be the reason Declan and I were able to do the things we could do.

If that was true, then I was very likely to be sentencing Lukas to an afterlife of reaping. Unless he could do the one thing Declan and I hadn't been capable of: flying under Silas's radar.

"You're not going to tell me?" he asked, raising his hand to his chest in mock injury.

"I don't know, Declan. So there's nothing to tell. The only reason I knew he was different is because his contract was different. His name has blue flecks inside the ink in his name. And I need to tell you," I took a deep breath before continuing on, "he's going to die soon."

"Well, that's convenient," he replied, reading over the contract once again while he tapped his finger lightly on the table. "This contract is good. Perfect, as far as I can tell. You've learned a lot in such a short time, but there's nothing different about the name on this contract compared to any other contract." His voice bordered on disappointed as he looked up at me.

"What?" My face scrunched as I leaned over the paper to examine it once again. There was clearly blue in that ink. I knew I hadn't imagined it, but before I could argue with him, I doubled over in pain. I clutched at my throat, feeling as if it had just been ripped open, but when I looked at my hands, there was nothing there.

"Are you okay?" Declan shouted, moving quickly around the table where he slid into the chair next to me. His strong hands gripped my arms, and even though I knew I wasn't physically hurt, I still found myself gasping for breath, feeling the fiery pain build until it almost consumed me.

"Anna, let him go," Declan soothed as realization relaxed the features of his face. "You've gotten yourself emotionally attached to this soul; you are going to experience his pain vicariously unless you let him go."

"Don't know how," I gasped through the ripping, burning pain that was still searing my throat.

"You have to forgive yourself," he explained as he smoothed my hair behind my ear. "You are not responsible for his choice to make this deal for his soul. Whatever decision he made, he did so willingly. You have to accept that."

I couldn't remember him pulling me into his lap, but his strong arms cradled me as he rocked me gently. I could feel the truth in his words, and as much as I wanted to deny it or be angry at him, I also didn't want to suffer through what Lukas was going through. It felt wrong, like I was a peeping tom to his trauma. I knew from my own experience that I wouldn't have wanted anyone to feel the pain and fear I'd felt that day in the bank. And Lukas's pain wasn't mine to hold onto.

Tears started flowing down my cheeks when the first sobs escaped my throat. They wracked my chest as I tried to forgive myself for what I had done, so that I might be free of the pain. After all, Declan was right; I hadn't forced Lukas to make that deal. He'd been the one to seek me out. He had followed me to the coffee shop with the sole purpose of making a deal with me.

He had willingly pressed his thumb to that dreadful contract to save someone he obviously cared for. Now, from what I could gather from my connection to him, he had sacrificed not only his soul but his own life for someone else. It was no wonder his was a selfless soul. It made me curious what Declan had made his own deal for, and I doubted the validity of the selflessness of my own soul.

After what felt like an eternity, my body finally stopped shaking, the pain fading into the background while I dried my tears with the back of my hand.

"I'm sorry you had to experience that," Declan said softly, brushing the red waves from my face, and a picture of the two of us surfaced in my mind. *I lay on the sofa, my head in his lap, and I laughed as he brushed my hair out of my face.* I shook away the picture, unsure if it was a memory or a daydream.

"I'm guessing you've had the unfortunate luck to have experienced that yourself," I croaked.

His beautiful blue eyes grew sad, and in a movement that was far too graceful, he stood, depositing me gently back onto my own chair.

"I did, yes, just once." He smoothed the almost invisible wrinkles from his soft charcoal sweater. I shivered as my body readjusted to the temperature of the room around me, trying to push away the sudden sorrow I felt at the loss of his warm, comforting embrace.

"We should go," he said, reaching out his hand for me to take. I looked at it lamely for a second before I realized he meant that we should go and reap Lukas's soul. In my overwhelmed state, I'd forgotten that there was still work left to be done, and I dreaded it almost as much as the thought of Rachel dying in that alley.

Shaking off the onslaught of overwhelming feelings, I took Declan's warm hand in mine. With a quick nod, he transported us to an old cabin in the middle of a wooded area where I spun around, trying to get my bearings as I registered the keening wail coming from inside.

CHAPTER 26

The night was cold enough that I could see my warm breath condense into puffs of smoke in front of me, and even though the air smelled crisp and clean, the faint odor of copper and iron lingered around us, the unmistakable scent of fresh blood.

"I'm guessing you're here to collect my soul," Lukas said, his soul manifesting between us and the cabin.

I nodded, unable to speak as tears welled up in my eyes, spilling down my cheeks in hot trails as I cried silently along with whoever was grieving him inside the small space. He turned to face the building, staring as if he could see through the walls before turning back to us.

"So, how does this work?" His translucent shoulders drooped in resignation.

"We have to take you for judgment," Declan explained. I was learning quickly that his demeanor changed with each soul, and I wondered why he was harsher with some than others. However, like so many other things recently, I knew it was a conversation for another day. Right now, we were about to take this selfless soul to be judged by Silas, and if he was like us, Silas would sentence him to an eternity of hell on Earth. Not here, of course, because it was too close to home, but he wouldn't be banished to the fiery pits of hell where Lucinda and Abigail had been imprisoned.

"Will this hurt?" he asked, and I was taken aback by how vulnerable he was compared to the afternoon before in the coffee shop when he had so confidently requested to sell me his soul.

"Not if you don't fight it," Declan replied, to which Lukas gave a curt nod.

As I stood there listening to them talk about the next steps, I watched a thin blue line appear. It was almost like a tendril of smoke that snaked its way across the cold ground from underneath the cabin door to where Lukas's soul stood. Once it reached him, it pooled at his feet, curling up and around his body as it began to coat his entire form in shimmering blue light.

"I think that's our cue to go." Declan stepped forward, deliberately wrapping one hand around mine and one around Lukas's. When nothing happened, I looked up at him, my eyebrows raised in question as he struggled to transport us to Silas.

"What happened?" I whispered.

"I don't know," he groaned, dropping both of our hands, and we watched as the blue film finished overtaking Lukas's soul.

Then, as suddenly as he had appeared, Lukas's soul dissipated right in front of our eyes.

"What in the hell just happened?" Declan hissed, his eyes accusing as he looked to me for answers.

I threw my hands in the air. "How should I know? You're the expert here," I whispered back. He turned away, pacing a few steps before bringing his fingertips to his forehead, shaking his head.

I kicked at the dirt with the toe of my sneaker, bringing my hands behind my back in an attempt to shove them into my back pockets. Instead, the fingertips of my right hand slid across the edge of the paper folded there neatly. I was positive it hadn't been there a few minutes before, and my stomach knotted.

"Shit," I cursed under my breath as I plucked the document from my pocket and stuck my index finger into my mouth. The metallic taste of blood coated my tongue while I fumbled with the sheet with the other hand. My eyes scanned across the paper in the fading light. It was Genevieve's contract. *Wait, Lukas is related to Genevieve?* "Double shit," I exclaimed, this time causing Declan to turn toward me, his eyes narrowing at the sight of the contract in my hands.

"What did you do?" he growled, stalking toward me like a predator towards its prey.

"This was not my fault," I stammered. Though, in all honesty, I guess it really was. To be fair, I'd forgotten about Genevieve's contract until it appeared in my pocket.

Snatching the paper from my hands, he read over it, shaking his head in denial as he paced back and forth. His eyes scanned the page again and again, probably looking for a loophole, but I knew there wouldn't be one, and I could almost hear Silas's laughter. He knew how to word a contract, that was for sure.

Grabbing my hand, he transported us back to Rachel's apartment, where we'd left Lukas's contract sitting on the coffee table in the living room.

"I cannot believe this. How could you be so careless?" He whirled on me, shaking his balled-up fists with one contract in each hand.

"It's not my fault," I argued, my voice cracking.

"These are your contracts," he hollered.

"Well then, maybe you should have taught me better," I barked angrily. "How was I supposed to know that this would happen?"

"This contract clearly states that none of her immediate family can be killed by vampires. Lukas was obviously killed by a vampire, which is why his soul was returned to his body," he roared at me.

"So why did her contract show up?" I asked my voice heavy with the annoyance that was starting to bubble over.

"It's been fulfilled."

"Well, why didn't Lucinda's contract show up?" I countered.

"Because Silas sent it to me. You had no training whatsoever, so it was up to me to teach you how to reap her soul," he said, closing his eyes as he allowed his head to fall back until he was looking toward the ceiling.

"So, then Silas knows that Genevieve's contract has been fulfilled?" I hedged. I had no idea what that meant for me, or the debt she now owed me.

"Of course he does."

"Then why didn't Lukas's contract show up?"

"Because it hasn't been fulfilled yet," he said. His words were clipped as he flopped into the chair Silas had occupied the morning all this had started.

"Okay..." I drawled. "But the contract is still valid, so that means you have to uphold your end of the deal and bring Rachel's soul back to her body," I reminded him. "Just because we didn't collect his soul today doesn't mean that we can't in the future."

Just then, the sheet in his right hand began to disintegrate before our eyes, leaving nothing behind but a faint glimmer of magic.

"Why did it do that?" I demanded, taking a step toward him. My breathing turned shallow as I started to panic.

"Because it's void."

He sighed loudly, his chest heaving as his jaw tensed.

"How? How can that be possible? You said it was perfect," I yelled.

"Because the first contract voided the second. He was never in any danger, and whatever he asked for is no longer in play because of it." Then, just like Lukas's contract, Declan disappeared before my eyes.

"Declan," I yelled at the top of my lungs. I couldn't care less who heard me, especially once I felt the power behind my words. Immediately, I had brought him hurtling back from wherever he had gone, almost as if by force.

He stared at me, his eyes glowing while his aura changed from its normal blue to an angry red. He was pissed.

"How dare you summon me that way!" he yelled, his fists clenched tightly at his sides.

"How dare you leave in the middle of a discussion?" I shot back.

"There's nothing left to discuss. We had an agreement, and you didn't fulfill your end of it. Your time is up, so there is nothing else to be done."

"Maybe you didn't understand me," I insisted. "I gave you a selfless soul. It was not my fault that you couldn't collect it," I sneered.

"She's going for judgment, Anna. Whether you like it or not, and since you were in such a hurry to summon me back instead of giving me some space, I guess there's no better time than the present."

He reached out, taking hold of my arm. He was going to transport us. I just wasn't sure where yet.

CHAPTER 27

Imagine my surprise when, instead of going straight to Rachel, we ended up standing in the middle of Silas's office. Declan's own expression mimicked mine for a fraction of a second before he recovered, as if this was exactly what he had expected to happen.

Silas sat regally in his chair behind the large mahogany desk, looking imposing, and even though Declan didn't seem at all surprised by our change in scenery now, it still took me a moment to get my bearings.

"Seems to me we have an issue," Silas remarked with a sigh, addressing the three of us as if we were delinquent children. I was not sure where Rachel had come from, but her soul was floating silently between Declan and me in the large space.

I turned to Declan, my lips pursed, eyes narrowed, as I dared him to explain what had happened.

"No issue. There was a misunderstanding, that's all," Declan said, slipping easily into the calm, cool demeanor I had come to know from him.

"Don't lie to me, Declan. It rarely happens that a deal is made regarding a soul that I'm not aware of, and I've let this charade go on long enough," he said with a flip of his wrist. "Besides, pouting is not a good look on you."

My eyes widened in surprise as I glanced at Declan out of the corner of my eye. He didn't even flinch. Instead, he opted to turn away, his long legs crossing the room to the door in a few strides where he leaned up against it, removing himself from the situation as much as it would be allowed.

"As for you," Silas said, addressing me next. "How did you know the Farrington boy was a selfless soul?"

"Just a lucky guess, I suppose," I lied without missing a beat as my heart thudded double time against my rib cage.

"That seems to be the case with you a lot lately." He cast an all too serious stare at me, and I shoved my hands into my pockets as they started to tremble. *Maybe this is why Declan always has his hands in his pockets.*

"Either way, I applaud you," he continued, his hands slapping together slowly in sarcastic applause as his dark eyes swept over me. "Even I would have taken you up on your offer for such a soul, and now that I know you can deliver, well, let's just say that I definitely will."

His eyes bore into mine, and it was almost as if he were searching for my secret. But he wouldn't find it, not unless he was a mind reader. And unless he could see auras the way I could, he would never be able to do what I had done so quickly and easily. After working for him for even a short time, I knew he couldn't; not even Declan could.

"So, does that mean Rachel can have her soul back?" I asked, shooting a glance at my friend who floated beside me. My voice was almost demanding, though I tempered myself because of the power emanating from him, and I was gaining a healthy respect for the authority of the man sitting in front of me.

"Well, that depends," he hedged as he steepled his fingers on the desk, laying his bottom lip up against them as he contemplated.

"On?"

"On you, of course," he replied, causing my heart to skip a beat. "But before you rush into any decision, I think that there are some things you should know," he drawled.

I was caught off guard by his tone, as it implied he thought he could change my mind. However, instead of dismissing him like I had initially wanted to, I gave a nod for him to continue, and out of the corner of my eye, I could have sworn that Rachel's translucent form shivered in fear.

"Would you like to enlighten Anna as to how you ended up in this predicament in the first place?" He turned his steely gaze to Rachel as his long fingers gestured toward me. I turned to face her, but instead of meeting my gaze, her own remained downcast. "Rachel wanted to make a deal with you, if I'm not mistaken?" he asked when the silence edged on uncomfortable. I wasn't sure why that mattered, but at the moment, I didn't see any reason to deny it, so I nodded in agreement.

"Did she tell you what it was she wanted?" he asked curiously.

"She wanted to live," I answered without hesitation.

"That was after you called on Declan," he insisted, shaking his head in disagreement.

I thought about it for a second, and he was right. Rachel had asked me about a deal a few days before she had been attacked in the alley. I had cut her off so quickly. I had no idea what she'd wanted then. I was loath to agree with him, but I gave him a curt nod, my lips pursed in annoyance at the fact that he knew about that in the first place. Though I wasn't all that surprised.

"I never gave her the opportunity to tell me," I replied.

I widened my stance, planting my feet squarely below my hips, as if that could protect me from whatever he was about to say next. Instead, I was shocked to hear Declan chime in from behind me.

"She wanted power. Specifically, she wanted to become the High Chair of the Southwest Coven. And once that happened, she was going to put you in the Prism where you would stay until people forgot what you could do," he stated, his voice thick with disdain.

My jaw dropped, and I felt as if all the air had suddenly left the room as I turned toward Rachel. "Is it true?" I demanded.

"No, I would never do that to you," she argued, her eyes pleading with me as she floated closer, her ghostly hand slightly outstretched but not close enough to reach me. I put up my hand to stop her, and she paused, floating just a few feet away.

"Then what were you going to ask me for?" I asked, my voice dripping with anger.

"I wanted to make a deal with you to lift my probation like he did for you," she said pointed to Silas.

"What else?" I demanded.

"Well, I wanted my full powers back..." she hedged, her eyes finding the carpet instead of mine once again, and I knew it in my gut that Declan was right.

"So, it's true," I said, my voice soft yet threatening.

"Of course, it's true," she sneered, her form taking on a smoky tinge I hadn't seen happen with a soul before. She didn't dare to attack me, though, not with Declan and Silas, both so close by. "You have the power to give people whatever they want, and instead of using it, you bitch and moan about it. Boohoo, I'm Anna, I'm going to walk the earth for eternity." She mocked me as she rubbed her fists against her eyes and floated around me in circles. "Boohoo, I can't leave this city. Boohoo, I made a deal with someone, and they got what they wanted, but then they died," she wiped away imaginary tears as she continued to make fun of me. "What did you expect would happen, *Anna*? They were all going to die eventually."

My heart clenched, and my head was spinning with the

knowledge that I had been so wrong. I assumed she was a good person, but as I stopped and thought back to our very first encounter in the alley when she saw what I'd done with that warlock's power, I should have known better. Every time she got a glimpse of what I could do, her irises had been ringed with red, but I had always attributed it to a reflection in her deep brown eyes. In reality, it was more to do with her own selfish nature.

"So then why not make a deal for power when you made your deal with Declan?" I asked her.

"Because when she paid her ex-boyfriend, dear Officer Martin from the Guard, to stab her in that alley behind Idir, he got a little too carried away. Instead of being injured, she ended up actually fighting for her life," Declan chimed in again with an unsurprised shake of his head.

"How do you know that?" she roared as she whirled to face him.

"Because he's been watching you since the moment Anna became my Intern," Silas admitted smugly. "Something about you offering up your personal space for her house arrest didn't sit well with me. You know, with all the animosity the witches and warlocks have toward myself and my wards. I figured there had to be something you wanted from her. I just didn't know what it was until she made her first contract. And even then, it was still just suspicion."

"You used me," I said incredulously to Rachel as all the pieces fell into place.

"Don't play the victim. You used me just as much as I used you. I was the only person in this hellhole you could even talk to about any of this," she said with a sweeping gesture. I felt bile rise in my throat. She was right, but I had also trusted her.

"So, what now?" I asked Silas, ignoring her comment.

"So now you have a decision to make. Either I can release her soul back to her body where she can live out the rest of her life, and you can go back to serving your sentence without the ability to make another deal. Or you can leave her where she clearly belongs. Allow me to sentence her, and you can become my Apprentice with the freedom I promised you in the first place. You did earn it, after all," he said, leaning back in his chair to wait as if it would take me time to deliberate.

"What if there's something else I want?" I asked, thinking on my feet.

"What's that?"

"Freedom for my own soul," I said without skipping a beat. I did not want to give myself time to talk me out of it.

Unfortunately, just like that fateful day in Rachel's apartment, he laughed. This time not quite so enthusiastically, but it still made me cringe.

"I give you credit for your persistence, but I've told you I don't make deals for souls I already own. Especially ones that are as unique as yours."

"Then why are you willing to let Rachel's go?" I demanded, thinking I had found a loophole in his reasoning.

"Because this wasn't my deal, this was Declan's deal, so I will uphold it. Plus, she's not really of much value to me," he admitted.

Rachel practically growled at that, but she didn't move from where she floated.

"Then, I'll take your offer. I want to become your apprentice," I said with a decisive nod.

Just then, Rachel let out a scream and rushed toward me, her fingers elongating into sharp claws as I stepped back, throwing my arms up to block her. In less than a moment, I heard her shrill scream begin to fade far more quickly than it should have.

By the time I opened my eyes again, the floor was already knitting itself back together. Declan was standing directly in the path between me and where Rachel had been, smoothing out the sleeves of his sweater before turning toward me and Silas. He had saved me from her attack, which, by my count, was now two specters he had saved me from. *I suppose I'll have to thank him for that later*, I thought with a grudging sigh.

"I'll need your signature," Silas said, motioning me toward the desk to where a new contract sat.

I strode purposefully to it, taking the pin he now held out to me and pricking my thumb with it. Then I allowed a fat, crimson drop of blood to well to the surface before pressing it to the paper. I felt the slight sting of the magic as it sealed my mark to the page, but it was so subtle now, I would have missed it had I not been thinking about it.

"So, what now?" I pulled a tissue from the box on the edge of the desk and applied pressure to stop the last of the blood before tossing it into the silver trash can nearby.

"Now you go do what you've been doing. I've lifted the boundaries of your sentence, so you're free to roam where you want. Declan will continue your training, and you'll be paid a salary with a fee for each soul you deliver. However, in order to continue working as my Apprentice, you will have to deliver me at least one selfless soul per year." He shrugged casually.

"What?" I demanded, my eyes wide with surprise at this new stipulation. "That wasn't part of the agreement."

"Actually, it was. If you had stopped to read the contract you just signed, you might have known that." He smirked.

I kicked myself mentally for thinking he wouldn't add anything to my contract we hadn't already discussed, but I should have known better. "And what if I don't?" I asked defiantly.

"Then you break your contract, and I will sentence you how I see fit."

"Ugh," I groaned, throwing my hands up in the air in frustration. "Are we done here?"

"As long as you understand your terms," he replied, his

voice heavy with annoyance. I and turned toward Declan, who was leaning against the heavy oak double doors leading out of the office. I didn't have to say a word before he strode forward to take my outstretched hand. He knew I was ready to go home.

"You'll find a copy of your newest contract, along with any contract you make from now on, filed in the cabinet of your new office down the hall. Two doors to the right—should you ever want to peruse them," he managed to say with a laugh just before Declan and I traveled to the park outside of the church, and I shivered at the sound of it once we were well away from him.

"Why didn't you bring me to my room?" I asked, realizing for the first time that he hadn't ever traveled to me in the rectory after I had moved back. With the exception of Idir that first day, he had always brought me inside places. So it struck me as odd that we were standing across the street.

"I can't go inside the church grounds." He shrugged. "Honestly, I'm shocked that you can. Not that I should be. You seem to be able to do a lot of things that I'm not capable of. But, a word of advice, you should find a new place to live. One that's not here, and soon. Because as you saw, Silas will exploit any anomaly you seem to have and use it to his advantage."

I nodded slowly as I moved toward the wrought iron bench under a nearby tree. The seat was cold when I sat down, and it took everything I had not to shiver violently until my butt adjusted to the change in temperature. Declan followed closely behind, but instead of sitting, he leaned against the tree, his hands shoved deep into the pockets of his jeans while he gave me some time to think.

"So you knew Rachel was using me?"

He nodded but didn't elaborate. "Why didn't you say anything to me?"

"Silas wanted to find out if it went higher up than her." The wind gusted, and he looked up, bracing himself with his hand on my shoulder as a dozen or so leaves floated down around him in the dark. The contact sent a tingle down my body, rousing another image in my mind of Declan and I on a fall day, watching leaves fall as we lounged under a tall oak.

He squeezed my shoulder, bringing me back to the present as his eyes met mine. "Don't worry, it seems she was acting alone. I thought maybe Melinda was involved after you were attacked by the vampire, too, but you were just collateral damage."

Maybe. Maybe not.

"Do you have an office?" I asked.

"Of course. I'm sure yours is right across the hall from mine," he said with a shake of his head, and I was surprised by the sad tone of his voice.

When I looked up, he was staring down at me, his blue eyes sad and tired, but for the life of me, I could not fathom why.

"What's wrong?"

"You should have just said no," he replied, and I was taken aback.

"Said no to what? Silas's deal?" I asked incredulously. *Easier said than done, isn't that what you told me?*

He nodded, his blonde hair falling across his forehead as if he heard my thoughts. "Yes."

"Why in the world would I have done that?"

"Because now he owns you," he said with a sigh.

"He owned me before," I laughed bitterly.

"Maybe, but not like this," he said, his lips pursed.

I blew out a breath, watching as the steam floated away from me. "Why do I feel like there's something you're not telling me?"

"There's a lot I'm not telling you. But it's not by choice, it's out of necessity. You forgot me once. I don't want to go through that again." He shook his head, taking another long look at me before he vanished without another word.

What the fuck? What was that supposed to mean? Seriously? My eyes searched the park, knowing he wasn't there but unwilling to believe he was gone. *You've got to be kidding me! You can't be all cryptic and then leave!* I knew I could summon him back, but truth be told, I was scared of what he'd said.

"I hate that you can do that," I called out to the darkness, disappointed when he didn't reply. Now that I was officially an Apprentice, he would have to teach me that trick.

After a few more minutes, I got up from the bench and crossed the empty street to the church, bypassing the main building and heading straight for my room in the rectory. He was right, I was going to need to find a new place to live, but that was going to have to wait. After all, I still had a body to move, and I was sure he would be back bright and early to show me how to do that.

As I closed the thin wooden door behind me, I sagged heavily against it, my brain and body weary from everything that transpired. Reluctantly, I climbed into bed after kicking off my shoes and waited for the ghosts to come haunt me. I knew they weren't real, but in that moment, my brain was almost begging them to visit. I wanted to feel the torment of those souls, almost as a penance for what I had done and would continue doing now that I was officially the Devil's apprentice.

Staring at the ceiling, I thought for a moment that I might be dreaming as a slip of paper floated down toward me, manifesting out of thin air. I reached up and took it, feeling the weight of it as I examined it before turning it over to read the neatly printed message.

It was on the same paper we used for contracts, so I wasn't surprised to see Declan's cramped print scrawled across it. *I tied up the loose ends from my deal. Consider it a welcome gift to my new colleague. The next part of your training will start soon. Take a few days to stretch your legs. You've earned it,* it said. I knew that he knew I was dying to get out of the city. So if that was the case, I would take him up on that. I figured he would find me wherever I was. *I'm going to have to see about renegotiating that with Silas.* But first, I had stuff to take care of in the city, my own loose ends to tie up. First things first, I would find a new place to live, and I would worry about the next round of training later.

CHAPTER 28

The sun was setting, and I glanced at my watch for the hundredth time before wiping a clean white towel over the glossy surface of the bar. It was dead, it had been all day, and I knew it was because of Rachel's memorial.

"Are you sure you don't want to go?" Matt asked, watching me out of the corner of his eye.

"For the tenth time today, I'm sure."

"She was your roommate," he said as if I had somehow forgotten.

"It's not open to just anyone," I replied with a huff.

He opened his mouth as if to speak, then went silent, not bothering to refute my statement because what I'd meant was that it wasn't open to me. I wasn't part of the coven, and I wasn't exactly in Melinda's good graces. Both of which were things he was well aware of.

"Why aren't you there?" I asked, turning to him as it dawned on me that he was probably the only one other than myself not there paying their respects.

"Fairies don't believe in funerals." he shrugged, and I tilted my head at him as my brows knit themselves together.

"Seriously?"

"Seriously. We're all made of energy, and that means that we never really die because our energy is just returned to the earth to wait until it is reborn into something new." His logic took me by surprise, and I had to swipe away a tear before it fell. *I hope that's true.* The thought of my parents' energy out there in brand new bodies somewhere brought me a sense of comfort.

Just then, Nate came through the door, his eyes red from crying, and I poured him a glass of whiskey that he finished in one gulp.

"Brace yourselves; we're about to be overrun." He slammed the glass down before grabbing an apron and taking up his place beside me.

He wasn't wrong because in less time than it took him to pour himself another, we were overwhelmed with grief-stricken supernaturals who were ready to drink. So, I did what I did best: poured drink after drink until Matt finally kicked everyone out well after closing.

Surprisingly enough, I hadn't had one bad encounter the entire night, even with Officer Martin, who stared daggers at me but didn't say a word other than to order his drinks. I figured it was like an unspoken truce that would only last until the grieving was over. Either way, I'd take it. After all, I'd had enough trouble with the supernatural community recently to last a lifetime, and soon enough, I would leave them all behind.

Well, just as soon as I worked up the courage to do it, anyway. Until then, I said goodbye to Nate and Matt and headed out the door.

The air was cold, and I pulled my jacket around me as I meandered my way down the darkened streets, passing by the alley where I had helped Rachel. It was hard to believe it was the same place she died only a few months later, and I tried to push away the emotions warring inside me, fighting for attention the way they had all day.

I wasn't ready to deal with them yet, mostly because I hated that I was grieving for her even though she had betrayed me. It had been a hard pill to swallow, and I wished I was able to get blackout drunk like some people at the bar had earlier.

When I got back to my room, I noticed a small, plain brown box tied with white satin ribbon propped against the door. I glanced down the hall, but there was no one, so I picked it up and carried it inside with me, where I sat it on the desk while I shrugged out of my light down coat.

Carefully, I untied the ribbon, removing the lid to find a perfect, light pink peony blossom and a bottle of rum along with a card that had my name printed neatly on the front.

Immediately, I thought of Matt, my heart starting to flutter at the idea that he had thought enough to send me my favorite flower and a way to drown my sorrows on a day that had been so emotional already.

Sliding my finger under the flap of the envelope, I tore it open and pulled the card from inside only to find myself shocked once again.

Someone wise once told me that there are two important things one needs to survive the death of a loved one. Alcohol to help you forget when it's too hard to remember, and something beautiful to remind you that it's worth it to keep going.
I wanted you to have a way to forget, and to escape the guilt I know you are undoubtedly feeling. I also wanted you to have something beautiful to remind you that there are still good things in the afterlife.
I promise it will get easier.
Declan

Tears slipped from the corners of my eyes, splashing onto the paper before I wiped them away with the back of my hand. I closed my eyes, suddenly remembering my mother embracing me and telling me almost that exact same thing. For some reason, I couldn't remember who it had been about, but I remembered that conversation like it was yesterday.

Sitting on the bed, I picked up the bottle of rum and broke the seal. He was right. I wanted to forget. Forget about the witches and warlocks who hated me so much. Forget about my new contract with Silas, forget about Matt, and forget about Declan. And maybe when I was done drowning my sorrows, I would want to remember.

ACKNOWLEDGMENTS

I would like to start off by saying a big thank you to my parents. I know if they were here today to see this, they would be so proud. Nothing I have accomplished thus far in life would have been possible without them. I would also like to thank my siblings, who have been my foundation since the beginning; your love and support still amaze me every single day. Never have there been a closer set of siblings. I especially want to thank my big sister Julia; without you, I would be lost. You mean the world to me.

To my husband, Brett, thank you for encouraging me, listening to me whine, and reading my books, and most importantly, being on my team. It means so much that you find value in my words. I love that you believe in me even when I don't. Thank you for being my biggest fan. To my children Kristopher, Justin, and Tyler thank you for being so genuinely proud of me; you will never understand how much that means to me. No matter what I do in this lifetime, you three will always be my greatest creation.

Deanna, who took me under her wing, answered every silly question I had, offered me advice, and most importantly, the support that only a fellow writer can; I thank you. You are my inspiration to continue writing. For Rosemary, who is the best beta reader and friend a writer could ask for. This one's for you! Thank you for reading every single draft, being my sounding board, and encouraging me to pursue publishing.

To Allie Doherty and Brittany Weisrock, thank you for the

many hours of hard work you put into editing and making this story what it is today. Anna could only reach her full badass potential because of you. I am eternally grateful for the two of you.

And last but not least, thank you to Lake Country Press and Reviews for seeing the potential in my story and bringing Devil's Intern to the world. I couldn't have asked for a better publisher; I am thrilled to have this opportunity to be a part of what you are creating. Thank you for taking a chance on me and allowing me to be a part of this family.

ABOUT THE AUTHOR

Jayme Phelps is a wife and mother of three awesome boys who are her biggest fans and greatest support system in following her dreams with debut book—Devil's Intern. Jayme is accomplished in more than storytelling; she's the proud holder of a Bachelor of Science degree in Signed Language Interpreting from the University of New Mexico. She grew up with her nose stuck in a book because there are no better adventures than the ones she's found on the page. She now lives in Albuquerque, New Mexico where she writes every chance she gets. Jayme loves bringing her own adventures to life and sharing them with others.

CPSIA information can be obtained
at www.ICGtesting.com
Printed in the USA
JSHW052257200222
23157JS00001B/11